Extreme,
    exquisite,
        unspeakable
            agony.

Pain everywhere. Behind my knees, between my toes. In my ears, up my arse. My knees, my fingers, my scalp. And inside I could feel every organ boiling. Spleen, pancreas, liver, gall bladder, kidneys – all had acquired the acute sensitivity of a tubercular poet dying in Rome. Everything screamed with pain. The noise of my pain filled the universe. The universe became my pain and formed around me. My pain made a world and I am in it.

This is Hell.

Welcome.

Also available by Anthony McGowan:

Henry Tumour

Hellbent

ANTHONY McGOWAN

Definitions

HELLBENT
A DEFINITIONS BOOK 978 0 099 48213 0 (from January 2007)
0 099 48213 4

First published in Great Britain by Doubleday,
an imprint of Random House Children's Books

Doubleday edition published 2005
Definitions edition published 2006

1 3 5 7 9 10 8 6 4 2

Papers used by Random House Children's Books are natural, recyclable products
made from wood grown in sustainable forests. The manufacturing processes
conform to the environmental regulations of the country of origin.

Set in 11/14pt Sabon by
Falcon Oast Graphic Art Ltd.

Corgi Books are published by Random House Children's Books,
61–63 Uxbridge Road, London W5 5SA,
a division of The Random House Group Ltd,
in Australia by Random House Australia (Pty) Ltd,
20 Alfred Street, Milsons Point, Sydney, NSW 2061, Australia,
in New Zealand by Random House New Zealand Ltd,
18 Poland Road, Glenfield, Auckland 10, New Zealand,
and in South Africa by Random House (Pty) Ltd,
Isle of Houghton, Corner Boundary Road & Carse O'Gowrie,
Houghton 2198, South Africa

THE RANDOM HOUSE GROUP Limited Reg. No. 954009
www.kidsatrandomhouse.co.uk

A CIP catalogue record for this book is available from the British Library.

Printed and bound in Great Britain by
Cox & Wyman Ltd, Reading, Berkshire

For
patrickmargaretcatrionamoyaniallmaggiemcgowan

My thanks also to Alex Antscherl and
Annie Eaton for pulling this one out of the fire

Abandon hope all ye who enter here.

Dante, *The Divine Comedy*, *Inferno*, Canto III, l.9

Part One
Crime and Punishment

Chapter 1
The Ice-cream Van of the Apocalypse

OK, so you've probably been told that there's nothing to be scared of about dying. And as for being dead, well who the Hell cares? In school you either get some happy-clappy, failed priest of an RE teacher with moist hands and greasy trousers who tells you that everyone gets to go to Heaven; or there's Mr Hep Cat Sociology with a wisp of Rizla stuck to his lip, who thinks he's shocking the kids when he says that when we go we go, no God, no Devil, no bullshit about punishment or reward – not even the hippie stuff about joining the stars or becoming one with the universe, just a big black nothing, for ever.

Well, they only say that because they don't know. But let me tell you something. Let me tell you right now. I *do*. Dying hurts. And being dead hurts.

Hurts like Hell.

I know.

So how do I know?

Let me go back a bit. Back to The Fart. The Fart of Ill Omen. The Fart of Doom.

I sit behind Phil Gilroy in biology. I say 'sit', but I mean '*sat*'. Phil's a fat boy. A proper fat boy. Fat from his toes to his ears. In some places his fat is soft and doughy; in some places solid as a melon. But everywhere his fat is fat. He talks about his 'glands', but the reason Phil is fat is because he eats too much, and what he eats is fat. Phil's a pie man: steak and kidney, mince and potato, cheese and onion, whale and bacon, lemur – put it in a pie and Phil eats it – toying with it first perhaps, as if it was a mouth organ or a fine cigar, but then down she goes. No one's ever seen Phil eat anything except pies. His favourite is a pork pie heated in a microwave until the filling liquefies to the consistency of warm snot. He then nibbles a hole in the crust, throws back his head and drinks the jellied slime like a South Sea islander gulping fresh coconut milk. Nothing green, nothing hinting at goodness, vitamins, minerals or roughage, has ever, to anyone's direct knowledge, passed those glistening, greasy lips. You don't need an A-level in biology to realize that the delicate coils and intricate curlicues of the human digestive system aren't made to take that kind of punishment.

Hence The Fart.

Well, I'm all for farts but there are limits. Sadly there are also limits to how many Tangerine Tossheads with cider chasers you can drink. My limit is one, but the night before, me and Johnny Hall, heavy mascara thickening our bumfluff into an entirely unconvincing imitation of maturity, had conned ourselves into a pocket-money-draining three and a half down at the Spleen and Marrow. It was great. I wasn't even sick. Then.

So the next day I'm feeling a might squiffy, but milking it for whatever kudos I can. I've spent all morning bragging about my hangover, which impresses the boys and, whatever they say, the girls too – perhaps even the pure and lovely Melissa Curtain, delicate as a snowdrop, gentle as a fawn and with the largest breasts not only in 4J, but also in the *whole of Year 10*. I'm feeling a bit rough, as I say, but it's all under control. Mr Akroyd's droning on about the formation of cartilage, or photosynthesis, or Charles Darwin's favourite finch, or something equally fascinating, and I'm sketching out an elaborate chariot drawn by a team of harnessed sperm when I realize that something is happening in front of me.

One of Phil's enormous buttocks is beginning to rise, like some grotesque Zeppelin. The cheek itself seems to expand: a great black sail slowly filling in a freshening breeze. A black sail as fatal to me as the black sail of the returning Theseus was to his father Aegeus. (Get used to it, I'm full of that kind of shit, as you'll find out.)

Everything slows down. I want to shout 'No, Phil, no!' but all that comes out is a whimper, a *mneu, mneu, mneu*. And then it begins.

This was not the usual fat-boy's fart, that familiar piping piccolo, a strangulated whine that has the local dogs running in circles. At first there comes a low murmur – a rumble from the double basses. Then the cellos join in, and the violas. This was going to be big. And then comes a great, crashing crescendo from the brass, a bellowing, braying dissonance, and a hammering from the timpani, booming like the End of Everything. And then she dies away, the roaring tempest now a gentle lapping of waves on the shore, the sucking and sighing of passion spent.

Another time I would have led the applause, called out '*Encore, maestro*', carried the bouquet, offered to manage him: together we'd break America, tour Japan. But for my hangover and, as I feared, the stench. The air became hazy; eyes began to water. There was a palpable wave of heat just before the stink reached us. A connoisseur would have found cabbage, egg and possibly asparagus underneath the too-brash, mouth-puckering tang of shite, but I smelled only death, decay and madness. I was losing control. It was coming. It was here.

Yaaaargh chggh chggh yaaaargh.

I puked on Phil Gilroy.

The Body of Christ is a dump. We all know that: kids, parents, teachers, the rats in the beck that runs along the side of the school, the pigeons that shit on the roof. Built for the massive council estate that surrounds it like a foetid womb, The Body gets the kids nobody else wants: the thugs, spacks, drongos, bozos, dildos, queers, Cnuts and killers. And that's just the girls. It also happens to be the only Catholic school in the town, so it also gets a few relatively normal kids whose parents were stupid enough to put RE lessons and saints' days above such fripperies and foibles as GCSEs. I suppose I'm one of those: aberrantly normal, brutally unaggressive and idiotically unstupid. My friends are the same and we live in the top set. It's all relative, of course. Our top set, 4J, would have any other school calling in the riot squad with tear gas and rubber bullets.

The Body looks like a Bulgarian nuclear reprocessing plant. The bits that aren't stained concrete are asbestos. It lies alongside the beck like a squalid drunk, breathing in the stinking air that drifts off the brown foamy water. But it was my school, and I carried for it the sort of fondness that you can develop for a trusted and faithful verruca of long acquaintance. And it had, of course, the advantage of not being home.

So I've puked on the boy Phil. A full-blown late-period Jackson Pollock. Black and yellow bile flecked with the usual vivid greens and intense orange. You could read anger in there. Perhaps a yearning for the lost mother. Pain; vulnerability; carrots.

You could tell that Akroyd wanted to hit me. Veins stood out on his forehead; his hands, as if of their own will, felt for my neck, and a brown fang showed beneath his slack lip. But I was safe – I'd puked, and that meant I was ill, and that meant that he couldn't touch me. The rest was easy: the sick bay and then home for me; the launderette and a bottle of Dettol for Phil; to be followed for both of us by a place in school folklore. Phil knew that immortality was his, and if he hadn't still been in a state of shock I think he would have thanked me.

So I'm walking home, replaying the morning's events. Chucking up has made me feel a lot better and I'm contemplating the Snickers bar in my hand. I live a dreary two kilometres from the school. It's raining. It's always raining. The houses all along the streets had once been council-owned but were now all bought up and pathetically customized. Once a decent and honourable uniform red brick, they now disport themselves in obscene variety: pastel colours, stone cladding, mock Tudor beams, wattle and daub effects, battlements, even the occasional moat.

It's probably about now that I should mention Scrote. Scrote's my dog. To say that he's a mongrel only hints at the bizarre mix of genes that made him what he is. Part Jack Russell, part Doberman, part poodle and part wombat. I've always thought that at some time in his ancestry a dog-owner became altogether too friendly with his pooch, so perhaps part person too. That would explain a lot.

We used to let Scrote roam the street during the day. There wasn't a bitch in the town he hadn't sniffed, shagged and dumped; not a dog that hadn't lost an ear, or an eye, or a testicle to Scrote. What a guy. He should have gone to our school. But he could sometimes be an affectionate dog, waving a paw and wagging his tail, snuffling up for a kiss, licking enthusiastically at your face.

Now Scrote could smell a Snickers from two or three kilometres away; he could hear the rustle and tear of the wrapper from even further – through brick, lead, concrete, even the thick and smoky air of our town. To me he flew. Over walls, across roads, through gardens he came, swift as a greyhound, relentless and dogged (if you'll excuse the piss poor pun) as a pitbull with a child's leg in its mouth.

So. I'm walking along with a mouth full of sugary chemical goodness when I see Scrote tearing towards me. *He's not having it* is all I can think. I turn, step out into the road. Then I see it. The shame, the horror, the ignominy. I'm about to be run down, flattened, squished and well and truly shafted by an ice-cream van. Give me a Morris Minor, a Citroën 2CV, a milk float, a bastard Sinclair C5, but please, God, no, not an ice-cream van.

Chapter 2

Me, My Mum, My Dad, My Sister and the Angels of Avalon

Before I tell you what it's like to die I should tell you a bit more about who I am . . . who I was. Bugger, this tenses thing is starting to annoy me. You'll have to cut me a little slack on my nows and my thens, which are all mixed up, with new thoughts and old memories squished together like breasts in a Wonderbra.

But whatever else has changed, I still have a name: Conor. Conor O'Neil, if you want the whole thing complete with a folderol bow and a hey-ninny flourish of my elaborately be-plumed hat. I'm sixteen years old and still a virgin. Now that *really* hurts, and I know what hurting means. I'm quite tall, quite thin and quite good-looking. Well, of course I think I'm gorgeous but I don't want you to think that I'm vain.

I'm also dead, but we'll come on to that later.

So, what am I like?

It might help if I tell you about my mum and dad, and my sister. So what does my dad do?

My dad's a failure. He fails. He's a loser. He loses. Don't get me wrong, he's a nice bloke and I sort of love him, but for all that he's useless. He used to be a college lecturer – he was a philosopher or something. Mum tells me he was brilliant, had stuff published – articles in magazines called things like *Phenomenology Now!* or *The British Journal of Aesthetics* or *What's New in Hermeneutics*. The house is still full of his old books, the pages all scored with multiple underlinings and cryptic notes ('half-arsed neo-Hegelian obfuscation' sticks in my mind for some reason).

But it all went completely poo-shaped for Dad somewhere in the early nineties. It might have been me. Dad started to go a bit funny after I was born – post-natal depression or something. He carried on, getting gradually stranger, losing the friends he had, letting people down, generally screwing up. Then, a couple of years ago, he gave a lecture to two hundred students stark bollock naked and got the sack. Well, not really the sack – retirement on the grounds of ill health. Now he makes things out of wood and cries a lot.

My mum's a different kettle of ballgames. She's a fox, or so my mates tell me. She's got blonde hair and wears nice clothes – sexy clothes. She's a solicitor and earns megabucks. She probably has affairs – I would if I was married to Dad.

Dad never hit me when I was a kid. Mum took care of that, like she took care of everything. She didn't hit us very hard, but she did something worse than that – they call it 'withdrawing affection'. She had a look she used to give us that could do serious damage – I'm telling you; that look could knock planes out of the sky.

My sister Cathy is like all sisters everywhere. A sweet-natured innocent child, exquisite in taste and sensitivity, ever solicitous, kind, generous, eager, faithful, loving. Yeah. That *was* sarcasm, in case you were wondering. She's two years younger than me and a complete squealer. Mum loves her more than me because she's just like her.

Cathy doesn't go to my school. Mum decided to pay for her to go to a posh school. That was a blessing in one way, but a slap in the face in another. Not that it bothers me.

We live in the last of the decent houses before you get to the estate. It's only a tiny notch up, but a notch is a notch. Dad was brought up on the estate and he doesn't want to move. Mum hates it so they'll probably move quite soon. You can't really blame her. There's not much point in burgling the houses on the estate. The only things worth nicking are the tellies and videos, and everyone's got them already, so why go to the bother of thieving another? So all the local lads go for the houses like ours – people rich enough to have *some* decent gear, but too poor, too lazy and too stupid to get a burglar alarm system. We've been done three times. It wouldn't be so bad if they didn't routinely shit on the carpet. All you ever find is the one pristine turd, as neat and delicate as the first one ever laid.

What else about me? Well, there's always the Angels of Avalon. A touch ironic now, that name. The Angels were me on rhythm guitar, John Moody on drums, 'Fingers' Fairs on keyboards and Paul Conway on bass and vocals. Paul owned all the gear and we practised in his cellar. John was good-looking but, in the way of all drummers from the dawn of time, not very bright (One drum short of a roll? One stick short of a pair – why not make up one of your own?). Fingers had funny, tufty blond hair that made him look like a puppet from a Saturday morning kids' programme. Paul was plain ugly: his chin receded so much he could scratch the back of his neck with his bottom teeth. But he was cleverer and funnier than anyone else I'd ever met.

The main thing to remember about the Angels is that we were shite. We only ever played one gig. The school disco. What a disaster – the *Titanic*, Lockerbie, the First World War – forget it, you're just not in the running.

The Angels started out as a punk band called Simple Harmonic Motion. After a couple of albums (we're talking virtual albums here, not the real thing) we turned reggae. Then it was jungle, acid jazz, hip hop. It all sounded the same – shit. God knows how we managed to talk the headmaster into letting us play at the Year Ten disco. He must have thought he was being particularly *progressive*. And therein lay the problem. Paul had just discovered his dad's prog-rock record collection – Emerson, Lake and Palmer, Pink Floyd, and yes, Yes. The rest of the band were against it, but Paul insisted that we perform his rock symphony *Scenes from the Tapestry of Life's Rich Ocean, Parts I–III*. This was supposed to form sides five and six of our ground-breaking triple album *Sheathing the Sword of Nemesis in the Body of Woman*. The idea was that we should all record our solo parts in a different country. I bagged Switzerland. Fingers was stuck with England, and only agreed if he was allowed a purpose-built château and a female butler specially trained 'to please'.

Anyway, *Scenes* was originally scored for a full symphony orchestra with a chorus of two thousand naked virgins, but we had to make do with the school brass band and my sister Cathy (fully clothed) on backing vocals. As soon as the opening trombone and triangle duet began, the missiles started to land. The school disco was a big deal for us and there must have been a hundred and fifty kids there, and that means a lot of Coke cans, oranges, hairbrushes, knives and used condoms. We knew that time was short and that this was the only chance we'd ever have to play our instruments at full blast, so that's what we did. Cacophony is a lovely word. Imagine it being screamed into your ear by a tone-deaf elephant with a lion chewing its bollocks. We got detention and the band split up, but it was good for us while it lasted and good for the world once it stopped.

So there you have me. I'm quite brainy, quite funny, a bit of a tosser – but you're supposed to love me. If you don't, then either my lying isn't as good as I thought it was or you're cleverer than I think you are. Oh yes, there's something else about me. I touched on it earlier. I'm dead.

Chapter 3

What It Feels Like to Get Knocked Down by an Ice-cream Van Playing the Theme from *Neighbours*

So then, what *does* it feel like to get knocked down by an ice-cream float playing the theme from *Neighbours*? Not funny. So far I've tried to make you laugh. Not now. What's the worst pain you've ever had? Don't give me any gumph about burning the roof of your mouth on a pizza.

Boys, you must have had a kick in the goolies. Imagine your whole body is one huge testicle. Now imagine a steel-toe-capped Doc Marten the size of a buffalo stomping on you. That's not close.

Girls. Well I don't know what the girl equivalent is – but imagine the feeling you get when you go for a piss at school and you tuck your skirt into the back of your knickers and walk round the school with everyone laughing at you and you don't know why until you get home and your mum tells you. Now imagine that embarrassment as a *physical* pain. Not in the same *universe*.

The dentist? Child's play.

Trapping your foreskin in your zip? As nothing.

Laying your gentle cheek down upon the electric hob? *Pah!*

Having your haemorrhoids chewed by a weasel?

A cricket bat smashed into your nose fifty times?

My last sight on Earth was a blur of pink-and-blue van; my last sound the baleful tinkering of *Neighbours*; my last smell the acrid stink of chemical-warfare-grade ice cream – fifty per cent water, thirty per cent lard and twenty per cent DDT.

Well, not quite the last smell. One of the things they *don't* tell you about dying is that you shit your pants. And my last feeling on earth? The same as my first feeling in Hell.

Extreme,
    exquisite,
        unspeakable
            agony.

Pain everywhere. Behind my eyes, between my toes. In my ears, up my arse. My knees, my fingers, my scalp. And inside I could feel every organ boiling. Spleen, pancreas, liver, gall bladder, kidneys – all had acquired the acute sensitivity of a tubercular poet dying in Rome. Everything screamed with pain. The noise of my pain filled the universe. The universe became my pain and formed around me. My pain made a world and I am in it.

This is Hell.

Welcome.

With the pain there is a sensation of falling. No, not falling. A sensation of being sucked. The universe is a great plughole and I'm going down it. A million shades of black. The silent trumpets blare, silent thunder roars, silent cannons blast.

Still the pain, the burning torment, grips me. I cannot think or breathe for the pain. It must stop. I will wake up, sweating from my nightmare. The fart, the ice-cream van, Scrote coming – all a dream.

All this stuff about pain. None of it gets close. How can you trap a thing like pain – a thing that isn't really a thing at all – in words? And how do I know that what you call a pain is anything like what I call a pain. It's all so private. True, I can see your face, see you writhe, hear you yelp. But I can't feel your pain. If I did, it would be my pain, and not yours any more. Maybe a picture.

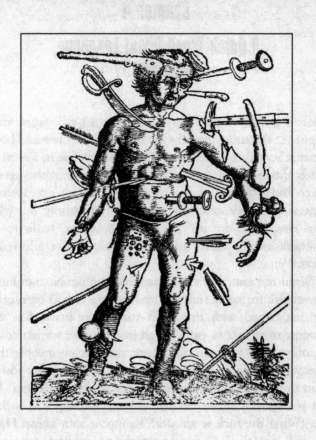

Chapter 4
A Quick Word About Language, Foul, Mostly

Before I go any further I want to have a quick word about language. The thing they always get wrong in films and books about school is the swearing. I'd guess that one in five of the words uttered by a typical school kid between the ages of eleven and sixteen is a swear word, or a reference to a feature of male or female anatomy, or a bodily function. But whatever else kids do on the telly, however realistic the programmes are meant to be, they're just not allowed to swear.

Given the fact that swearing was commoner than pus at our school, for some time me and my mates had been growing dissatisfied with the usual stuff. You swear for three reasons: to shock, to get a laugh and because sometimes it's the only thing you can do. There aren't many people these days who are going to break down in tears because you tell them to fuck off – you really do need sticks and stones. Nor is it particularly funny. So you can see why any kid with an iota (What the fuck is an iota? I suppose iota know. Ha ha ha. Well, actually I do: it's the eighth and smallest letter in the Greek alphabet) of originality might get a smidge bored with the traditional repertoire.

The standard response to any form of irritation began with 'fuck off' and concluded with, in an escalating order of unpleasantness, 'you wanker', 'you bastard', or 'you c**t'. The nuclear option, the one to be used only when the target was defenceless, or too far away to retaliate with lethal force, was 'you poof'. Every sentence had at least one, often two, and sometimes all of the following: prick, knob, bollocks, arse, spunk, piss, shit, tits, fanny, shag, hump, honk, Blair. 'Shit' – the almost invariable expression of concern, annoyance or exasperation – was the commonest of all, infesting every conversation like fleas in a sofa.

Some of these I had no quarrel with, for all their lack of imagination. 'Wanker' and 'bastard', although stale with overuse, retained some of their Olde Worlde charm. 'Wanker', in particular, had become almost a term of endearment, something to utter along with a groan after some particularly poor joke. (*How many ears did Captain Kirk have? Three: a left ear, a right ear, and space, the final front-ear* – that kind of thing.)

'Shit', I just couldn't make my mind up about. There were times when it was the only word that would do: stubbed toes, crap music, school food, trodden dog turds all seemed to cry out for the sudden, explosive 'Shit!'. But I argued long and hard for the old pretender 'shite', either plain, as a direct substitute for shit, or drawn-out into a plangent 'she-ite' which could, depending on the context and precise emphasis, represent amazement, admiration, or disgust.

I was also very keen on interesting variations on the theme of shit. Two favourites that gained a certain popularity at school were 'shit-legs' and 'shite-hawk'. I have no idea of the origins of these: no doubt Dad could have told me how they went back to the Restoration or something. Or maybe I made them up.

I *did* once bring up the subject with Dad, saying that I was trying to widen my vocabulary so I could get away from 'damn' and 'bloody' (two words that were just about respectable in our house, even in front of Mum) without going the whole hog. We were in the kitchen. I was watching our kitchen telly, and he was making some kind of stew thing

for dinner. Dad got quite into the idea of colourful language
– he was, after all, always going on about how kids today just
grunt at each other, like Neanderthals or Homo Erectus (that
always made me snigger which pissed him off all the more).

He rattled off all kinds of stuff from Shakespeare and
Jonathan Swift and Alexander Pope, some of it quite funny –
that bloke Swift was *obsessed* with cack – but none of it
much use in the modern playground. Then he went off to get
one of his old books. He came back ten minutes later, saying,
'Listen to this. This is cursing as an art form.' I was
moderately impressed with what he came out with, even to
the point of writing it down. The book was *Gargantua and
Pantagruel*, by some mad monk called Rabelais.

The good bit went like this:

*Pratling gablers, lickorus gluttons, freckled bittors, mangie
rascals, shiteabed scoundrels, drunken roysters, slie knaves,
drowsie loiterers, slapsauce fellows, slabberdegullion druggels,
lubbarly lowts, cosening foxes, ruffian rogues, paultrie
customers, sycophant-varlets, drawlatch hoydens, flouting
milksops, jeering companions, staring clowns, forlorn snakes,
ninnie lobcocks, scurvie snakesbies, fondling fops, base lowns,
sawcie coxcombs, idle lusks, scoffing Braggards, noddie
meacocks, blockish grutnols, doddi-pol-jolt-heads, jobernol
goosecaps, foolish loggerheads, slutch calf-lollies, grouthead
gnat-snappers, lob-dotterels, gaping changelings, codshead
loobies, woodcock slanghams, ninnie-hammer flycathcatchers,
noddiepeak simpletons, turdie gut, shitten shepherds.*

I thought some of the things on Rabelais' list were pretty
cool, but I couldn't see how we could use them. Picture it.
One of the school mutants is chasing you round the playground with a used johnny on the end of a stick. You turn
and face him:

'Hold fast there, thou ninnie lobcock, jobernol goosecap, grouthead gnat-snapper, ninnie-hammer flycathcatcher.'

Yeah, that's really gonna stop 'em. Get ready to eat condom.

This all reminds me about sticks. In my experience of these things (which is wide), you can be chased by three sorts of stick. The first sort of stick is a stick-stick, i.e.: a stick with nothing on the end of it except for more stick. The worst that can happen to you is that you get hit with the stick. The second sort of stick is the shit-stick. A shit-stick is a stick with shit on the end of it. The worst thing that can happen to you if you get caught by a shit-stick is that you get daubed with shite. And that's a bad thing.

The third kind of stick is, of course, the johnny-stick. Used johnnies turn up in all kinds of strange places: on lampposts, in trees, threaded through wire fences. Wherever it is deposited, you can guarantee that some twat will find it, mount it on the end of a stick like a lady's favour on a lance in a tournament, and chase us poor fuckers about the place. For some reason a johnny-stick, or fuck-stick as it is often called, is deemed to be worse than the shit-stick. But neither of them is especially nice.

Where was I? Swearing. In our campaign for real swearing, perhaps our greatest innovation was the substitution of 'Cnut' for the useful, ever popular, but profoundly uncorrect 'c**t'. The c-word, although theoretically the final taboo, had become so common in our school that it barely registered. It could still get you a punch in the guts, or worse, if you let it slip at the wrong moment, but amongst ourselves it had ceased to have any real impact. Calling someone a Cnut, on the other hand, had one of four, generally gratifying, results:

1. complete bafflement
2. bemusement, followed by rage

3. puzzlement, followed by laughter
4. laughter

I got the idea after a history lesson about the Saxons and Vikings in which I found out the happy fact that good old King Canute of turning-back-the-waves fame was now generally called Cnut. Not the hardest anagram in the world, that one.

'Cnut' had the real advantage that you could use it within earshot of a teacher, making you look like a hero in front of your mates, who were all in the know, but without risking any real comeback in the form of lines, detention etc. Some of the teachers caught on pretty quickly, but they were split between the ones that found it funny and the ones who, although enraged, could think of nothing to do about it. The rest were thrown off the scent, and indeed often rather pleased with the explanation that Simon Boxer was a Cnut because of his overweening pride and taste for Danish bacon.

Chapter 5
The Corridor of Uncertainty

I have woken up.

But what is this place? A grey corridor. Blue plastic chairs. A dim, yellow light seeping from the walls, like slime. And there are thousands like me in this corridor. Millions. All paralysed by the pain and the fear. The long and lonely lines of the dead.

Every hour or so the line would shuffle down a place. No one spoke. Except me. I looked at the figure in front of me. He seemed to be about a thousand years old. A few wispy grey hairs, yellow spots, no teeth, a hearing aid, stinky piss-and-shit-stained pyjamas.

'Hello,' I said. Before he could reply I felt a crashing blow to the back of my head. I fell onto the hard lino and a scaly, three-toed foot landed on the back of my neck.

'No talking,' a voice bellowed. I craned round to see a huge figure looming over me. The head was like the product of some awful medical experiment – a pig's face moulded onto a human skull. Short sharp tusks curled up from the slavering mouth and two horns sprang from the bunched and knotted scalp. The massive body gave off a smell for which there can be no name, only a symbol – a skull and crossbones. It was swathed in leathery plates and I couldn't tell if they were part of the creature or some kind of protective clothing. A long naked tail slithered restlessly behind. He, she or it held a whip in one hand and an iron trident-cum-club in the other. I saw blood and hair and bits of bone stuck to the heavy pummel-end of the trident. Mine. He reminded me of our maths teacher, Mr McHale.

I now noticed that there were others like him patrolling the long corridor. Every now and then the whip would lash out or the club fall on a fragile skull. I crawled back into my place and spoke no more.

On the wall, there was a clock which seemed to follow me as I shuffled down the line, but it ran backwards and forwards randomly, the hands moving sometimes in opposite directions, sometimes in the same direction at the same speed, at other times stopping altogether. I could have been in that queue for days, weeks or years. However long it was I could feel myself drawing closer to something truly nasty. The background levels of pain intensified. I could hear muffled screams. There was a smell of burning flesh. Liquid oozed from the floor and the walls: sometimes yellow, sometimes brown, sometimes red.

Eventually I saw the source of the horror – a door guarded by two of the huge devils. The damned at the end of the queue entered, but none returned. The old man in the pyjamas was still ahead of me. He had been crying silently to himself for some time. He now began to tremble. His hearing aid fell from behind his ear. Some residual surge of deference made me stoop to pick it up for him. He took it from my hand without a word. A little later he mumbled to me under his breath.

'What are you here for, boy?'

I answered without thinking: 'I don't know. Must be some kind of mistake.'

I honestly hadn't thought what I'd done to deserve this. I wasn't even sure what 'this' was. I did have a pretty good idea that I was dead, and a sneaking suspicion that I was in trouble. But surely they had purgatory or limbo for people like me? Remember, I'd been to a Catholic school, so I knew about this kind of thing. I wasn't bad. I was just ordinary.

'What about you?' It only seemed polite to ask.

'Killed my wife,' he replied. 'Back there they thought it was a mercy killing – she had cancer. But I hated the bitch. Ugly as sin. Big wart on her thumb. Used to obsess me. Only got a suspended sentence. Pay for it now though.'

With that he stood up and was led by one of the devils through the door.

I looked back along the line. The corridor was perfectly straight and I could see for miles. Was there no end to the damned?

Chapter 6
Sentence

And now it's my turn to be led through the great door. Inside I expect to see something terrifying – scenes of torture, children roasted on spits, decapitation, bodies torn and ripped asunder. Instead there was a large desk and a small, bald man in a bad suit and worse tie. The room was windowless, and wooden panels covered the walls. After the bleak horror of the corridor, the room felt almost cosy.

'Take a seat please, Mister, er, O'Neil,' said the man, who I began to think of as my judge, although he looked more like a clerk in a benefit office, or a supermarket manager. I liked this *Mister O'Neil* stuff. I'd never been called Mister before. I began to think that maybe there had been a mistake and it was all going to be cleared up, or that everyone – the damned and the saved – went through that awful corridor before being sent on to their final destination – a Luton Airport of the afterlife.

'I'd like to confirm some details,' the judge went on, looking at a large ledger and a stack of computer printouts.

'Full name?'

'Conor O'Neil.'

'I think I said full name.'

'Conor Quentin O'Neil.'

Yeah, I know. I'll never forgive them for that. What was wrong with 'John' or 'Robert' or any other sodding name you care to mention? When word leaked out at school (sister to blame, naturally) it took two years for the novelty of calling me 'Quentin' or 'Quent' to pall.

'Religion?'

'Catholic.'

I said it without thinking much. I was a Catholic in the same way I had brown hair. It wasn't my choice and it would have taken some effort to change it.

The judge gave me a long, searching look, as if my answer was inadequate. I had a flash of inspiration.

'Catholic atheist.'

I'd got that from my dad. Wish I hadn't bothered. The judge smirked.

'Date of birth?'

I told him.

'Date of death?'

I told him that that, too.

Annoying how these people ask you what they already know. Power trip, I suppose.

'Cause of death?'

'Traffic accident.'

Again the penetrating look.

'I was run over by an ice-cream van.'

Was that a smile that flickered across those thin lips? The Cnut.

He cleared his throat and looked down at his ledger.

'I suppose you know why you are here?' Without waiting for an answer, he went on, 'I have here a list of very serious offences. This is not a trial. You have already been found guilty. All that remains is to determine the severity of your punishment. Have you anything to say in mitigation?'

Already found guilty! I'm a kid of sixteen. What can I have done to end up in a place like this?

'I don't understand. Why *am* I here? What have I done?' I could feel myself whining, my voice moving unerringly to that unappealing falsetto that warbles 'slap me'.

'*What have you done?*' the judge replied with a look of incredulity on his desiccated, inscrutable face. 'Perhaps I should read out some of the things that you have *done*. Number one, lying: two hundred and thirty-four thousand individual episodes of mendacity.'

'But that's only lying. Everybody lies. It's normal,' I squeaked.

'Surely you're not trying to tell me that lying is *good*? That really shows a terrible lack of ethical understanding, a crippling of the moral sentiment. This may be more serious than we thought.'

'But lying does no harm. Surely sometimes it *is* good – you know, telling someone that they're not really ugly when you know they are. Or pretending that you still want to be friends when you dump your girlfriend. Where would we be without lies?'

'I see. So you are trying to posit a humanist, utilitarian ethic in place of the stern categorical imperatives of religion or, indeed, any other variety of moral objectivism?'

'Eh?'

He sighed and went on. 'Let me explain. There are basically two ways of looking at the whole subject of good and evil. Either things are right or wrong in themselves – simply by virtue of what they are. Murder is wrong. Lying is wrong. Full stop, end of story, no need to explain any further. Or things are right or wrong insofar as they contribute to some greater good – happiness, in your scheme of things. One's focus here is on the consequences of an action, not on the action itself. So lying or murder could be considered good if they contribute to an increase in the sum of human happiness. I simplify, of course, but you get my meaning. Sounds plausible, I admit. But that's not the way things work down here. Down here we like things to be straightforward. There is no room for ambiguity in Hell, my boy. Right and wrong;

black and white; life and death. But of course the Authorities are not unreasonable. It is accepted that even a saint might occasionally commit him- or herself to an indiscreet untruth. And so you are permitted an allowance, a *quota* if you will.'

'What is the allowance?'

'Well the formula is a little complicated. A certain number per year, with a correction dependent on certain circumstances. Sisters, and so forth and so on.'

'So how many was I allowed?'

The judge ran his finger along a row and down a column of figures.

'*Yeeeees* . . . just a moment . . . here we are. Two hundred and thirty-*three* thousand, nine hundred and ninety- . . . seven. Well,' he said dryly, 'you must be pleased that you didn't miss it by just the one. That would have been *most* unfortunate.'

Three lies over the limit. Just my luck. I thought about the last three lies I'd told.

– *No, Phil, I haven't got any left.*
– *Seven inches and still growing.*
– *So* what*, I've got the first ever Batman comic, but it's so valuable it has to be kept in a bank vault in Switzerland.*

Worth it? Tough call, but probably not.

'Two,' he continued, before I had time to scroll back and marshal some powerful arguments in favour of what at least I now knew was called utilitarianism, 'stealing. One hundred and twenty-eight episodes. Shops, I see. Mother's purse, father's trousers, school friend's rucksack. Not an edifying record.'

'But that's barely anything. Anyway, the shops can afford it. What's the big deal?'

'I must refer you to the answer I gave a moment ago. You must not fall back on these tired excuses. I suggest you show

27

a little more grace in accepting the inevitable.'

Things were sounding, well, *grave*.

'Number three, wanton cruelty. Eight thousand, three hundred and forty-five separate episodes.'

'You must be joking. I'm nice. When have I been cruel? Who to? My dog? I love my dog.'

The judge checked a computer printout. 'Fourteenth December 1993. Pushed sister to the floor. Knelt on chest. Produced thick line of drool, repeatedly allowed it to drip towards the sister's face before sucking it back into his mouth. Finally allowed drool to fall onto the sister's face.' He looked up at me. 'We admired that one here. We've incorporated it into our training programme.'

'Yeah, it's a killer – the Conor Special, I call it. But that's only my *sister*. Boys are supposed to do that. Anyway, she put the skin from her verruca in my cornflakes and then told me about it after I'd eaten it. What would you have done?'

He ignored my outburst and referred again to his printout.

It had all been pretty rough up until then. What could I say? The bald bastard had a point. How could I justify lying, bullying Sis, stealing? They all seemed so normal at the time. I always thought I was one of the good guys, and now here I was, about to spend eternity in torment. This sucked. It was all about to get a lot worse.

'Number four. Murder.'

'What?'

'Murder. One episode. The victim: Jason Roberts.'

No.

This was seriously bad news.

Erco, I thought.

'Erco,' I said.

'Yes, "Erco", as you called him,' said the judge, staring into my soul as if I were a piece of mould on his breakfast crumpet.

'A word or two of kindness. Perhaps informing the teachers what was going on. There was no need for heroics. But I'm afraid you did nothing. In parentheses, I should state that we take a very stern view of acts of omission here. Causing misery by failing to act is no better than causing misery directly, by your own actions. I am relieved to be able to confirm that all that is necessary for the triumph of evil, is for good men, and boys, to do nothing. But if you had only stood aside . . . Well, who knows? We might have allowed you to slip through the net. But that isn't all, is it, Conor?'

I looked at my feet. I noticed that my newish Nikes had been changed into a pair of tatty Dunlop Greenflash. Nice touch, I thought.

'You didn't simply stand aside, did you, Conor?'

I didn't say anything. There was nothing to say.

'Need I go on?' asked the judge.

I shook my head.

There was a pause, and I could clearly hear the breathing of the judge and the scratching of his pen.

'There remains, therefore,' he said at last, 'only the task of assigning your personal tormentor before we send you on to your allotted place.' He pressed a buzzer on his desk and a moment later a devil came in through the door.

This one was not like the scary guard-devils I'd already seen. This one was short – shorter than me. His face was more human, his horns and teeth smaller, his tail furry, more like a squirrel's than a rat's. The tail emerged through a hole in the back of a sort of one-piece romper suit in stretchy red fabric. He carried a toy trident and was obviously trying hard to look mean. And along with the devil came trotting, of all things, a dog.

My dog.

Scrote!

'Clarence,' said the judge in a businesslike way (he was

already looking at the papers on the next in line), 'take O'Neil to his place of torment.'

Before I had the chance to smile at the prospect of being tortured for all eternity by a stumpy devil called Clarence, the little bastard speared me on the end of his trident and shunted me through the door at the back of the room.

As I left I looked back to see the long, scaly tail of the judge sweep the floor contentedly.

Chapter 7
Orientation

A chamber of horrors; a dungeon; a furnace; a pit of vipers, scorpions and tarantulas. All these would have left me unsurprised. But this I hadn't expected. The door from the room of grim judgement led out onto a bleak railway platform. When I say bleak, I don't mean the desolate bleakness of the rural station in East Anglia where my Aunty Maureen lives, with its two trains a day and no shelter. I mean the teeming human horror of Crewe or Doncaster, with trains delayed, tannoys babbling in Latvian and drunken Scotsmen puking Tartan Export into litter bins.

Lost souls, each accompanied by a devil, stood about: ashen-faced, stunned, silent. I probably wasn't looking great myself. I was still in my school uniform. The arse of my trousers was caked in cack, and the purple and gold of my blazer was torn and muddy. I wished I had a mirror to check my hair (there'll be more, much more, about my hair later on). And then those trainers screamed out to all the world, or at least to Hell: 'Unclean! Unclean! All ye who remain untainted, shun this boy.'

The station itself was formed of concrete and zinc singing in perfect discord. It stank of all things excremental built onto a solid aromatic framework of vomit and urine. A scary red sky glowered down and there seemed to be mountains away in the distance, jagged peaks surrounded by clouds of deep purple. Then I looked down at the floor. Staggering in horror, I saw that the floor was made up of countless faces, flattened and worn smooth – almost, but not quite, beyond the point of recognition. They were clearly conscious, blinking and cringing silently at the feet that stomped down on them.

'Wanker,' said someone close by. I looked around. My fellow damned all seemed too preoccupied with their own thoughts, their own pain, to take any interest in the world about them.

'Wanker,' came the voice again, hoarse, sinister and – I realized – close to the ground. I looked down at Scrote. Scrote looked up at me.

'Wanker.'

'What?'

'You heard.'

'What is this? Can you talk?'

'What does it sound like?'

'What are you doing here? How can you speak? This is fantastic. I thought I was going to be on my own. And you can talk. This is so cool. My mates will never believe it.'

'You're dead, shitnick. And your mates don't give a toss. And my name's not Scrote – it's Achilles Herculeus Giganticus.'

Clarence, my devil, had been listening to all this with a half smile on his face.

'It might help if I explain a few things. As you've probably worked out, Scrote here – forget the Achilles business, just a touch of canine self-aggrandisement, all the mongrels seem to have it – met his end at the same time as you. A box of chocolate flakes fell out of the ice-cream van and as you were lying there, bleeding and broken, your faithful hound gorged himself too quickly and choked to death. HQ decided it presented interesting possibilities for torment, so we allowed you to stay together. It's not normal, of course – animals in this circle of Hell – but, you know, management always like to try out new initiatives. You'll soon come to understand the thinking behind it.'

Clarence had a nervous way of talking, with what threatened to be a stammer without actually being one. You could see him close his eyes with the effort of overcoming a troublesome *p* or *t*. He was prone to wringing his hands and nodding idiotically as he listened to you, and he had a way of helpfully finishing your sentences along with you, as if to offer encouragement or support. It made you want to kick him. But for all that, he seemed desperately keen to please, and I found myself warming to him in the overall context of hating his guts.

'Can you tell me a bit more about this place? I mean, it seems in some ways like home, but in other ways so different. Is this real, or am I dreaming all this? Will the pain ever go away? Can I change my underpants?'

'Well, answering your second question first, we're not really that big on actual physical pain any more in the *outer* circles of Hell. Things have moved on a bit since the lakes of fire, brimstone (whatever that is – I always meant to ask), impalements, dismembering and so on. Now don't get me wrong, pain has its place – the traditionalists aren't completely wrong – but we like to think that we're a little bit more sophisticated now. We've commissioned research on this. Physical pain seems to take the customer's mind off the mental aspects of damnation.'

'*Customers?*'

'Yes, awful, isn't it? Really makes me cringe. But it's all part of giving a good service. We like to think that we can deliver torment more efficiently than anywhere else. And we're fully committed to equal opportunities – there's no discrimination down here. Man, woman, black, white, gay, straight – we guarantee maximum suffering, minimum fuss! I've got a business card somewhere,' he added, tapping his pockets.

'So what's in store for me?' I asked, still a little bemused.

'Well, you'll always have the background pain – that's a

freebie. But we've devised a long-term torment package tailored to your needs. We emphasize torment here rather than torture. All sorts of mental discomfiture from mild irritation to full-blown anguish. I suppose that's where Scrote comes in. You'd be surprised how much dogs hate people and the lengths they'll go to inconvenience and annoy you. And when you think they're being affectionate, that's when they really get you. Scrote ever licked your face?'

'Yes, all the time.'

'Well what do you suppose he was licking before that? If you're lucky it was just his, um . . . organs of reproduction.'

Scrote sniggered. I gagged.

'And my job,' Clarence continued, 'is to make sure you get all the torment you deserve. I'll be by your side, or at least close by, every minute of the day. We'll really get to know each other before we're finished. I should say that you're my first assignment. I want to make a good impression. You get some of these old devils, and although they really know their stuff, they just can't be bothered with the details – and the devil is in the detail, you know.'

'So what's with the train station?'

'We've found that a really bad train journey – over-crowded carriages, screaming kids, ancient rolling stock, cancellations, everything running late, people continually walking up and down the aisle for no good reason, you know the kind of thing – is just the best possible start to our customers' new life in Hell. It all really came together when we privatized the system, of course. There *was* a small problem with condemned trainspotters and other rail enthusiasts. We discovered that some of them were actually *enjoying* all this. We fly them out now. But you wanted to hear more about the sort of place Hell is, and what you'll be doing for the rest of eternity.

'First a little geography. Hell is divided into a number of

administrative districts. Some people call these the circles of Hell, but they aren't really circles at all – just regions, with their own particular customers and administration. It might be best to think of them as states of mind. We actually call them *Themes*. You've been assigned to a unit on the Islets of Langerhans in the outer circle, in the district of Sheol. I'm afraid you weren't important or interesting enough to warrant anything nearer the centre of things. We're not talking top-notch torment here – we haven't got all the hi-tech gadgets and gizmos they have for the first-class guests. But we like to think that we can make up in ingenuity and guile what we lack in technology. Each person – and this is the important bit, so listen carefully – each person has his or her own *private* Hell. We've had all eternity to get it just right.'

'But how could you have all eternity? I'm only sixteen years old!'

'Well, it's not really my subject – I always found theology boring – but I think they call it predestination. You see, when the Old Fellow made you, or *conceived* you, or whatever, he must have known how you were going to end up. That's the thing, you see – he knows everything – omniscience is the word, I believe. How could he not know? And if he knew how you would end up, it must have been – what's the word? – pre-ordained. You can't have had much of a say in it.'

'But that's just plain unfair. What chance did I stand? What if I turned out to be good? What about free will?'

'Just an illusion, or so they taught us in college. Everything is determined. There are various theories about the mechanism – environment, genes, Original Sin – all amounts to the same thing. Anyway, it makes life a lot easier for us down here. No last-minute panics, no unexpected visitors.'

'I was shafted.'

'Well, p-perhaps I'd put it a little differently, but that about sums it up. Anyway, as I was saying, you have a nice little place, fits you like a glove, or a death mask. And then there's us – demons, devils, ogres, fallen angels, tempters, teasers, tantalizers. We are here to make your life Hell. As you may have noticed, we come in various forms, or grades. I'm an Executive Devil, the basic entry-level grade for tormentors. We do most of the routine casework. Below me there are Administrative Devils who take care of the simple clerical stuff – filing, fiddling with the photocopier, bending paperclips out of shape, that sort of thing. Not a particularly bright lot on the whole but harmless enough. And then, at the bottom, there are the Bruisers, the security staff. They march around guarding things and stabbing people, and they hunt down runners, and they do whatever manual torturing is required. As I've said, we don't do much of that these days, but there *is* still a call for it in some places. You don't want to get mixed up with them. Nasty bunch. Chew your head off soon as look at you.'

I thought about the pig-faced guards in the corridor and made a mental note not to get my head chewed off.

'Above me, of course, there are the Higher Executive Devils. They deal with the more interesting casework: murderers, drug dealers, paedophiles, accountants. Once you get past HEDs you're really into the management grades. Senior Executive Devils hardly have any face-to-face contact with customers. It takes eight or nine million years to get that far – if you ever do. Above SEDs I get a bit vague – all Very Important Devils. We never get to meet them. And then at the top or, I suppose, the bottom, comes the main man himself, Satan. Now none of us have ever seen him. Some of us,' said Clarence, dropping his voice to a whisper, 'suspect that he might not exist at all. Sometimes I think it could all just be a silly superstition. I mean, the concept of Satan doesn't really help to explain anything, does it? Some philosophers say that evil must come from somewhere. Nothing comes from nothing, everything has a cause, so there must be an original cause of evil. But then other philosophers say it's all just part of being human, or diabolic. It's all a bit beyond me. But I've spoken too much – and look, here comes the train. By the way, all that stuff about Satan not existing – that's just between the two of us. If that sort of thing gets back to my boss, that's the end of my career.'

Chapter 8
The Tracks of My Tears

We all shuffled onto the train: some kind of smelly diesel, coated in the filth of ages. It oozed oil like pus, and clouds of stinking gas enveloped us. It had been bitterly cold on the platform, but the inside of the train was stifling. Me and Scrote were forced onto one seat in an old-fashioned compartment and squashed against a window by the press of foetid, decaying humanity. Clarence floated up to the baggage rack and seemed to fall asleep there. The other guardian devils did the same. They all looked more or less like Clarence, dressed in the same silly costumes. But I couldn't help but think that my devil seemed a little bit nicer than the others. They all appeared more brutal, more inclined to snarl and cuff, to spit out an acid, burning saliva or prod their charges in some soft and tender part.

My train companions were the usual lot: shattered old folk, misers, misanthropes, murderers. None dared talk openly. Some mumbled to themselves. Some wept. Some jabbered. They were all so ugly, their faces subtly distorted into caricatures. It was as if they had all become stock types, illustrations of the effects of vice in some textbook. I was the only young person there and I guessed it was because, on the whole, kids don't die, or if they do they're usually too young to have done anything really bad.

The train stayed in the station for what felt like days: it was impossible to tell from the light outside, which shifted randomly from a hammering purple to a neuralgic orange.

The heat grew ever worse. The foul breath of the damned commuters hung in layers of yellow stink. Scrote sat on my lap, adding sly, meaty farts to the general miasma. He was chewing my knee, contentedly. That reminded me: I was hungry.

How can the dead be hungry?

How can the dead think: *How can I be hungry?*

'I'm hungry,' I moaned, looking hopefully up towards Clarence. 'And thirsty. Do you have food in this place? I could kill for some pizza and a can of Coke. I don't suppose there's a buffet car?'

Clarence opened an eye.

'Yes, gluttony. We like that one here. And kill for it? Perfect. I'm afraid you'll have to wait until we get . . . *home*. But food we'll have, and drink too. Yes, a surfeit. And if you can't wait, there is actually a buffet carriage. But take it from me, you really, *really* don't want to go there.'

I didn't like the sound of any of that. Clarence had lost some of his bumbling pleasantness. Perhaps the food was really bad. But I could take it. I had eaten school dinners for ten years. And then there was Dad's cooking. Lentil bake, anyone?

The train began to move. A low moan filled the compartment. I couldn't decide whether I should be relieved or terrified to be underway. The scenery changed with alarming rapidity. One moment we were amid scenes of sublime grandeur: huge mountains towering over the tracks; torrential rivers that seemed to part like legs as the train approached; lakes of fire that boiled the air in the carriages. And then we passed through decaying cityscapes: tenements filled with starving children and flayed adults; steepling tower blocks that twisted and snaked into the red sky. But everywhere – pain and suffering without end: bat-winged devils goading the damned, whipping, piercing, taunting them from above. Women and men screamed, filling the air with the rapture of the damned.

Obviously sleep was out of the question.

'Can't say I really approve of all this,' tutted Clarence. 'Terrible waste of energy. And all that *noise* – it just dissipates the suffering. You get more real suffering in the average city office than we manage to produce with all this . . . this . . . sound and fury.'

Hours or days or weeks later we arrived at the *terminal*. And yes, I choose my words carefully. The Islets form a loose chain – like snot blown from a footballer's nose – off the coast of the mainland. The train pulled in at a station and a group of us, perhaps fifty or so – not the most wretched-looking, but bad enough – shuffled off. Flogged, screamed at, already broken by the journey, we were herded towards a rickety jetty to which was moored a raft of fragile, splintered wood. Someone had painted letters on the planks. I could make out M-E-D-something-something-A. The water was thick and brown and smelled of poo.

It *was* poo.

This was worse than Blackpool: the ratio of turd to sea water was exactly reversed. I could see the archipelago rising from the sea of diarrhoea some miles away.

'We'll never all fit on that raft,' I muttered.

Clarence was fluttering above me.

'That's all part of the fun,' he replied.

Sharp tridents and burning whips forced us onto the raft. Fifty souls on something the size of a large dining table. There was a scramble to get to the relative safety of the middle. Two souls fell into the stinking brown sea and sank, their anguished cries choking on the swallowed ordure.

'Don't worry, they'll wash up in time,' laughed one devil. 'Nothing wasted here – everything gets recycled.'

And so for an hour we fought, scratching, punching, biting each other in a desperate struggle to stay on the raft. Eyes gouged, hair pulled out in handfuls. I fought as hard as anyone. I was younger, fitter than the rest, and I stayed at the centre. Throughout, Scrote held fast to my leg, as immovable as a bloodstain.

It didn't take a genius to work out that this was some kind of a lesson. Or a warning. We were all on our own. We could find no help, no solace, in our companions in Hell.

Some writer once said that Hell is other people. Well that isn't quite right, apart from Man United fans. On the whole, other people are quite nice really. Hell is only other people when people stop being *people* at all, when the ties that bind us together become weaker than the forces that tear us apart. Then other people become just things that get in our way – vague shapes that move but have no inner life. And so it becomes all right to use them to give you pleasure, or to shield you from pain – or, in this instance, to throw them into a sea of boiling shite.

And so, a writhing mass of hating, ruined humanity wafted by the wings of demons, we passed over to the Islets of Langerhans, there to spend eternity in torment.

Bummer.

Chapter 9
My New Home

Our little raft with its cargo of poo-soaked, dull-eyed zombies finally drifted ashore on the black sand of our desolate devils' island. It looked like a huge lump of jagged coal. I couldn't see any sign of vegetation: just the harsh black rock floating in the sea of shit beneath a purple sky. Steam or smoke poured from the centre of the island, flowing down its sides like dry ice.

Clarence fluttered down, like a huge moth engendered by the sleep of reason, and led me away with half-hearted prods from his little trident. Scrote followed. Even he looked cowed, his customary air of belligerence replaced by a sullen resignation.

'Rubbish,' he muttered. I couldn't disagree.

'Your place should be ready,' Clarence crooned. 'I hope you like it. You'll certainly appreciate all the effort we've put into it.'

Black sand became black rock and I saw that the island was honeycombed with caves. The damned, it seemed, like rabbits, hobbits and *Homo Neanderthalis*, lived in holes in the ground. Pale, anguished faces peered out at the new-comers. Were they afraid that we had come to evict them? Or that we hadn't?

It was unbearably hot and I was covered in crap. The ocean slime had worked its way into my pores, into my mouth and eyes and ears and for the first time ever in my life I actually wanted to have a bath. I tried for a bit of

no-nonsense, stand-up-for-yourself, take-no-bullshit postur-
ing, but as usual it came out as a whinge:

'I thought you said you preferred torment to torture. This
place feels like proper old-fashioned Hell to me. I stink and I
hurt. I thought you were going to be all enlightened with me?
I thought I was just going to have the mental stuff – you
know, anguish and all that? People have rights, you know.'

'My friend,' began the stumpy be-tighted one, 'perhaps the
time will come when you will get the chance to pay a visit to
one of the less enlightened regions of Hell. Coach trips can be
arranged . . . Then, I think, you might look a little more
fondly on these gentle rocks, on that fragrant sea and on
these lovely skies. But anyway, we're nearly home, and I think
you'll find it interesting.'

I soon realized that my new home was going to be in one of
the caves. Would it be cold and damp, filled with creepy
crawlies and torture stuff – you know, like racks and thumb-
screws? Or was it going to be a furnace, where I would be left
to cook until I was done in about nine million years' time,
and then cooked some more? Could hardly wait.

Actually, both were off beam. I had underestimated the
cunning of these devils.

We shuffled into the mouth of what was evidently 'my'
cave. It was pitch black inside, but Clarence felt along the
wall until he found, to my surprise, a light switch. The single,
naked, forty-watt bulb cast its glum little light on a green
wooden door, evidently separating the inner from the outer
parts of the cave.

'Go on in,' said Clarence, acting for all the world like an
estate agent showing a property to a reluctant punter. 'It's not
locked.'

I pushed the door, still wondering what was waiting for
me. Freezing or boiling? Hanging or crushing? Red-hot

pincers tearing at my flesh, or leeches, giant fleas and lice feeding on me?

No.

It was books.

Books everywhere.

The walls were lined from floor to ceiling with leather-bound volumes. More lay in piles on the floor. There was a huge old desk in one corner; a popping gas fire; a couple of lamps; a saggy sofa; and an armchair that looked like my granny asleep. On a table near the armchair there was an old-fashioned radio with a big, dimly glowing dial and, ominously, just one knob. It looked like it must have weighed as much as a pregnant hippo. The floor had some sort of hard plasticky covering that, from somewhere deep in my psyche, I knew must be lino. Perhaps once it was white, perhaps yellow. Now it was brown as a tramp's underpants. There was a faint sickly smell from the room. The same part of me that knew what lino was told me that the smell was a mixture of talcum powder and old lady. The sly bastards.

'What's going on?' I asked Clarence.

'I'm very proud of this,' he grinned. 'You can probably work out the thinking behind it.'

'Tell me,' I said, but the rough outline of the horror had already formed in my mind.

'Well, what do you like?' he said, getting ready to count things off with his fingers. 'You like loud pop music, comics, violent films, video games. What do you *hate*? Peace, quiet, Radio Four, classical music, reading, high culture, middle culture, any culture a millimetre above low culture; stuffiness. What do you fear most? Boredom. Here, my friend Conor, you will find a boredom so acute, so penetrating, so all-encompassing that it will torment you beyond endurance.'

Scrote yawned, pissed on the granny-armchair, turned round one-and-a-half times and went to sleep.

So this was it. An eternity of tedium.

Bad, I thought, but could be worse.

Chapter 10
Cosy?

'So,' said a smug-looking Clarence, 'what do you think? Cosy, isn't it?'

'Mmm,' was all I could manage. The awful tedium and torpor of the place had already saturated my bones, like radiation.

Clarence was clearly pleased with the effect.

'You may have noticed that we've turned down the background pain levels a touch. We find that too much explicit agony can take the client's mind off the boredom.'

It was true. A drowsy numbness had taken the place of the pain. I still hurt all over, but now it was more like the day after a really tough football match than the full-body toothache I'd had up to now.

'Thanks,' I murmured.

'Oh, you're more than welcome.'

'By the way, what's with the "client"? I thought I was a customer.'

'Oh, yes. New directive. Just came through. You're all clients now. Suggests a more professional, rather than narrowly commercial, relationship.'

'How reassuring.'

'You'll also note,' said Clarence, continuing his estate agent tour of the property, 'that there isn't a bedroom. Sleep, even a sleep filled with our best quality nightmares, might be too much of a relief from the dullness of your days. We might allow you the odd nap in the armchair, perhaps let you imagine for a few moments that you are back on Earth, with all life going on, its joy, its ecstasy, its intensity, and you part of it. But then we'll jerk you back and all you'll have gained is dribble on your chin and a new edge to your misery.

'Well, I'll leave you to settle in. I've got a devilish amount of paperwork to do – you wouldn't believe the forms I've got to fill in. One day we'll get a decent computerized filing system, but for now it's all manual and the clerical support is next door to useless – they're all either young bimbos, straight out of devil school, without the faintest idea about spelling or arithmetic, heads full of pop music and fashion, or ancient crones, gone-in-the-head dodderers and dullards. Mind you, I don't know what the Administration expects, given the wages and conditions. See you later on, perhaps, for tea.'

With that he fluttered away, squeezing under the space below the door, like a tea tray or playing card. But he caught the leg of his tights on a splinter, causing a lovely long ladder. That was the best thing that had happened since I died.

I began to explore the room. My first impression of over-whelming stuffiness was confirmed, in the way that hitting the ground confirms your opinion that you might have fallen off your bike. There was nothing here that could offer any amusement, diversion or entertainment to a sixteen-year-old boy. The room was a distillation of millions of old people's homes; of fusty academic dens; of beardy pipe smokers (or smikepopers as I always, for no good reason, want to call them); of overheard conversations beginning 'and ninthly'; of Open University programmes on Euclid; of all things old and dull and dead, and dull and dead, and dead and dull.

I looked through the books. There were books in Greek, in Latin, in Sanskrit, in languages I'd never heard of. There were treatises on dead poets, dead philosophers and dead civilizations; anatomies of melancholy; textbooks of knitting.

There were shelves full of histories of times and places I didn't care about. My eye was caught by one book, some loser's PhD thesis, by the look of it, on beauty. I thought it might have some good pictures in it but it turned out to be about statues and paintings and art, and all written in the usual academic gibberish that I knew too well from listening to my dad.

Above all there were works on and of religion: volume after volume detailing doctrinal differences in the Byzantine Church. Was Jesus a man or a god, or both? If both, how much man and how much god? Was he a god made temporarily into a man, and then back into a god? Or a man temporarily suffused with godliness? There were books by and about St Augustine, Thomas Aquinas, Martin Luther, John Calvin. To my surprise, I found two shelves filled with different translations of the Bible; but all of them were unreadable: awful modern hippie bullshit, or full of impossible words and old-fashioned talk.

There were a few other surprises for me. Every now and then I'd open a book and something nasty would happen: a hand would come out and slap me hard across the face; or a foul smell would rush out, engulfing me in a stinky cloud; or I'd find a photograph, or a short video clip, taking me back to some acutely embarrassing moment from my life – the time I wet my pants on the football field at junior school, or the night my parents called me and my sister down from bed to meet some friends they had round to dinner, and after we said hello and answered the usual questions (How old are you now? How are you getting on at school? Would you like to join me and my wife on the yacht for an orgy?) I looked down to see my willy hanging *completely outside my pyjamas*, like a day-old bluetit fallen from the nest.

Even worse than the books was the music. The radio had only one station. It played a mixture of classical music, from the lute twiddlings of Fernando de Poncey (OK, not a real composer, just one I made up to stand for everything with a folderol, a hey-ninny, or a sackbut in it), to the thundering modern awfulness of Otto Shitehausen, and earnest documentaries about European Culture in the Age of Enlightenment, or James Joyce's use of the apostrophe (I could certainly tell him where to stick it).

This was very bad. There is a special kind of yawn that begins somewhere around your knees, gathers momentum as it travels up through your goolies, rattles through your guts, possibly picking up a comet's tail of wind, before exploding out of your mouth and nose with a noise like a million wildebeest gnuing. In my life on earth I had reserved that yawn for very special occasions: the night Dad took us all to Opera North in Leeds to see *Ariadne auf Naxos* – yes, the name is branded by the hot iron of excruciating boredom on my brain; visits to Granny Elseworth, Mum's mum, who'd give me and Cathy a boiled sweet out of a moist paper bag – a boiled sweet that we somehow knew had been sucked by Granny and then put back in the bag; the car journey up to the Holyhead ferry on our annual holiday to Ireland – six hours in a car with no radio, listening to my dad sing crappy made-up songs while my mum smoked and hit us; maths lessons; Sundays. Well, now everything was all of those, and worse.

So all this I discovered in the time that Clarence was away. But one thing further I discovered, something entirely unexpected.

Hope.

Chapter II
The Carnal

I don't know how long I spent moving among the books and the dust and the dull radio waves. Not because I didn't have an idea about the time. Quite the opposite: I had too many ideas about time. There were four clocks in the room. One – a huge, malignant old grandfather clock – did not, if you went by the cobwebbed hands stuck perpetually at a quarter to three, appear to be working. But it still managed to tut at me with a severe and disapproving tick. Another, above the fireplace, went backwards. The third looked like it might be more sensible until I realized that the hour, minute and second hands all went round at the same speed. The fourth was the strangest of all – too weird to describe. All I can say is that instead of time going forwards, or even backwards, both of which would have been comprehensible, this clock time went *sideways*. So the best I can do is to say that I was there for *a while*, my flesh turning slowly to stone with the tedium of it all, like a prince in the world's most boring fairytale.

Sometimes I'd find myself reading the books: strange and yet drab works on Hell's geography and cosmology by people with names like Antonio Manetti (1423–1497, as if you care), and Alessandro Vellutello.

I did almost become interested in one tome, grandly entitled *The Infernal Encyclopaedia* (eleventh edition), (University of Golgotha Press, 1963). This, it turned out, was the latest edition of the standard reference work down here.

Clarence tells me they've been promising a CD-ROM version for ages now, with on-line links to the internet, but it's all bollocks – we'll come onto the pathetic state of communications and IT in this shithole in due course. The book was over a metre tall and as thick as a Manchester United supporter, and it emanated a fusty evil. It was from *The Infernal Encyclopaedia* that I learned about the theory underlying the practice of Hell.

First a bit of physics. What was there before the Big Bang (or 'the Creation' in God-squad language)? Not quite nothing. Not quite something. The same stuff, in fact, that you get inside a black hole. As Stephen Hawking discovered, the formation of a black hole is much like the creation of the universe, but run backwards. With a black hole you get a massive body collapsing in on itself, taking everything else within reach along with it. What you end up with is a state of 'singularity'. No time, no space, just a dense ball of what? – stuff? Sorry, this is all Hebrew to me. Well anyway, the creation of the universe happened when one of those singularities exploded out to form the discrete and organized matter of the universe. Yep, yer basic Big Bang. Turns out the Big Bang theory was right. Also turns out that someone pulled the trigger.

Back to Hell. Hell is that singularity in the heart of a black hole and before the creation of anything. Hell contains everything that ever was or could have been, but all squashed and warped and twisted. Everything is possible in Hell. Time and space exist only as endless possibilities for inflicting pain. The space of Hell bends in on itself, curving, twisting back, threading itself into a knot. The space of Hell is the space of pure thought. Moving through Hell is like moving through a dream. Sometimes it's like dragging yourself through treacle; sometimes racing across voids at the speed of light. Time follows the twists of space, and so you can seem to have experienced years, only to find yourself back at a point before you began. But it has a logic. Hell is the most complicated equation you've ever seen; there aren't enough chalkboards in the universe to chalk it on.

I tell you all this to help you to understand my world. Everything that follows is my nightmare and, like all nightmares, it's true.

So, by Hell's standards, *The Infernal Encyclopaedia* was quite interesting, but only in as much as it made me even more depressed about the hole I was in.

To escape from the general crapness of the reading material, I'd simply stare into space, the monotony humming in my ears like one of those blue electric fly-killers. But soon, without the giddy distraction of the books, the radio would come into focus and I'd have to listen to some twat telling me, with fascinating excerpts from the great recordings, about Claudio Monteverdi's *L'Orfeo*, which, believe me, was as deadly as it sounds. Boring, yes, but solely on account of what followed, and in spite of the way it was all to end, bathed in a pale reflected beauty and wonder.

You see, it was as the tooting and luting of Monteverdi came to a close that She came to me.

In that moment of partial relief, just as the Monteverdi had dribbled to its thrilling climax and before the bossy woman who was going to tell me all about the tempera technique of Sandro Botticelli (tempera, as far as I was able to make out, was some kind of paint made out of scrambled eggs) had done more than clear her throat, the air began to shimmer and take on a heavy, liquid quality like a supernaturally clear shampoo, or vodka left to chill into viscosity in the freezer. I guessed that this heralded the arrival of more pain, of some new horror or some yet higher, more exquisite level of boredom – a Premiership

52

boredom complete with sponsorship deals and executive boxes.

And then the heavy water of my apparition seemed to take on the shape of a girl – or no, not a girl, a *woman*, a proper *woman*. Colour came into her parts, first to her hair: a dark-glowing, glorious red, curling, curving, carving the air about her shoulders. Then to her eyes, green and grey; and then to her skin, pale, pure; and then to her lips, a gaudier, bloodier red than her hair.

She was lovely.

And she was naked.

Well, nearly: naked but for a filmy, gauzy scarf flowing from her thin pale neck to her fragile ankles. I wanted to say something beautiful to match her beauty.

What I said was: 'Corrrrrr.'

I've always loved the way that girls look and smell and walk and smile. People sometimes say that girls are just as disgusting as boys, just as violent, dirty, selfish and greedy. Part of me knows that to be true. Women can be vulgar. They swear, drink, flirt, shag, gorge themselves on fatty food and then jag their fingers down their throats until they spew. They hack up green sputum; they fart, shit, piss. Part of me knows this. And part of me denies it absolutely.

But whatever dreams of beauty I've clung to, whatever illusions, fantasies, lies I have entertained, none could match this woman with me now, floating like the body of a drowned angel in my tiny corner of Hell. Although she was – but for that tantalizing scarf – naked, and I could see (and then not see) her breasts, her thighs, her *everything*, I could not feel desire. This opalescent, evanescent, deliquescent (I'm sorry, but *you* try to find words) being was above any base craving of the flesh. And yet I wanted to touch her, to take her in my arms and . . . what? Smooth away my pain with her beauty, and make her beauty real with my pain. There is a name for this, for the way I felt, an absurd, hopeless name, especially absurd and hopeless given the fact that I named it thus after exactly four seconds. The name is love.

She spoke to me. But how was this speech? This was the aural equivalent of that time in the evening when you've had a couple of swigs of sweet cider in the park and your friends are there and the world is at your feet, and everyone is beautiful and everything is possible. It only lasts for a few moments and you spend the rest of the evening and, I suppose, the rest of your life chasing it, but it sure as Hell makes sense of alcohol for those few moments.

But my lady.

Her voice.

Just a murmur in the air-like-water, just a sigh sending shudders of pleasure through my corpse, like a wind in the trees, like a ghost in a churchyard.

'Conor.'

How could my name sound so magical, so saturated with beauty?

'Who are you?' I stammered. 'What do you want?'

Next to her sublime cello, my voice sounded in my ears like a duck playing a tuba.

'My name is Francesca. I have come to you because, like me, you are an innocent among the guilty. You are a child, and you have been punished as if you were a man. I am here to help you.'

I wasn't entirely sure if I agreed with this 'child' business, but these were the first kind words, the first words not filled with hate, spite, malice, sarcasm or contempt I'd heard since I'd come to Hell.

'But how can you help me? This is Hell. I'm here for ever. This place has been designed specially for me, designed to cause maximum misery. I am beyond help.'

Despite these words, I could not help but feel the stirrings of hope inside me. The presence alone of beauty was enough to make Hell seem less nightmarish, or my nightmare less hellish.

'There is a way, and in your heart you know it. Tell me, Conor, are all people alike in what they love, in what they hate? In what moves them, in what leaves them cold? In whom they desire, in whom they shun?'

'No,' I said. 'I suppose we're all different.'

'And is not this place of torment made up of many chambers, each moulded by the particular fears of those who must dwell here?'

'Yes, it seems to be.'

She smiles a smile of impossible sadness and infinite mercy, and for a nanosecond the gauzy stuff drifts away from her breast, giving a tantalizing glimpse of exquisite pink. I almost black out.

'Is it not then possible that one soul's Hell might be another's Heaven?'

Too much beauty. I couldn't think. She was saying something important, but what? And then it hit me like a punch in the guts. The implications were astounding. People were different. Punishment to fit the criminal, not the crime. Could it be that in the vast expanse of Hell, somewhere in this land of terror and pain, there might be a place designed for another's torment that, by some miracle, might give *me* an eternity of bliss or contentment or, at the very least, *unpain*?

It was impossible, but somehow likely. I fell to my knees and tried to take one of her feet in my hands to kiss. But she was becoming insubstantial once more. It seemed almost as if she were being pulled away by some terrible wind. Her voice spoke to me, but now from a distance of miles, or millennia:

'I will come again, when you most need me. Call out my

name three times, and think of beauty. But I warn you, I can only come to you twice more.'

And she was gone, blown away like a leaf in a storm, leaving behind a faint smell of burnt rose petals.

Chapter 12
Some Lessons

And as she left so the horror and pain and misery came back redoubled. I had been given a glimpse of something wonderful (and I don't just mean that flash of tit) but then that wonder had been whipped away, like a bully stealing a kid's ice cream. Could this be another of the sophisticated torments Clarence was always droning on about, just a way to make me feel even worse? Or could it really be that Hell, though brutal, had its own flaws, its own inefficiencies and screw-ups? Could there be a way out to something better? And if so, how in Hell could I find it? I'd inherited my dad's sense of direction, and he needed a compass to go for a shit.

Before I had time to think through these questions – questions, in any case, well beyond the reach of some poor schmuck like me, someone normally preoccupied with nothing more taxing than deciding which finger to pick my nose with – Clarence came in through the keyhole, flowing like red mercury. Cool trick, I thought, despite myself.

'Only me, panic not,' said Clarence in a strangulated voice as he pulled himself back into shape. 'Time for tea, I think. What's that foul smell? Never mind, you must be famished. I think you'll appreciate where we're going.'

'What makes you think that?' I replied sulkily. 'I haven't appreciated much else about Hell. Hell's crap.'

'Rubbish,' said Scrote in gruff agreement.

Before I go any further I should explain Scrote. I'd guess that you're quite interested in the idea of a talking dog. You probably have a dog of your own: a cute Sheltie, all doe-eyed love and innocence; or a bonny Highland terrier, keen as mustard in his little tartan jacket; or a clever rollover-sit-liedown-playdead-fetchthestick mongrel. Even when he was alive Scrote wasn't like that. He wasn't a people-dog. He was a dog's dog: a fighting, shagging, bum-licking, postman-biting, in-yer-face, piss-on-yer-leg, all-night-barking, vomit-eating, bike-chasing, bad-breathed, flea-bitten bag of menace.

There was only one command that he responded to and that was: 'Kill'.

And as a dead dog? A dead dog with the power of speech? Were there wonders to report? New perspectives on people and their pets? Challenging new insights into language, perception, and the eternal dichotomy between nature and culture? Would Scrote turn out to be some kind of noble savage, unlettered but pure of heart, his innocent eye seeing more clearly and farther than his decadent master?

Er, no.

That first speech was a one-off. He must have been coached by Clarence. He never again reached that pitch of eloquence. It turned out that Scrote had a vocabulary of eight words: dinner, bum, shag, rubbish, nice, piss, shit, bite. Generally he would utter just one at a time, but occasionally he would string two together into a sort of sentence: Bum nice! Dinner rubbish! But I never heard him manage a three-worder. Still, there were kids at my school that couldn't do that.

'Oh! I'm disappointed,' said Clarence, in response to my 'crap' and Scrote's 'rubbish'. 'Surely at least part of you can see how well run everything is down here? Our efficiency has increased by two hundred and twenty per cent since the last round of reforms. We do more work with fewer staff. Full automation and full computerization are just around the corner.'

At this the little devil seemed to falter. From the beginning I'd got the impression that he was speaking less to me than to some other listener. What might automation and computerization mean for him? I thought. What do they do with unemployed imps down here? I didn't imagine that they had much in the way of a social security safety net.

But with these thoughts still forming, Clarence bustled me out through the door and on into the perpetual dull-red gloom of the hellish day. Scrote scratched and whimpered for a walk. I had no sympathy to spare, but Clarence let him come along.

'So what's this place you're taking me to?' I asked. 'What kind of food do they have?'

I was, as Clarence had reminded me, starving. I could feel the skin tight about my ribs. My stomach was writhing and clamouring like a junkie doing cold turkey. Bugger, why did I have to think of cold turkey? Oh for a sandwich. Oh for the turkey curry four days after Christmas; oh for the bloated beauty of a gut full of food and a crap film on the telly. I was on the verge of an embarrassing blub.

As I was thinking about the food I tripped over something on the rocky ground. Looking down, I saw to my amazement that it wasn't just another big stone. There were two heads, one behind the other, their bodies buried beneath them. It took me a couple of seconds to work out what they were doing.

My God it was sick.

The one behind had chewed away the back of the skull from the one in front and was tearing ravenously at the bared brain.

'What the fff—?' I stammered, gagging at the sight. The chewer rolled his terrible eyes towards me. Blood and brains dribbled from his mouth and his tongue played across his lips. He spat a ragged gobbet of brain matter at me, and laughed.

'Shag off, boy, or you're next.'

I was getting over my horror.

'You can spit, but it looks to me like you can't run,' I said, kicking dirt into the champing, ravening face. 'I see your diet hasn't made you any brainier.'

Scrote, padding along behind me, raised a casual leg and sprayed a golden shower on the two heads. He narrowly missed having his gristly knob chewed by the biter.

'Good lad, good lad. You're coming on nicely,' said Clarence indulgently, whether to me or to Scrote I wasn't sure.

'What do you mean?'

'Well, we can't be everywhere, you know. There's only so much tormenting that any one devil can do in a day. That means that if the job's going to be done properly, without leaving long gaps in between appointments, we have to fall back on care in the community. We rely on the punters . . . er, clients . . . to torment each other. We find it works very well.'

I should have learned that lesson on the pitiless raft across the poo-sea. When it comes to inflicting misery on the human race nothing comes close to other people. I don't just mean Belsen and Bosnia – I mean my sister. So I resolved to try to be nice to the hopeless and the feckless here in Hell. But how many times had I resolved to be nice to Cathy? Well, not that often. We walked on.

'Who were those two?' I asked. 'I seem to have gotten off lightly compared to them. They must have been really bad.'

'Not feeling *pity*, are you, Conor? We don't want you to feel *pity*. Sympathy, as you know, involves putting yourself into someone else's boots. If that's what you want, we can arrange it.'

There were times when Clarence seemed more than a touch sinister.

'Pity? No! Getting their just desserts, I imagine. But what did they do?'

'One was the head of a privatized industry. The other was the minister in charge of the privatization. I'll leave you to figure out which was which. They both did rather well out of it at the time.'

'I'm struggling to get a grip on what goes on here. I mean, I take what that judge bloke was saying about the bad things I did. I was a shit, I grant you that. But I was only being normal. Everyone tells lies and takes the piss. How come I get all this hassle?'

'What makes you think you're so special? How do you know everyone doesn't end up down here, except for a few boring saints and the odd eunuch?'

'But that can't be right. What was God playing at if zillions of ordinary people go to Hell? Where's His sense of fairness?'

'Well, think about life in general. You know, the bit before death. Didn't you find that the worst things always happened to the best people? Didn't the wicked always seem to prosper? Aren't there wars, famines, plagues, where millions of 'innocent' – quaint concept – people die? If the Old Boy really cared about people, wouldn't He put a stop to all that? No, God got fed up with the human race a long time ago. Rumour has it that He's given it another go in one of those countless parallel universes we hear about. Apparently the new lot are much better. Their version of Hell is almost empty – nothing for the staff to do but play bridge and fork each other with their tridents.

'It's all down to free will. Humans are able to choose between good and evil. God gave you the opportunity to be sinners or saints, and most of you, as we could have told Him, chose party-time. Well, God learned His lesson and the new lot don't have a choice. Takes some of the fun out of it, if you ask me. Makes you wonder why He bothered. Bit of an ego trip, I reckon. Must be nice to be worshipped.'

'Wait a second.' I was bloody annoyed. 'This is bollocks – you told me earlier that it was all predestined. You said there was no such thing as free will. You said it was all planned. You said free will was all rubbish. You're a liar!'

'Just four points,' replied Clarence. 'Firstly, for that little bout of impertinence I'm afraid we'll have to impose a correspondingly small penalty.' He clicked his fingers and from nowhere two Bruisers appeared, breathing their dog's breath all over me.

'Just hold him over here, please, if you would,' he said, pointing to a miniature volcano, about a metre in height. It was topped by a dustbin lid which Clarence flicked off with his trident, releasing a blast of pent-up superheated air and pumice.

The sniggering Bruisers unceremoniously grabbed my ankles, yanked me upside-down (in the process bashing my head on the volcano's rim) and dangled me above the bubbling molten lava within the crater. It wasn't going to be the last time that I was held to dangle above a Bad Thing. But we'll get to that when we get to that. For now, I felt and smelled my hair sizzle.

'Secondly, you have to get used to the occasional fib in Hell. Of course I'm a liar – what do you think I am here for?

'Thirdly, we *can* reconcile freedom and predetermination. It's all to do with chaos theory. Or the other one – what-do-you-call-it . . . *complexity*. Surely you've heard of *them*?'

Holding a civil conversation is tricky when each breath scorches your lungs and the red fire of Hell burns brightly through your eyelids. But I did my best.

'Ah, well, they sort of ring a bell. Something to do with a butterfly breaking wind in China causing a hurricane in Florida? They must have got that idea from Phil Gilroy. But I don't see what it can have to do with people going to Hell.'

'It's quite simple. It follows from the fact that on the one side you can get really complicated structures from just a few basic rules: a sort of limitless variety out of initial simplicity kind of thing. And then from the other end, you find that totally random, or random-seeming, events you might think ought to result in chaos and mayhem, produce beautiful big patterns that let you make predictions. At least if you have a powerful enough computer.'

'If it's all random, how come you get these patterns?'

'Good question. It's because of what are called . . . if I could remember . . . that's it, "strange attractors". These are mysterious forces that pull chaotic systems in certain directions. Evil, of course, is the ultimate strange attractor. Add evil, the joy, the allure, the power of evil, into that chaotic system you call life, and the outcome is all too simple to predict. Surely now you get it. What looks like randomness – no, what is, in fact, random, still conforms to certain laws. People are free, but they always end up doing the same sorts of things. We just wait here for you all to drop in. That's all perfectly clear, I take it?' he concluded, seeming rather proud of his performance.

'No . . . er . . . yes,' I corrected myself in the hope it might mean that I got out of the volcano before my head was baked like a pie.

'Good, good, good. That's enough, thanks, Boris and, er, Bradley.'

I was dragged out of the volcano and left gasping on the ground. B & B waited for a few moments in the hope of a tip and then trudged off gracelessly.

'Shake a leg,' said Clarence. 'Don't want to miss tea.'

What Clarence had said did make a *kind* of sense. But as we walked (my head gently steaming), an objection occurred to me.

'But what about temptation, Clarence? Don't you lot – you, Satan and that – go up into the world to lead us to evil? Aren't we bad because you make us bad?'

'Oh come on, Conor, my young friend. Do you blame the apple tree for giving forth fruit rather than the boy for stealing it? Would you want a world without nice things, just to keep you away from temptation?'

I wasn't entirely convinced by that one, but I couldn't think of a decent answer. We were walking along a narrow path, climbing ever upwards towards the centre of the island. The ground was still black and rocky, acned with more of the baby volcanos, and my legs were cut and torn from my frequent stumbles.

'What about fourthly?' I asked after a while, stupidly.

'Oh yes, fourthly,' smiled Clarence, and in a blink the long leather whip was in his hand. Flourishing it in the air, like a circus ringmaster, he brought it down with a crack across my back.

'OUCH!' I yelped. 'What was that for? I've already had my head boiled.'

'Ah yes, sorry. But you see punishment here is always capricious. There'll be things we let you get away with, and things we punish you for twice. And,' he whispered, 'we *are* monitored, you know. That's why I had to play about with the whip first – putting on a show. It can't have hurt that much. Anyway, this isn't supposed to be enjoyable.' And then, again in a whisper, he added another 'sorry'.

By now we were approaching the top of the mountainous ridge that formed the island's backbone. 'My' side of the island was for the most part lonely and desolate – the damned lived in burrows, largely isolated from each other, each person left to wallow in a very private misery. I supposed that this was because we had been crowd-lovers, chatterers, gang members, gregarious people-junkies. I assumed that the other

64

side of the island would be the same, but perhaps not quite as nice as my side – funny how we get possessive about the strangest things.

I assumed wrong.

Breasting the ridge my eyes fell upon an astonishing sight. What I had thought of as the dark side of the island was a big, bustling metropolis, teeming with the damned and their devils. Although we were still far away, I could see everything with a supernatural clarity.

All was motion: hectic, ceaseless motion. It was like the squirming of billions of bacteria, caught under a gigantic microscope. It was Tokyo, Mexico City, Cairo and Calcutta all crushed together and dumped on a volcanic island. Looking down from the ridge, I could see no pattern or structure to the streets or work out any logic to the buildings. Filthy tenements coiled around the knees of gleaming tower blocks; black factories belched out blacker smoke and a stench like burning hair. Oh. Sorry. That was *my* hair. Groups of people were harnessed together to pull huge loads as devils whipped and goaded them. Other people carried devils on their naked backs, the devils' claws digging into their sides.

The city was surrounded by an octagonal wall with a tall tower at each corner. Squat, evil-looking devils patrolled the wall, facing not outwards but in, towards the city. I saw one devil hurl a boulder at one of the souls who had strayed too close to the wall. The rock crushed and pinned him to the ground. Only his arms and legs stuck out from under the rock, and these twitched, roachlike. A low murmurous wail came up from the city, like the wave of stink you get when a tramp sits next to you.

'Nice place,' I said.

'Mm,' replied Clarence. 'Some people think it takes a bit of getting used to. A lot of my colleagues commute in from the country, but I like the bustle of the city – there's always

65

something going on: a new play, or a concert, or a disembowelling. After we've been to the Valhalla, I need to pop into the office – you're welcome to come along.'

Chapter 13
Teatime at the Valhalla Café

We trudged down towards the city, Scrote pausing to piss on anything bigger than a pebble. That was until one tree stump opened a mouth full of jagged teeth and snapped at his exposed undercarriage. Scrote managed to leap away, saving his 'nads but losing his dignity. From then on, after two assaults on his doghood, he did the canine equivalent of crossing his legs. But then I remembered something that my dad had told me. He said that when a dog had a slash it wasn't just relieving itself but taking part in a chemical conversation, full of nuance and complexity. A sort of peemail. That had been his idea of a joke.

We came up to a huge iron portcullis. From close up the walls seemed to reach for miles into the sky. A heavily fanged devil carrying a trident, a whip and a bazooka skulked behind the gate and bellowed out, 'Who the shag goes there, damned or devil?'

'Relax, Draghignazzo, it's only Clarence Slawkenbergius here with my new boy. I'm taking him to lunch at the Valhalla.'

He took out a plastic photo ID card, slipped it into a slot by the gateway and the portcullis rose creakily. We entered.

Up close, I found the horror and turmoil of the place multiplied a thousandfold. The souls here had no peace. They were hounded and driven through the streets in a manic frenzy. Any that paused for a moment were instantly set upon by devils more hideous and savage than any I had yet encountered. I shrank back against the wall and Clarence noticed my dismay.

'Yes, marvellous, aren't they, in their own fashion? I told you about the Bruisers earlier on, didn't I? Generally a shoddy lot, but these are an elite within their ranks. They're the Malebranche. It means the evil claws, or something. To be honest, they scare the heck out of me. No manners, either. But it's time we ate. Onwards to the Valhalla.'

We forced our way through the crowds, Clarence leading. The dead souls parted before him, cowering back, intimidated by his devilish mien. Scrote and I followed in his wake, surfing the wave of panic. I found myself kicking bodies aside as I tried to keep up with Clarence. Scrote did his bit by snarling and biting at anyone who came too close. The dead snarled and spat back, but they dared not touch us.

After an age in the chaos of the main streets, Clarence led us down a quieter back alley. It had grown dark and a creeping menace replaced the sound and fury of moments before. I had the impression that weird creatures with slithery shapes were moving in the shadows, watching us, licking their lips. Famished souls of the damned? New demons come to torment us?

A winking neon sign in front of us read:

The V lh l a C fé

A faint sound of screeching seeped from the doorway below it. We entered. It was rather nice.

The place was a perfectly normal-looking tea shop, complete with checked tablecloths and little vases of wilting flowers on the tables. The awful screeching sound turned out to be a string quartet playing a folderol by de Poncey. The odd thing was the people playing the instruments: four burly, bearded men in ludicrous Viking costumes, complete with the horned helmets that every school kid knows were never worn by *real* Vikings.

'Here we are,' said Clarence, rubbing his hands together. 'A little Heaven ... er, I mean *haven* of peace in all this bustle.'

Another bozo in Viking costume came up and asked, 'Table for two?' with a sweet smile. This was all getting very camp. 'But I'm afraid,' he added, 'the hound must stay outside – hygiene regulations.'

The café was about half full. Some devils were there alone, mobile phones placed proudly on the tables before them. Some were accompanied by their charges: grey lost souls like me. There were even a few of the damned alone – some covered in boils, some with a limb or a nose missing; one with a really, *really* bad haircut, like a Teletubby's aerial.

'What is it with the staff all done up like Vikings?' I asked Clarence as we were shown to our table. 'Is this some kind of fancy-dress joint?'

'*Dressed* as Vikings? Oh, I'm afraid they're not just *dressed* as Vikings – they *are* Vikings. You see the musicians? The first violin is Harald Bluetooth – nice record of murder, pillage, rape, sacrilege, neglecting dental hygiene. The viola is Eric Bloodaxe – didn't earn that name by staying at home doing his embroidery. Then there's Harald Hardrada on the cello – it's because of him that Willy the Bastard (a favourite of ours down here, by the way) did so well in 1066. And finally, on second violin, Olaf the Miserable, the one they call No-laugh Olaf in the sagas. You've probably worked out the deal. What do Vikings do? They roam around killing and stealing. Why do they do it? Well, apart from the genuine pleasure that these things can bring – and we certainly wouldn't want to downplay that – they do it because if they die in battle, they get to go to Valhalla. And what is Valhalla like? Feasting, getting pissed, bonking. The life of Riley. I think it was one of our best ideas to put them to work in places like this. Can you imagine the disappointment? The humiliation?' Clarence chuckled to himself maniacally, the little devil.

The quartet had stopped their nurdling. No-laugh Olaf donned a pinny and came over to our table.

'Are you ready to order?' he asked, sounding like he was auditioning for a part in Ibsen's lost masterpiece, *The Depressed Viking*.

'Just the usual for me, No-laugh,' said Clarence. 'And bring us a bottle of the house yellow.'

I got into a fluster – I hadn't even looked at the menu yet. So now I did. It was distinctly odd. It seemed to be a list of animals, some of which I recognized, but most of which were completely strange:

Moa
Dodo
Great Auk
Stella's Sea Cow
Passenger Pigeon
Giant Ground Sloth
Auroch
Thylacine
Khazar

'We've also got some fresh specials on the board,' moaned No-laugh, pointing at a distant wall. 'Bison, Oryx, Orang, Ne-Ne and Blue Whale. Or you can have our top value splatter-platter.'

I wasn't sure what to make of this, but it didn't sound too bad.

'I'll go for the platter. Thanks.'

No-laugh made to leave, but then turned back again with

a grimace: 'You're welcome,' he forced out, between pursed lips.

I asked Clarence to explain the menu.

'They're all extinct, of course, or going that way. Morally culpable or ethnically suspect, or otherwise unfit. I suppose that's why the Big Man got rid of them. Can you think of any other reason? That's why they've ended up down here.'

'So what are we talking about – steaks? Roast moa, whatever a moa is or was?'

'Steaks? No, no. *Products*, certainly. But I don't want to spoil the surprise.'

I didn't really care what it was, so long as it was edible. The awful, gnawing hunger had grown to the point where I would have eaten the tablecloth washed down with the brown water from the dead flowers.

I thought I knew what hunger was like after getting sent to bed without any supper. But this was something special – a man was hammering at my belly with a pickaxe. This was the worst pain I'd yet had in Hell. So much for the refinements of torment over the crude savagery of torture. I think I'd have swapped my hunger for a couple of million years in the lake of fire that burns but does not consume, or whatever.

'So what do you think of it all so far?' asked Clarence, in a pleasant, conversational tone.

What was I supposed to say? – *Oh, having the time of my life. Never been better!*

'Well, it's all quite bad, really. I never thought I'd die. At least not for hundreds of years. I never thought I'd go to Hell. I didn't really believe in Hell. I hardly even believed in Heaven. I remember the priest talking about purgatory, and I thought that if any of it really existed, I'd end up there. But having said all that, it could be worse. I mean it hurts, hurts like Hell, and the place is a mad house, but yes, it could be worse.'

Clarence looked a little disappointed. 'I don't think you've quite come to terms with the eternity business, Con,' he said urgently. 'That's the beauty of it. And that's why, in your case, we've gone for the boredom strategy. It probably hasn't quite kicked in yet. After all, you've had the excitement of arriving here. But wait until you've been here for a hundred thousand years, a million years – and those million years will be as a single second to the whole history of the world. And for all that time you will do nothing but gaze at dusty books, learning things you never wanted to know, listening to music you despise, conversing only with me and with a few listless, tortured souls like yourself. Don't tell me this does not dismay you. And I have to say that notwithstanding its impact on you, the system does have some advantages for us: it makes you a very low-maintenance client. You'll have noticed the mayhem out in the city?'

'Hard to miss.'

'Yes, well, some poor devils have to spend every moment pursuing, goading, gouging, burning, blasting and buggering their charges. Now *that's* a full-time job!'

I nodded sympathetically and said, 'Our Viking friend No-laugh Olaf doesn't exactly hide his misery, does he?'

'Never did. But he's got good reason for it now. You can't imagine how much he suffers. In his last moments on earth he disembowelled a monk and was just about to rape a nun when a big stone crucifix falls on his head. The next thing he knows he's playing second fiddle in a string quartet and waiting tables. Lovely. Pity things don't always work quite so well. There was another client I worked on as an apprentice just before I was assigned to you. Bit of bad luck. He tried to escape. Almost made it. We had to send him to the Annihilator. Hate it when that happens.'

'How do you mean, escape? And what's the Annihilator?'

The very sound of it was like a blade drawn across my throat.

72

'I shouldn't really tell you this, but I've grown fond of you – I feel that we're *mates* as well as having a, er, professional relationship. This chap was a masochist. You wouldn't believe the stuff he used to get up to – nails hammered into all sorts of places, razorblades, welding irons . . .'

'Nowt so queer as folk,' I said in a comical Northern accent.

'Quite. So you see our problem – the usual stuff wouldn't do at all; he lapped it up, yelled for more. So we had him on a pain-inflicting programme. I have to say, I wasn't convinced by it. Too neat. And often these people like dishing it out as much as they like getting it. But it seems that our man really was horribly squeamish. We put him to work at our dentistry practice, but it was there he met the sadist. They got to chatting over the drill. You can imagine the rest. They decided to swap. They were never going to get away with it. I know they were both under the low-maintenance regime but it was sheer folly – right under our noses. We really had to make an example out of them. Yes, the Annihilator.'

He paused and looked around him, holding up his hands. 'You've probably wondered where all the power comes from for the lights, furnaces etc.? No? Well, we haven't got much in the way of natural resources in Hell. Except souls. The soul contains a tremendous, almost incalculable amount of energy. Normally it's trapped in there. That's why souls are immortal – they just don't run down. But some time ago our scientists discovered how to split the soul. Splitting the soul releases all of that energy. Made a terrible mess the first time they did it. Some of the blast leaked through to the earth and blew the top off some mountain. So the difficult thing was harnessing the energy, controlling it, so that it could be put to good use, inflicting pain and torment. Hence the Annihilator. Our top brains worked on it for generations – every other project was put on hold. The economy suffered terribly, I can tell you. But finally it was revealed. The Annihilator of Souls: a vast engine that converts souls into usable energy.'

'And the souls?'

'Oh they're gone. Gone for ever. It's the only way a soul can be destroyed, the one exception to the soul's immortality. Of course such power requires great responsibility. Souls are a finite resource. There are many better things we can do with souls than burn them up for energy. It's against one of the fundamental objectives of our mission plan. Once you've destroyed a soul, it's not there for you to torment. So it's only in very special cases that we annihilate them.'

I thought for a while about annihilation, about the horror of that vast emptiness, about the tragedy of *not being*. It made me feel sick and dizzy.

'I don't know what's worse, being nothing or being tortured for ever.'

'Oh, the torture's much worse – that's the whole reason we are here. I think you keep imagining that being nothing is something you experience as a bad thing. But there is nothing there to have the experience. So it's not like being locked in a black room or buried alive. It's just nothing. If just nothing was enough to scare people, they'd never have needed Hell – death alone would have been sufficient to put the fear of God into you. As I've said before, theology was never my best subject – I was always good at natural history and English – but anyway, some of it went in. *Your* theologians have come up with all kinds of theories about Hell. I was always quite fond of the Ubiquitists, who thought that Hell was everywhere and that we, I mean you, carry your Hell around with you, like a tapeworm. And then there were some who thought you only got punished for a few million years and then you got out – Valentinian and his silly Gnostics and, I think, the Socinians, believed that. But as well as the nature of Hell, people have never managed to agree about the purpose of it. Some people have said that we're here to balance things up after what's gone on down on Earth. I mean, as we discussed earlier, you can hardly claim that the good always prosper, and the wicked lose out on Earth, can you? The opposite, if anything. No, more often than not, the bad guy wins. But we've been through all this.'

'Hang on,' I piped. 'If you're trying to say that you, Hell, are some kind of posthumous system of justice, wouldn't that make you a force for good? You wouldn't be evil at all, any more than any system of justice is evil.'

'Not so fast. I only said that some of your theologians have tried to explain us away like that. I didn't say that it was true. Humans are always trying to find reasons for things. Sometimes a thing doesn't have a reason – it just is. There seems to be something in people that makes them want to read the world as if it was a secret code that they can somehow crack. And they think God is the key. Things happen which seem to have no purpose, and then you invent a god and suddenly it has a purpose. Oh look, here comes dinner.'

True enough, No-laugh Olaf was trudging towards us, a large plate in each hand, an undextrous thumb smearing the gravy. A bottle of something was wedged under his sweaty armpit. I had never been so pleased to see a Viking waiter – my guts were jabbering and wailing by now. My mouth filled with saliva and I couldn't stop it from spilling down my chin.

And then the smell hit.

No-laugh put the plates down before us. I had dreamed, insanely, of choice cuts of prime quagga, succulent and savoury. I should have known better.

It was poo.

I'm not saying it wasn't nicely presented. The chef had clearly gone to enormous lengths to make it a work of art. Was this his punishment? Had some chef-*artiste* been condemned to work his magic with extinct animal turds? I hoped so. There were seven types of crap arranged beautifully on the plate in small, sculpted groups. A runny crap sauce had been drizzled across the whole and painted in a neat scallopy design around the edge. Adding insult to injury, it came with a side order of sprouts.

'Would you like to taste, sir?'

No-laugh was talking to me. I nodded dumbly. He poured a splash of viscous amber fluid into my glass. You can probably guess what the house yellow turned out to be.

Clarence licked his lips.

'*Mmmmmmmmm*, smell that! I know it's boring, but I always order the auk – you can really taste the sea in it.'

Clarence's plate was splattered with white-and-black bird poo reeking of fish. The odd blank, fishy eye returned his avid, monkey gaze.

'What? You like this . . . this . . . *shit*? Are you mad?'

'I was brought up on it. Try some – you never know, you might like it.'

I was torn between my hunger and my revulsion.

I took a forkful.

'Good lad, that's moa – big bird from New Zealand. Hunted to extinction in a few years after the Maoris got there.'

I ate of the moa shite. I found it bad. I ate also of the quagga, of the sea cow, and of the giant ground sloth. I found them all bad. But how did I do it at all? How could I sink so low? I mean, *what could possibly be worse than eating poo*? Only someone who has known the agony of Hell's hunger could answer that. My hunger was just too great. I forced down the first acrid, stinking mouthful, shaking with the horror and degradation of it, but then my eating accelerated until I was cramming the stuff into my mouth as fast as I could. Crap besmeared my face; dung was in my ears; faeces greased my hair like Brylcreem. Yes, I was debased, I was a human dung beetle, but at least I wasn't hungry. For now.

'Did I ever tell you about the great auk?' asked Clarence, politely ignoring the hideous spectacle I presented.

'Nnngh,' I replied, spraying sea cow cack (green and kelpy, the constituency of overboiled spinach).

'Always makes me laugh, the great auk. They used to be quite common. Looked a bit like a penguin. Couldn't fly. Lived on rocks and islands and remote bits of coast up in the northern seas. People used to eat them, and especially their eggs. They used auk oil for lamps and auk feathers for pillows. Loads of uses – sort of a Swiss Army bird. Look, it tells you all about them on the back of the menu. Here we are,' he continued, the text now before him. 'The great auk, or garefowl, *Pinguinus impennis*, mmm . . . extinct around eighteen fifty blah blah blah, often herded into corrals or driven on board for slaughter by sailors, fishermen and sealers who visited the nesting colonies. The feathers were used for bedding, the carcasses for oil and the eggs for food or fish bait. The colonies dwindled rapidly before eighteen hundred and the last two known specimens were captured on Eldey Island off the coast of Iceland on June the fourth, eighteen forty-four. The bit I like though,' he said, looking up at me, 'is that the last colony took refuge on an isolated rock off Iceland. No one could reach them there, and anyway, they were protected by then, so it looked as if they might pull through. And what happens? Go on, guess.'

'Oh, I don't know. The island blows up and they all die,' I tried, at random.

Clarence was crestfallen: his horns drooped like dead flowers. 'Er, yes.' But he soon cheered up at the thought.

'Imagine that. Just blows up. They could have picked any other island, anywhere else in the world, and they wouldn't have become extinct. Priceless. And people say there's no Satan.'

With that he picked up his plate and licked it with relish.

'Time to go,' he said brightly, daintily wiping the shite and slobber from his lips with a napkin. 'On the tab, Olaf,' he called over his shoulder as we left.

We didn't leave a tip.

Back into the streets, back into the rush and horror, back into the purple-orange twilight. Faces contorted with rage and pain pressed against me, screaming silently. One old man, hampered in his movement by a broken foot, its bones and tendons flapping loose, whispered as he passed:

'They lie, they lie. Remember that they lie.'

I had to pull Scrote away from the trail of blood and ragged flesh the man left behind.

'We're just popping into the office, if that's OK,' chirped Clarence. I followed silently through the streets. The buildings looming on either side of us changed as we passed along – from new gleaming towers to ruined, crumbling tenements, to stained concrete.

'Here we are,' said Clarence, suddenly. 'Tie the dog outside, will you? And I should warn you that there's a no smoking policy inside, so if anyone sets fire to you, please leave the building. Only joking.'

Clarence showed his pass to two ugly security guards, sitting chewing squirrels behind a desk. I had to sign in and wear a pass, agonizingly pinned to my nipple, declaring that I was a 'guest', and stating in bold capitals PLEASE KICK.

We took the lift up to the fourth floor. Clarence again had to slide his pass through a reader to get us through another set of doors and into the main office. It was open plan with big windows giving a fantastic view of the city. We walked along through the room to what was labelled as the West Wing. About half a dozen pale wooden desks, each with a computer and a stack of beige folders. Some desks were unnaturally tidy, everything from paperclips to thesaurus squared and regular. Some were hopelessly cluttered, looking like they'd been mounted by a randy tractor, leaving papers scattered and chewed pens strewn about, with rubber bands tangled and matted and spilling like intestines after a battle.

'Hi,' said Clarence generally to the devils two-finger-tapping at their keyboards. Six faces looked up:

'Yo!'

'Hey!'

'Clarey!'

'Wanker!'

'Main man!'

'Hello!'

'Guys and gal, I'd like you to meet my new client, Conor. Conor, this is Col, Nick, Simon, Trixie, Jez and Beelzebub, Lord of the Flies the Third. This is the Ennui Team in Hell Admin HQ, to give us our full title.'

I looked out for the one called Trixie. I hadn't seen any girl devils yet and I wondered what they looked like. The boys were all built on the same plan as Clarence: basically human, with the odd devilish element – horns, sharp pointy teeth, tails. One was bald with a doughnut of sandy hair and a couple of sad strands pasted over the top between his blunt and stumpy horns. He wore a tweed jacket and a frayed polyester and egg-yolk tie. Another was sharply dressed in a shiny suit, no tie, and a buttoned-up purple shirt. His short hair was combed forward and he sported a couple of neat sideburns. One had long, shaggy hair, an open collarless shirt and a woolly waistcoat.

And there, ah, Trixie. Standing up by the photocopier. Not bad. Not bad at all. Tight white blouse. I could see the dark, stabbing nipples though the thin material. Tight, very, very short skirt. Red lips, white teeth, a long, black forked tongue. Two needle-sharp horns and scything black talons. Her tail was coiled around her left leg, teasing her ankle.

'Nick's shagging her, lucky devil,' whispered Clarence in my ear.

The walls and the low dividers between the desks were covered in photocopied cartoons and posters saying things like: '*You don't have to be evil to work here, but it helps*', or '*I love pain – I could sit and watch it all day*'.

After a few seconds of scrutiny, the others lost interest in me. Clarence went to his desk and rummaged about in a drawer. His desk was the most untidy, with papers scrunched up and shoved into every available space. He really didn't have a clue. My mum could have sorted him out. She had a mind so coldly logical and ordered that me and my sister used to go to a pocket calculator for human warmth when we were little.

'Time to go,' called Clarence. 'See you lot later – I'll be in all day tomorrow. Don't do anything I wouldn't do.'

They all shrugged their goodbyes. As we walked away, Trixie called out, 'Oh, Conor,' in a cutie-girlie voice. I turned, surprised that she had spoken to me. As I faced her, I felt, or heard a hiss, and just saw the blur as she flicked her tail towards me. It whipped up between my legs, catching me an agonizing cuff in the bollocks. I fell to my knees, clutching at my throbbing pods. The bitch. The 'gang' all fell about laughing. Clarence seemed rather annoyed.

'No call for that, Trixie – I've got my own programme worked out. I never interfere with your clients.'

'Come on, Clarey, chill out,' she replied, her voice now deep and mellow. 'You know, people have been saying that you're just a little bit too much of a softie for this work. Not going to get ... involved, are you? Not losing your objectivity? The brat was having naughty thoughts.' She turned and faced me. 'Isn't that right, lover-boy?'

I swallowed air like a beached guppy, and blushed.

'And what kind of devil would I be if I let him get away

with that?' She put on a face of angelic innocence, widening her eyes and forming her mouth into a surprised little 'o'.

I had some more naughty thoughts and crawled away towards the lift, out of range of that tail.

Part Two
The Devils

Chapter 14
Everybody Needs a Plan

On the way back home, through the torrent and turmoil of the streets, through the scorched and parched misery of the trek over the mountain, I found a place in which to take refuge: that inglenook of hope, first illumined by the lovely Francesca, but grown now to something greater, something real:

A PLAN

A plan. Everybody needs a plan. I've always thought that what was wrong with most people – my dad, my sister, my friends (but not Mum, who planned everything, thereby giving planning a bad name) – was that they never had a decent plan. People seem to blunder through their lives, never knowing what they want, or where they are going. Fix a goal, work out a route, and you're more than halfway there. Talk to anyone. Ask them what they want. I bet you a million quid that, if they answer at all, rather than staring dumbly at you, blowing spit bubbles, they'll answer vaguely, something about just being happy, or fulfilled. I mean it – go and ask them. I'll wait here for ten minutes.

You back? See, told you. Now ask them, the ones that didn't dribble, how they intend to get it – happiness, fulfilment, whatever. Go on, I'll mind the shop. And, by the way, that's bollocks about the seventeen-point plan to combat global warming, reform the health service and conquer Mars.

You'll have to do better than that to earn your million quid. I'll pay out when I see it on the news. Some people!

That was quick. Didn't have a clue, eh? But I don't mean to look down on the rest of you bumbling, buck-toothed, brainless bozos from a great height. I'm just as bad. The only plan I ever had involved Miranda Prim's knickers, and I never got anywhere near them. Miranda Prim, by the way, went to church three times a week, never missed confession and wanted to marry a martyr. Now that would be a self-fulfilling prophecy. But she was pretty, and the combination of piety and puberty, Mass and mammaries, made her well nigh irresistible, if utterly unattainable.

So, I had a plan now. Far-fetched, odds against – as improbable, futile and doomed, in its own way, as the assault on Miranda's knickers – but a plan, for all that.

A sudden jagging pain pulled me from my reverie.

'Ouch! What was that for?'

Clarence had stuck his trident in my arse, where it remained, quivering. We were almost back at my own private hell-hole.

'Oh, er, umm, sorry,' he stammered. 'But you seemed to be daydreaming – you had a smile on your face. That's not really allowed. This *is* Hell, you know. I'm supposed to make things uncomfortable. At least try to look as if you're having a bad time. I could get into all sorts of trouble if they find out you're not suffering enough. You heard Trixie. I have enemies, you know. And you'd be a lot worse off if they got rid of me. How would you like some Bruiser playing ping-pong with your testicles?'

He put one neatly cloven foot on my left buttock and pulled out the trident from the right. The wicked barbs at the end of the three little prongs meant that, like our local council estate, getting in was a lot easier than getting out. Three ragged, bloody holes were left in my trousers, with strips of my poor bum hanging out like cat tongues. But almost straight away I felt the healing begin.

That's one of the things about Hell. They keep fixing you up so they can keep knocking you down. Something in the air or the water makes the wounds we get seal themselves: the sides of great gashes close together; burns form pink new skin; teeth and limbs re-form, re-grow (though it could take some time, as that bloke we'd seen on the way back from the Valhalla proved). They don't stop hurting, but at least it gives a nice clean canvas for the next artist to work on with tongs and whip.

Home. I was quite pleased to see my burrow again after the stress of the city. But as I closed the door on my cell, and surveyed the gloomy, drab interior and heard the dull voice on the radio talk about some eighteenth-century clergyman who once wrote a book in which the hero only gets born on page nine hundred, I was lost again in the torpid brown everything of death.

Gnu.

So what, you must be wondering (assuming that you've been paying attention), is this great plan? What ingenious scheme has the young maestro cooked up? What complex ruses, double crosses, feints, dummy runs, nutmegs, googlies?

Well, so maybe it's not that great a plan. The two bits – or rather, this being a plan and me being, whether you like it or not, a writer, and having the time to look up the right word, *elements* – were the realization that there might be a place in Hell where I could be comfortable, and the vague feeling that I could find out where that place was – and how to get there – from information in Clarence's office.

OK, so it's not really a plan at all, just a wish list. But wait till you get to Hell. See if you can do any better.

The problem was to get inside that office. I needed

Clarence's pass, and I needed to find my way into the city. Now these things required all my powers of analysis and concentration. But the awful dullness of life back in this grey hole of Calcutta was sapping my horribly limited supplies of both. It would not be much longer, I guessed, before I became indistinguishable from the granny-armchair, caked in cobwebs, rotten, honeycombed, crumbling: like a piece of breakfast-bed toast lost and forgotten down the back of the headboard.

And time, in its bizarre, hellish way, was passing. How long had I been here? What I needed was a clock giving Earth time, not the crazy clocks in my room – the backwards/sideways clocks. Perhaps this was another exquisite form of torture. Have you ever needed to know the time really badly and found that the battery on your watch has gone, and nobody else has a watch, and the town hall clock has been stopped by roosting auks, and the sun's run down and the stars have lost the plot, so there's no way in the universe of telling how late you are, or if you're even late at all? Even when I was alive, I was obsessed with time: where it came from, where it went, why it was sometimes heavy, sometimes light, why when I wanted loads of it, there was never enough, and when I wanted shot of it, it clung like shit on your shoe.

The thing is that I was torn between my psychopathic fear of lateness and a constitutional inability to be on time. If only I could have been laid back about being late, or good at being on time: a chilled dude wandering up half an hour after the appointed time, so loved, so cool that friends actually *enjoyed* the chance to stand around and talk about me. Or if not that, then a Teutonic anal retentive, someone the good burghers of my town could set their carriage clocks by. But no, I had to be a frantic hurrier, always just missing the bus: a sweaty, wild-eyed, gasping buffoon, getting there as everybody else was leaving.

I hated it, but I couldn't get it right. And cursed, boy was

I cursed. The only time public transport ever ran on time was when I had to catch it. Other chronic latecomers would always, by sheer fluke, arrive on time if I was part of the group, showing *me* up as the spoiler. The only time I was ever early, nobody else turned up.

All this made me think of my friends down, or up, or across, on Earth. Were they thinking of me? Did they cry at my funeral? Or did they take the piss because of the mode of my unfortunate but admittedly comic demise?

– 'I bet the angels didn't play trumpets when Conor died – they played *cornets*! D'yer geddit – *cornets*!' HA HA.

– 'Yeah. Poor old Conor, his number was up – *number ninety-nine*! Geddit, like the ice cream?' HA HA HA.

– 'I was really upset when I heard Conor had died – I screamed. Geddit? GEDDIT – *ice-creamed*!' HA HA HA HA.

But I don't mind that stuff so much. What I can't even begin to think about is the effect on Mum, Dad and Cathy.

Dying was the most stupid thing I ever did.

Chapter 15
Hitting the Bottom

You, like me, are probably too young to remember when space was exciting, when the sight of a man in a heavy white suit and bubble helmet walking on a drab rock under a black sky could fill the whole world with wonder and amazement. But my dad told me that, back then, one question dominated the thoughts of the watching millions. No, not the precise proportions of oxygen, hydrogen and plutonium required to fuel the giant Titan rocket. No, not the type of rigorous training undergone by the brave astronauts, nor the special food they consumed, although that brings us closer. No, the question that teased and tantalized the watching millions, as Apollos 1–17 went about their pointless business in the sky, a question for ever framed, but too seldom asked, was: *How do they go to the toilet?*

Did it involve bags, vacuums, pumps, tubes, nappies, pads? Where did it all go – the pee, the poo, the paper – when they finished? Or did they just hold it all in until they got home, to occupy their bogs for days after, groaning and screaming for epidurals and gas?

Well anyway, if I were you, just about the first thing I'd want to know is how the toilet stuff works in Hell. I admit that I am, just maybe, a tiny bit obsessed with things cloacal. But then, as every psychoanalyst knows and every stand-up comedian loves to point out, so are most boys. We all know that men spend an awful lot longer about their business than women. And let's not beat about the bush (I'm not sure, but

90

I think that might be a joke), I'm talking about shitting, not the general tarting up and poncing about that goes on in bathrooms. But nobody seems to know why. For most of the differences between girls and boys there'll be some weird-looking American scientist (odd patches of beard scattered randomly about his face, glasses on crooked) or English boffin (tweed jacket, bald, cross-eyed) to give you an explanation of the genetic origins of the difference. So, for example, male superiority at ball games is something to do with flinging missiles at woolly mammoths. I should say I know a lot about this stuff because there were several thousand yellowing scientific journals neatly piled around my room – light diversion from the causes of the Peloponnesian War.

But nobody has ever come up with a good evolutionary explanation for the fact that I liked to spend a good forty minutes on the bog, with *Judge Dredd* and a bag of wine gums, but Cathy is in and out in the time it takes to say 'plop'. Surely, you'd have thought, it would have made primitive man, sitting for all that time behind his bush with that look of concentration and awakening wisdom (mmm . . . fire . . . meat . . . meat-fire . . . meat-fire GOOD!), an easy meal for any passing sabretooth?

This has gone on long enough. I've been procrastinating. In fact, I meant to procrastinate earlier but I kept putting it off. The thing is, nobody likes talking about their own bottom, or the terrible, terrible things that come out of it. But here goes.

You remember, we were discussing the toilet arrangements here in Hell. Poor, very poor, is the answer. I had, in one corner of my apartment, concealed behind a heavy curtain, appropriately decorated with scenes of the most hideous torture, a lavatory. It looked at first glance like a most inoffensive water closet – clean white porcelain, a utilitarian black seat matching the black plastic handle on the charmingly old-fashioned chain. But oh! the misery; oh! the agony; oh! the humiliation that that barbarous instrument had in store for me.

The problems began, of course, before you got anywhere near the thing. After our trip to the Valhalla (hours ago? months? years?), my diet consisted entirely of a grey mush that dripped from the walls, like pus from a septic wound, to which I was directed by Clarence. I was hungry the whole time, and tried tasting everything in the room, from the books to the granny-chair, to the radio, but only that oozing, utterly tasteless slop turned out to be remotely edible. It's very tastelessness was, doubtless, part of the point – any kind of flavour might have proved a diversion. Nor did it even satisfy my hunger – it just suggested for a few brief moments what it might be like not to be famished. Bit unimaginative, you might think, this slop stuff – surely the scientists in Hell could have come up with something a little better than just *tasteless*? Well, firstly remember that boredom *was* my sentence but, and here it gets good, *it didn't stop there*. Roughage was the thing. The lack of it. In the old days, although the comics, the wine gums and me spent many a long hour together, they were happy times, and never, never, without ultimate issue. I'd always get there in the end. Weetabix, Shredded Wheat, the occasional bowl of muesli, the odd carrot or pea. There was always enough. Not, perhaps, a surfeit, but bowel-wise, I was sound, not bound.

Not now, *oooooh* no. The goo had the effect of wallpaper paste (of course! That's it – it *was* wallpaper paste). It would have taken a grappling hook attached to a team of Shire horses to get anything out of me. Not that I didn't feel the urge. And there's the rub. I'd think to myself, 'Now, it's happening, go, go, go,' and I'd rush to my innocent-looking bowl. Pants down, hit the seat and then, just as I began to squeeze, the surface of the water would boil and froth and from the dark world beyond the U-bend would burst a savage, eyeless head like that of some deformed child, with white, pointed teeth gnashing, grinding, chattering.

You can probably imagine how unnerving this was, the first time it happened. I screamed and, propelled solely by buttock contraction, flew at least a metre into the air. But I soon learned that Vincent, as I decided to call him, was pretty harmless. His main function seemed to be to remove the remotest possibility of pleasure or relaxation from the whole toilet business. I even began to feel sorry for the poor fellow. Was he a sinner, too, and condemned like me? Another reason to think that I'd got off pretty lightly.

And Vincent, this savage, bum-biting, bollock-chewing, haemorrhoid-eating (yep, me, the coolest guy in our school; the unkindest cut of all) demon wasn't the worst. No, for the truly awful feature we must move on to the grim horror that is the bum-wipe in Hell. Each time I managed to squeeze out my meagre allowance I'd reach for the paper, and each day a new trial would confront me. It was as if the black powers of Hell were trying, or experimenting with fiendish ingenuity, to find the most painful and uncomfortable substance with which to wipe the poor, delicate bottom of Conor O'Neil. Let me count the ways:

- barbed wire
- gravel
- a wild cat
- a trombone
- a cheese-grater
- a hot poker
- a bunch of thistles
- a set of dentures
- a microwave oven

- a fiddle bow
- a bunch of keys
- a wasps' nest
- a tennis racket
- a hacksaw
- a pan-scourer
- a turnip
- a hairbrush
- a hedgehog
- a jellyfish
- a viper
- the jawbone of an ass
- a three-bar electric fire
- a coat hanger
- shiny school toilet paper

Now, if I was trying to be funny, and not in the business of enunciating eternal truths, I would claim that the school toilet paper, that supernaturally tough fibre used widely outside the state education system in bulletproof vests and on the nose cone of the space shuttle, was the worst. But it would be a lie. I suppose it was Clarence's little joke. Not bad for a tit.

No, I'd have to say that the jellyfish was the worst. And I cannot help but feel a tiny shimmer of pride at the thought that I am perhaps the only person who can, with proper justification, with the authority of experience, assert that it is more comfortable to wipe your bum on a hedgehog than a jellyfish, and that a fiddle bow drawn slowly across a winking haemorrhoid beats a trombone any day.

Chapter 16
A Wake

So, my plan – elegant and impossible – hung in the heavy air of my cell like the fading after-image of the fortune, or the girl, or the cool car, that you were dreaming about before your mum woke you up with a threat or a promise. I'm sitting there vegetating and fretting at the same time (picture a parsnip with a worried expression), absorbing mush about the not-that-impressive conquests of Charles the Something of Scandawegia from a bad eighteenth-century translation of an original work by some ferret-faced nonentity in a wig, when in floats Clarence, as bright and irritating as a puppy with fleas.

'Conor, mate! Nice to see you. Sorry I haven't popped in for a while.'

It did seem to have been some time since the little *tosseur* had paid me one of his visits. Were the powers that be concerned that I might look forward to them? That they might be a break from the boredom?

'What do you want?' I asked, sullenly. I could almost hear my mum's stiletto of a voice saying, 'Conor, manners,' so cold it made your teeth hurt.

'Conor, manners,' replied Clarence and, with a casual wave, he made my teeth hurt. 'I'm doing you a favour. I've brought a video round. You'll like it. You're the star.'

He'd got me. My curiosity won out over my all-too-rational fear.

'What do you mean? The only video I've ever been in was

for my fat cousin Oonagh's wedding. Mum made me wear a vomit-coloured suit the texture of pig bristle. I'm only in one shot and I've managed to pull the front of my shirt out through my zip so it looks like I've got a white floppy tongue hanging out. Oh how they laughed.'

I told it deadpan, but I could see that it tickled Clarence.

'No – I like the sound of that, but in this one I'm afraid you're a . . . a little less animated.'

'It's my funeral, isn't it?'

'Mmm.'

'Let's get on with it.'

Clarence put his two little fingers, with their well-manicured talons, in his mouth and whistled. A stupid-looking devil in grimy overalls came in, carrying a TV on one shoulder and a video recorder under his other arm. His head looked like a turnip which had been rudely shaped with a spade.

'Where ye want it, guv?' he asked, like a labourer in a sit-com.

'Just in the corner'll do fine. See the match last night?'

'Din arf. Fuckin . . . er, scuse, er, bit of a massacre, won't it? Bitsa body left all ovah duh pitch.' He chuckled, a sound like bones being crushed. He set the stuff down and shambled out, scratching his balls.

'What match?' I asked.

'Oh, just a weekend kick-about,' replied Clarence as he fiddled with the connections at the back of the set. 'We have quite a few old footballers down here. Bad lot, on the whole, sportsmen. Footballers all drunks and fornicators, athletes all drug-users. Cricketers gluttons. And they're all totally selfish, their minds fixed on the gratification of their desire to win. I suppose that's how they made it in the first place. We actually invented sport, you know. Think about it. It's the one way in which inflicting misery, humiliation, and often pain, on other people is completely acceptable. Indeed worshipped. But any-way, as you know, we like to make the most of people's talents and so we stage games. And what do sportsmen and -women hate most? Losing. So in our football matches, *both sides lose*, often by huge margins. And of course we remove any ability that the players had – they fall over their feet, miss the ball more often than not, cry like babies when they get tackled. All good fun. And, naturally, we throw in a few extras – exploding balls, snipers in the crowd, doggy-do all over the pitch – you should know the sort of thing I mean by now.'

'Yes, I think I do.'

'Got it!' said Clarence, emerging from behind the set. 'Now where the Hell's the remote control? That reminds me,' he went on, 'of another of our inventions: the disappearing remote control. We smuggled a couple of million upstairs. Every hour or so they're programmed to slip into a different dimension. You wouldn't believe the numbers of domestic murders, not to mention the lesser crimes against the person, it's triggered. And all kinds of blasphemy. The designer was a friend of mine from college. He won an award. Hasn't done much since. The Ugly Mirror™ wasn't bad, but the Bad Hair™ hairbrush flopped like a, er . . .'

'New Romantic's fringe?' I suggested.

'Whatever. Here we are,' he said, pulling the remote from under Scrote's slumbering, boil-covered mass. 'Let's have some fun.'

Up to this point Hell had been bad. There's no getting round it. Even a congenital optimist who might see losing a leg as a good chance to catch up on some hopping, or terminal cancer as a way of shedding those excess pounds, or who might believe that this – yes, *this* – is the year that Man City won't be rubbish, even he (or she) would find it hard to think of something good to say about Hell. But, for all that, I felt I was holding up. Everything hurt; the food stank; things came out of the toilet and bit me on the bum; my dog was a misanthrope and a bore; I was subject to every kind of humiliation and embarrassment. But I had my little shred of hope.

And I hadn't blubbed. And that's something. That *was* something.

The video began. It was my house. Our living room. My mum and dad were there, and Cathy. My dad had on his suit and a black tie. He never wore his suit. Mum was wearing a black dress and a hat with a veil. She looked good. Cathy was in a silly red coat, buttoned-up. The doorbell rang.

'Car's here,' said Dad.

'I don't want to go,' said Cathy.

'It'll soon be over,' said Mum.

They all got up. Dad put his arms out and all three of them hugged. Now *that* had never happened when I was around. The next scene was in the church. The camera-work was a bit crappy here. It was like Erco's funeral: the whole school was there. And that must be my coffin, in front of the altar. Pale wood and brass handles. Quite nice, really. It was closed. The ice-cream van must have made a right mess out of me. Raspberry ripple all over the place. The camera panned shakily along a row of my friends: Phil, Johnny, Mick, then the Angels: Moody, Fairs and Conway; then some girls: Penelope Weaver, Ursula Curtain, Lucy Jordan (still no ballumbas). A teacher sat at the end of each row: Mr Plenty (fat as a tuba, but with none of the traditional fat man's good humour); Mr Harker (ineffectual, listless); Mr Conlon (brutal Irish games teacher, bow-legged, humpety-backed, rubbish at all sports); Miss Oldridge (pale and lovely, controlled classes by pitiless use of beauty); Sister Eugenia (called Mister Sister by everyone, as pale and lovely as a goitre). They had all donned suitably solemn faces. But on the screen, under each face, subtitles appeared. They seemed to be the thoughts of my friends.

Thoughts of love? Sad thoughts of loss? Happy thoughts of friendship? No, not really.

Phil

Crust. Meat. Crust. Crust. Meat. Fat. Crust.

Johnny

BBC 1: *Watchdog*; *EastEnders*; *Animal Hospital*; news. That's all shit. BBC2: All shit. ITV: *The Bill*; some girl drama thing; news. All shit. Channel 4: NHS documentary. Gardening shit. Girl drama thing. Mucky thing. Nearly all shit.

Mick

GOOOOOAAAAAL! And the young genius, plucked out of obscurity to play for his country in this moment of national crisis, has hammered in his fourth goal against the Brazilians. The whole stadium is on its feet. And what's this? The pitch has been invaded by beautiful nudie girlies. They have surrounded him. They are smothering him with kisses. They are rubbing their bare titties all over him!

Penelope

and cactuses and Gibraltar as a girl where I was a Flower of the mountain yes when I put the rose in my hair like the Andalusian girls used or shall I wear a red yes and how he kissed me under the Moorish wall and I thought well as well him as another and then I asked him with my eyes to ask again yes and then he asked me would I yes to say yes my mountain flower and first I put my arms around him yes and drew him down to me so he could feel my breasts all perfume yes and his heart was going like mad and yes I said yes I will Yes

Sister Eugenia
I'll knock that fecken smile off of his face Jesus that incense makes me fecken ache for a fag nice arse on that lad.

That all went on for a bit. The message was clear enough: your mates aren't really bothered about you. They've all got more important things to think about than me. And yes, I was pissed off. It's not like I wanted them to be tearing their hair out and rending their garments and pouring ashes over their heads and all that. But they just didn't seem bothered. Could it be true that no one really liked me very much? But that's stupid. Everyone likes me.

Don't you?

Then the camera zoomed onto the priest, a smug and shiny man dressed head to foot in drip-dry polyester robes. 'Conor O'Neil, blah blah blah, nice boy, blah blah, his friends have told me how much he loved and admired the singers . . .' (the priest here hurriedly checks his notes) '. . . George Michael and Boy George and how he wanted to be just like them.'

BOY GEORGE AND GEORGE MICHAEL! The Cnuts. The camera returned to the faces of my 'friends', who were all trying – and failing – to swallow their guffaws, tears rolling down their evil faces. And the teachers thought they were crying at the sadness of it all. This one had the stamp of Moody all over it. He, after all, was the one who had once swapped a tube of Deep Heat for his dad's Rectumese piles cream.

The priest went on: 'And now we are going to play what was Conor's favourite song. You may all join in. I'm sure

Conor is up there watching and listening. He may even join in on the harp, which I believe was his favourite instrument.' And Culture Club's *Do You Really Want to Hurt Me?* followed, Boy George's vocals as camp and sickly as a Mr Kipling's French Fancy. It was all too much. Of course I blubbed. My friends saw my death as nothing more than an opportunity to have a laugh at my expense, and the whole school now thought that I was a ponce with shite taste in music.

The video rolled on, remorselessly. A wake afterwards for my aunts, uncles and cousins, and a few teachers and half a dozen of my so-called friends. Ham sandwiches. A bottle of whisky. All pretty drab. No one said anything very nice or insightful about me. No one deplored the tragic loss to humanity. Cathy looked quite pleased with herself, and played *Danny Boy* on our old sit-up-and-beg piano. A couple of aunties sniffed and dabbed at their eyes. Then it was all over. People drifted away, like cows when they realize you have nothing to give them. In the end just Mum, Dad and Cathy were left. They stood together: alone, grey, grim, silent. And then I cried some more, but for different reasons.

The tape ran on into a home video of a group of devils lounging round a pool, with a barbecue smoking in the background. Then it stopped.

'Must be getting along – I've some spreadsheets to prepare before I get into the office tomorrow. Then I've got to whip my PowerPoint presentation into shape,' said Clarence.

'Isn't that all just bullshit? My dad says people use PowerPoint as a way of avoiding communicating. And he should know.'

I noticed that Scrote had woken up and was trying to get at his balls. But his neck had shrunk, or his body stretched, and the desired objects kept whipping out of reach.

'What do you think, Scrote?' I asked him.

'Rubbish,' came his satisfying, if predictable, reply.

'I can see that modern business methods are lost on you. I have to say that I'm a little disappointed. And you really don't want to disappoint me – I am here to make things miserable for you, after all.'

Despite the fact that he'd certainly done some bad things to me, somehow I couldn't quite manage to summon up any authentic fear. But I still wasn't stupid enough to push my luck.

'Sorry, Clarence.'

'Mmm. Apology accepted. But I must be off. See you soon.'

He did his puff-of-smoke disappearing act, which usually meant he was in a bad mood. In his haste the little devil had left one or two sheets of paper behind.

And something else: a small plastic card. A plastic card with a particularly unappealing photo of its owner.

Chapter 17
Pass Go

This was too good to be true. I knew that Clarence was borderline incompetent: inexperienced, careless, absent-minded. But how could he have been stupid enough to leave his security pass behind, the very thing that I needed to set my plan in motion? I trembled with excitement and fear. Fate had given me the key; but could I find the door? Tragically, as a result of my diet of brainy books, I now knew how to put the problem into the correct philosophical jargon. Having the pass was a *necessary* condition of carrying out my plan. That means that without the pass, I was screwed. However, having the pass was not a *sufficient* condition for carrying out the plan – that means that I needed to do all kinds of other things as well.

Impressed? Well you'd know all about necessary and sufficient conditions if you'd had to read Plato and Aristotle and Plotinus and Aquinas and Leibniz and Spinoza and Descartes and Locke and Berkeley and Hume and Kant and Hegel and Schopenhauer and Kierkegaard and Nietzsche and Russell and Wittgenstein and Popper and Ayer and Husserl and Heidegger and Sartre and Merleau-Ponty and Derrida and Lyotard and Baudrillard.

Sorry. Got a bit carried away there.

It *was* too good to be true, but it was the only chance I had.

Preparations. I was about to set out on a journey: firstly to the awful city; and secondly? Well, only God and the Devil could know. What would I need? Maps, compasses, ropes, All-Terrain Attack Sandals, Kendal mint cake, plastic explosives, a Bowie knife, clean underpants and all sorts of other things I didn't have. I just had to go for it. And time was everything. Clarence would soon find out that he'd lost his pass, and even he could put two and two together. I had to go right now.

The first problem was getting out of my cell. Clarence entered and exited in a variety of ways – the puff of smoke, the sliding under the door, the walking through the door as if it were liquid. I tried the knob. It turned. The door swung open. Had it ever been locked? Had I just been too sapped of energy to try it, too weak, too fearful? How many of the cells and prisons we inhabit are illusions of our own making? (Just how many profound-sounding questions can I get into this paragraph?)

'Come on, Scrote, freedom beckons,' I said to my boil-covered, emaciated, battered but still unbowed companion. He looked at me doubtfully.

'Bum,' he replied, but followed.

Outside, Hell had entered one of its randomly occurring dark-purple nights. I could just make out the massive shape of the black mountain before me. Here and there flames burned, but illuminated nothing beyond themselves, like a wit who has insight only into his own character. Sporadic screams rent the air, and moans and gurgles: sounds from nightmares.

Worse still were the sounds of scuttling feet and the scraping of scaled bellies across the pumice and rock, as if big lizards were patrolling the gloom. I hoped they were part of some other sinner's torment, that they would leave me to my own devils. But I wasn't waiting to find out. I set off up the mountain, talking to Scrote as I went in a feeble attempt to keep up my courage.

'So the plan is we get into the city, use Clarence's pass to get into his office, hack into his computer to find out how to get to this other bit of Hell where we can live the life of Riley. All quite simple.'

'Piss.'

'Well, you say that. And you do have a point. But what's the alternative? We just stay here and rot?'

'Rubbish.'

'I know it's rubbish being here. But the beautiful lady' (long, drawn-out sigh emitted at this point from the boy Conor) 'Francesca. She promised me there was a way out. Something that beautiful . . . you just have to trust it.'

'Shag?'

'Bloody Hell, Scrote. Is that all you think about? I love her. I *think* I love her. No, I definitely love her. Love is like pain: you don't think you've got a pain, you either have or you haven't. Same with love. It's a feeling. Either you feel it or you don't. And I feel it. I feel it all over. I just want to be near her. I want to breathe her in. I want to drink her.'

'Nice. Piss.'

'Scrote, you're a dog. You've got no idea about the finer feelings humans are capable of. It's what makes us different from you. All you think about is your knob and your gob, in that order.'

'Shag. Dinner.'

'I don't know why I bother talking to you. But it isn't true that all that people think about is eating and sex. Granted, we think about those things a lot. But all of this stuff they've made me read and listen to. It's not all about humping and chomping. I know you're gonna say that the only reason Beethoven wrote his symphonies was to impress girls, and that Keats was just trying to get inside Fanny Brawne's knickers when he wrote "Ode to a Nightingale", but that'd be mad. There's miles easier ways to cop off than by writing symphonies and operas and poems and that. Now, don't get me wrong. I think they're all shite. I'd swap them all for a Prodigy album, and to see Leeds beat Man U six–nil. But it can't all just be about shagging. And Hell? What'd be the point of Hell if we were all just animals?'

In reply, Scrote coughed up a block of black vomit, sniffed it and trotted on. But in its own way that puke had an eloquence. What if we were all in Hell? it seemed to say. What if Hell was everywhere, all the time? What if life on Earth was just part of the same Hell as where we were now? Perhaps life was just one long remorseless struggle for existence: a battle unto, and beyond death, a war of all against all? But then there was a bloke I read, Kropotkin, or something. Some kind of anarchist. But he wasn't a blowing-things-up-with-bombs kind of anarchist. He said that if you just leave ordinary people alone, we'll all get along and love each other and co-operate, and that nature was full of co-operation as well, and that the struggle stuff in Darwin was just because of capitalism, and living under capitalism makes you see fighting everywhere because that's what capitalism's like, and that's what it wants you to think the world has to be like. So maybe Hell's just capitalism? I wished I knew what capitalism was.

'Arse.'

'What?'

Scrote had stopped dead in his tracks. I froze too.

'Shit.'

Scrote was peering into the darkness. He was trembling, the strong muscles of his flanks fluttering like eyelashes. I caught his fear. The sounds of slithering and scuttling I'd heard earlier were drawing closer, mixed now with a sly hissing. '*Shh, sssseeee, sshushhh,*' they seemed to say. But I could still see nothing but shadows, and shadows within shadows. I stumbled in the darkness and my hand touched something cold, dry and scaly. It moved and I saw a flash of white and felt the agony of teeth in my arm. I screamed like a girly girl and tried to pull away, but the teeth held fast. I put my foot against the beast's head and kicked out. The mouth opened and I pulled my arm free. Scrote cowered between my legs, cringing and whining. Eyes – slow blinking, yellow, unknowable – opened all around us, forming a closed circle. Tongues flickered; long tails coiled, and the hissing and shushing grew to a quiet crescendo.

And then I thought I could make out words in the hissing. '*Sssssmell blood.*' '*Sssoft ssskin.*' '*Taaaasssty.*' '*Warm flesssh.*' '*Musssst eat.*'

They were going to eat us.

They were going to eat us.

I very much didn't want to be eaten. I cuffed Scrote. 'Kill, boy,' I tried, pointing at the circle of eyes, but Scrote just hunkered down further as if he were trying to enter the rock like a seal melts into water. My arm sizzled and stung. I peered at it. I could make out the dark of the blood against the paleness of my skin, and the wound burned with poison; even as I looked I felt the evil work its way up my arm, paralysing as it went. Soon I would be unable to move, and then the creatures would gorge on me, and I would live through it all, feeling each tearing bite, each slavering lick.

And even worse than this fear was the knowledge that my bid for freedom was now doomed to end before it had properly begun, that I would never see Francesca again.

Francesca. Of course! Francesca's promise. Francesca would help. What had she said? Something about calling three times, and thinking of beauty. But I only had two more goes. Bastard. Too early, but there was nothing for it. I was going to have to use up one right now. The lizard things were coming closer as they sensed my growing paralysis.

Thinking of beauty was easy: I just imagined Francesca.

Mmmmmmmm. And then I cried out, 'Francesca Francesca Francesca,' perhaps the first howl of hope, rather than despair, that this place had ever heard.

To begin with it seemed that nothing was going to happen. I began to think that the whole Francesca business had just been another trick, to lure me out here. But then, as before, the air become dense and scented, and my heart leaped with the dual ecstasies of escape and desire. Somehow in the place of dread, surrounded as we were by darkness and by the beasts of darkness, Francesca seemed yet more beautiful than she had before. I could think only of the hackneyed images of angels in my infant school RE books, angels haplessly copied by fat-fingered kids with fatter crayons.

And, as before, she spoke without speaking, whispering her words into my soul. And she caressed my face with hands that did not move. And then she saw the ragged wound on my arm, and she touched that also and it was healed and the poison left me like mist driven by the sun.

She spoke: 'Conor. You called and I am here and it is good: these guardians of our night could not be passed without my help.' And then, handing me a burning candle, she said, 'Take this light. It will show your path, and these beasts cannot come within its annulus.'

Now, I didn't know what an 'annulus' was, but as long as it meant that the lizards were kept out of biting range I was happy. I'm easily pleased.

'And,' she went on, 'as you can only call on me one more time, I must tell you now how to enter the city. As you stand with the Great Gate before you, walk to your right and you will find a low culvert through which the filth of the city flows. It is the only way you will ever be able to gain entrance.'

Culvert? Sounded a bit too much like a sewer. I had the feeling that I was going to be crawling through some bad shit.

'Thanks,' I said, inadequately, adding in my suavist, sophisticatist, elegantist manner, 'Er, and you're lovely.'

For some reason she seemed to enjoy the compliment. She bowed her head with impossible grace and smiled. And then she was gone, again drawn away as if by some powerful wind.

Something wet ran down my leg. I thought I'd pissed myself. But it was only Scrote – he'd drooled on me. I held up the long, thin candle. It was the kind that we used to use to light the big candles on the altar.

Oh – didn't I tell you? I used to be an altar boy. Not cool, I know. And a fat lot of good it did me, Heaven-wise. I started when I was six or seven, and I was still doing it at fifteen – I was the oldest altar boy in the church. I even used to go and serve on Thursday nights, when there'd only be four old women there with me and Father Abbotsley. My reward was a bag of chips on the way home after Mass, eaten scalding hot, drenched in vinegar and crusted with salt.

To be honest, it wasn't so much the altar-boying that I didn't like. It was being in church. If anything, the ritualized choreography of the job quite appealed to me. And the starched white cotta over a heavy red cassock. But why didn't I just give up, wave goodbye to the cotta and cassock? Inertia plays a part. Sometimes it's just plain easier to carry on doing what you're doing, even when you know that change is the right thing. And then I was frightened of hurting my parents, that vague sense of letting people down. So much for the great rebel.

Taper. That's the name of the long thin candle. And here is a taper to light you to bed. And here is a chopper to chop off your head.

So, I held up the taper. The lizards backed away from the flickering circle of light, but the flame drew forth a yet more malicious gleam from their yellow eyes.

'Come on, boy, let's go to work,' I said to Scrote with all the confidence I could muster. With the taper I could at least see where I was walking, but the comfort it gave was more heartening than the light it shed. The lizards stayed with us until we reached the top of the mountain slope, circling, hissing. But they dared not come within the reach of the light, and they melted away to look for easier pickings before we began our descent.

Chapter 18
Some Dull Opiate

The city at night was a thing wondrous and fearful to behold. It looked like a huge iron foundry, all glowing metal, showering sparks, pouring fire. If the frantic pace of the day had slowed, it had been replaced by something more sinister: a creeping horror, the feeling that terrible things were happening – a quiet butchery, a slow, inescapable murder.

On the way down voices called to us piteously: 'Bring the light. Please, bring the light. Only let us into the light.'

But we did not stop, or slow our pace, and soon we were before the massive gate. The gate was quiet. Moving around to our right along the wall, we soon found the arched drain that must be the culvert of which Francesca spoke. We couldn't miss it. The stink was fearful. A thick green and brown paste oozed from the drain. Solid matter bobbed in the unholy minestrone. Scrote whimpered and shied away – and remember, Scrote has had his nose in some pretty unpleasant substances.

The culvert was about a metre high. The slime filled the first third.

'Here we go,' I said cheerfully to Scrote.

'Rubbish,' his inevitable reply.

But, brave and hardy mongrel that he was, he pushed his way into the filth. It came up to his ears, and he had to point his nose in the air like a snooty poodle to breathe. I half crawled, half hunched my way forward. The sewer was filled with things you don't want to hear about, such as:

- condoms, used (Who was getting screwed down here? And who would use a johnny?)
- excrement: all sizes, all textures
- limbs
- unrecognizable internal organs
- pop tarts
- dogs (Scrote greeted each one with a growl and looked smug when they floated off, unable to meet his challenge)
- rats (dead and alive)
- big brown cockroaches (alive)
- sprouts (fresh)
- false teeth (chattering)
- cancerous growths
- a Duke and Duchess of York Royal Wedding commemorative mug
- a pork pie.

Scrote chewed at the pork pie, but then spat it out and cleansed his palate with a rat carcass.

The taper, which had lasted us well, was burning low, and soon it flickered, dimmed and darkened for ever, leaving us to feel our way along the slimy brick of the culvert walls. Hell knows how long we were in that foul tunnel: it seemed like years. At one point a great flush of thick filth surged over our heads. I thought I would choke, gag and be washed back down those agonizing miles of sewer. But the surge passed, leaving us pocked with thick gobbets of slime, latticeworks of tissue paper, women's sanitary products and soft turdy torpedoes. Shortly after, a dull ochre lightening of the gloom showed that we were near to the end, of something.

Scrote, who had suffered almost as much as I had, forged ahead, but then stopped and looked up, the faint light reflecting in his dead eyes. The light came through a grate above us. I could just reach it. I pushed. It moved. I dragged myself up and pulled Scrote after me, his jaws clamped resolutely, but unmaliciously, around my wrist.

We emerged into a quiet alleyway. I had only seen the city during its daylight hours. The impression I had got from a distance, that feeling of slow horror, was magnified infinitely here in its midst. It was as if the atmosphere itself had congealed: we moved as if underwater, or as in a dream when you're chased by some scary thing but you just can't make your legs move quickly enough and your scream comes out as *nnngf*.

'You're a dog, aren't you, Scrote?' I asked. 'Can't you find the way to Clarence's office? You know, sniff your way there?'

'Bum.'

It would have to do. He limped off. I followed, having sod-all other choice, but with hope dying in me as surely as our guinea pig Snuffy had perished under the not very loving care of me and Cathy. (Poor Snuffy. Alternately nursed and neglected, stuffed and starved; dressed in doll's clothes one day, shaved naked the next. And finally strangled to death, accidentally, by Cathy as she carried him upstairs by the neck. This earned her the local nickname of the Hamster Strangler, despite her earnest rebuttal that Snuffy wasn't a hamster but a guinea pig.)

It was as if the scenes of mutilation and torture that had filled the streets before had now somehow *become* the streets. The walls of the buildings, the gentle sucking ground on which we trod, were the souls of the damned, the tongs, whips, goads, knives, chains of the tormentors. Our bodies cast huge shadows onto the buildings we passed, but only for moments, and then the shadows were absorbed into the walls, eaten by them. How I yearned for my cosy cell, for my death by boredom. In the city at night I found madness, or the image of madness, and it was bad.

Scrote, at least, had a clear sense of purpose. He did a passable impersonation of a bloodhound, keeping his nose close to the ground, just occasionally raising his head to sniff the air. I was convinced that we'd end up at some particularly alluring lamppost, recently sprayed by a juicy bitch. I was wrong. The stained concrete of Clarence's office soon loomed before us, its windows dark, its corridors – we prayed – empty.

Chapter 19
Office Politics

There was nothing for it but to stroll up to the main entrance and put Clarence's pass to the test. The door had been open on my previous visit with Clarence, two Bruisers checking passes. Now the door was shut, but there were no guards. I slid the pass through a black box on the wall. A small green light came on, and the door made the satisfying *tchik-tchik-clunk* I'd been hoping for. We were in. The lift to the fourth floor; another slider. This was all so easy.

All too easy.

I did not dare to put on the lights but I found Clarence's desk readily enough by the mess and clutter. My big fear was that they'd use some kind of weirdo operating system, but it turned out just to be Windoze. And not Windoze Millennium, NT, or 98, or even 95, but Windoze 3.1.

Now *that's* a disgrace.

The computer itself wasn't much better – an ancient 386. So, it was all true. Windows and Intel really were the spawn of the Devil. Those Mac and Unix bores were right all along.

First problem was guessing Clarence's password. It's a bit of a cliché to say it now, after we've seen it so many times on films and the telly, but it really is easy. People are amazingly predictable. It's always a wife or girlfriend, or the name of a kid. I read about it somewhere. Unless people pick something obvious, they always forget it. Same with PIN numbers. It's always their birthday. Some people, the really stupid ones, the ones lacking any spark of imagination, any inkling of *nous* just use their own names, sticking a numeral on the end to baffle any fiendish hackers. I tried *Clarence 1*. Zip. *Clarence 2*. Arse. *Clarence 3*. Balls. *Clarence 4*. Yes. Yes. Yes. So devils were the same as people on Earth. Just as stupid. I was starting to enjoy myself. There was all the usual stuff on there, the useless stuff that comes with Windoze: you know, Cardfile, Write and all that, plus Word and Excel (but still antique versions – I don't suppose the creaky old 386 was up to anything newer), and a copy of *Tetris*. I had a quick play on that, but I didn't get on the high score table, which was a bad blow. The top ten, by the way, were:

1. Le Grand Tosseur 27,657
2. Sex machine Gez 25,998
3. The Name's Bond 21,342
4. Seymour Fanny 19,004
5. Arse! Feck! Drink! 19,001
6. Juan Kerr 17,581
7. Conan the Librarian 12,867
8. Funky Chicken 12,849
9. Mmmmmmm Donuts 12,811
10. P. Kness 12,595

My guess was that numbers 1, 4, 6 and 10 were the same guy, which was quite impressive. I always call myself 'The Eventual Winner', a signature I've left on computers and games machines the length and breadth of, well, our high street, and which really pisses people off.

Back to work. I checked in at the File Manager. I still wasn't sure quite what I was looking for. Clarence had his own directory. There were about twenty files in it. I guessed I must be oneilc.doc. I double clicked, and Word opened, creakily, like the legs of a ninety-year-old hooker. Yeah, like how would I know? Just thought it sounded clever.

And this is what I found, all of it familiar:

Subject	O'Neil, Conor
Age at death	15
Sins	Lying; theft; polymorphous perversity (eh?); spitting; being a smart aleck (fair point); murder (not fair)
Mode of dispatch	Multiple injuries caused by ice-cream van
Punishment	Acute boredom; assessment after 400,000,000 years
Location	Cell 63, Islets of Langerhans. Map reference C89076.6765
Personal Tormentor	Clarence Slawkenbergius, Executive Devil
Notes	Must be watched carefully — possible recidivist

Appended to this was a log of my 'treatment': all the humiliations and punishments I had undergone, e.g.:

*No. 467. Made to misremember first date with
Monica Thornton. In place of mildly erotic kissing
and fondling, subject recalls only utter rejection and
returning home to find huge bogey stuck to lip.
Subject responded to new implanted memory by
writhing on floor of cell, moaning and slapping
forehead.*

Well, that was all quite dull. Good news about Monica though. So I really did get a snog after all. But the tricky bit was what to do next. I checked through Clarence's other files. There didn't seem to be any other clients – just general office rubbish: a report that Clarence seemed to be drafting written on 'Advanced Methods of Inducing Catatonia in Hyperactive Adolescents', a shopping list (milk, Pringles, cheese slices, talon polish, hydrochloric acid, etc.), a letter replying to a complaint about a Senior Executive Devil ('Dear Mrs Walsh, As you may be aware, our policy on mutilation is determined by the provisions of the Sixth Satanic Directive, which require that . . .'), a bid for a larger stationery budget ('the current plastic pencil-sharpener is woefully inadequate, and needs to be upgraded to aluminium') and loads of dazzlingly unhelpful spreadsheets.

I realized that I needed to get into the files of some of the other devils. Only there could I hope to find what I was after. I know this sounds stupid, but I was actually quite enjoying myself. I like farting about with computers and this was almost like a decent adventure/puzzle game – a bit like Everquest®, but without the cool graphics. Even Scrote seemed to be chilling out. He'd pissed on all the chairs and tables, laid a satisfying brown dog-egg by the photocopier and settled down to sleep on someone's swivel chair. There was something comforting in the green glow from the monitor. I wasn't bored, and I didn't hurt.

'Ffnnuuuuuck!'

The crack had come out of nowhere, and the pain followed a nanosecond behind. A red cloud burst in my eyes and I felt as if my head was going to splat like a melon hit by a bus. I was on the floor looking up into the exquisite pouting lips and black eyes of Trixie. She flicked her tail into her hand, brought it to her mouth, circled the end with her tongue and sucked it. She then let it coil down to my throat, and chest, and belly, where it played in curlicues like a sharp, teasing finger.

'Conor,' she cooed, 'you really are a naughty, naughty boy, but then I've always liked naughty boys the best. Isn't it lucky I forgot my lipstick, or we'd never have had this chance to get acquainted. I really can't believe my good fortune. It's considered very unprofessional to become ... involved with another devil's client. But you are so succulent, so toothsome, so ... fresh, I really can't resist. And now I have you here all alone, and all to myself.'

She licked her lips with her long, black, forked tongue and then drew it deliberately across her sharp white teeth as though she were sharpening a scalpel. Despite the pain (I guessed she must have whipped the back of my head with that tail of hers) I could feel only a rising excitement. I knew that she was evil, evil beyond the reach of poor old Clarence, but I didn't care. Something strange and wonderful was going to happen to me, and I was bursting, dripping, drooling with desire. Trixie ran her hands over her body, and the end of her tail, writhing sinuously, snaked up between her legs before it struck like a viper and caught me by the nape of my neck. Then I was dragged up onto my toes and her tail coiled around me, holding me so tightly I could not breathe. She pulled me close and my whole body was suffused with sensations new to me, new to the world: pleasure and pain so commingled that they could not be distinguished. This is it. This is it!

She took my face in her hands. I felt her lips close on mine. I felt her tongue slide into my mouth. Its twin forks encircled my tongue, moving backwards and forwards along its length. I almost blacked out, but struggled desperately to stay conscious. Then her tongue moved on, moved down, gathering speed. It slithered down my throat. I felt it in my stomach. And the rushing, pulsing speed of it was in me, through me.

She'd stuck her tongue all the way through me and out of my arse.

What followed can only be told in the plainest terms. To think about it now makes me shake and sweat, despite all that I've been through, all that I've seen. But tell it I must. She pulled me, with her tongue, inside out, bum first, through my own mouth. There. Said it. You won't believe me. You can't believe me. But it happened. I've been trying to think of things in your own lives that might give you an idea of what it's like. Of course there is nothing. I'm going to ask you to spend a few minutes (I recommend between ten and fifteen) just thinking about what it might have been like for me. I've provided a blank box for you to stare at while you do so.

There. If you don't now need some kind of therapy or a stiff drink, there's something wrong with you.

Anyway, so there I am: a sloppy pile of organs, shiny connective tissue, bony bits and general all-purpose body slime. I can't see anything, because I'm inside out, but I can hear Trixie softly cooing to herself, the bitch, and I have a feeling that the fun has only just begun.

But then I heard a muffled scream and a thud. Scrote? Had my faithful hound leaped, at long last, to my aid? Well, something very strange was happening. And I can now tell you that there is one thing worse than being turned inside out – and that's being turned back outside out and inside in again. Just when I had started to get used to it! So, with a slither and a pop, I was back to my old self, minus one or two internal thingies that seemed to have dropped off in the process. But I felt OK, so they couldn't have been that important – pancreas or spleen perhaps?

The first thing I saw was Trixie, tied neatly to a chair and gagged with her own fishnet tights. She seemed to be unconscious. Now that was certainly beyond Scrote.

And then I saw Clarence.

'Clarence! What the Hell is going on?' I said, although it came out as 'Carnce! Ot da ell id gorn?' as I was still a touch zonked by my recent reversal.

'Oh shut up, you stupid little shit. Do you have any idea about the trouble you've caused?'

I'd never seen Clarence so angry. His head had swelled up to twice its normal size and blue flames were coming out of his ears and nostrils.

I thought quickly. What could I say?

'I just wanted to play on your computer. I was only mucking about.' It was the best I could manage.

'Don't don't *don't*,' he spat, with a camp and melo-dramatic emphasis. 'Tell me now, before it's too late, exactly what you're doing here. This is some kind of pathetic attempt at escape, isn't it? Come on. I might be able help you. I'm certainly your only chance. And let me tell you, you – *we* – are so deep in the crap we already need a periscope.'

Something about Clarence's manner made me believe that he wanted to help. For some reason Clarence clearly felt that our interests lay, for the time being, in the same direction. But I wasn't going to tell him about Francesca.

'Well I had this idea that I might be able to swap with some other bloke. You know, one who likes the things I hate and hates the things I like. I thought I might be able to change us round on the computer.'

Clarence looked grim.

'So you came here to find some sordid little hidey-hole where you could bathe in every kind of depravity: pop music, girls, videos – you got the idea from the dentist chap I told you about, didn't you? We're not stupid here, you know. How did you think you would get away with it? You were bound to be caught and then it would be straight to the Annihilator. And I wouldn't give a damn if it wasn't for the fact that now you've dragged me down with you. You took advantage of my one little mistake. Did you even pause to think what would happen to me, if you had escaped? Mmm? Well?'

'Er, no, not really.'

'Well I'll tell you. *I'd* be Annihilated. It's one strike and you're out here. One lousy mistake, and my whole career screwed. All I had to do was to keep my nose clean, get reasonable box markings and I'd have been up for promotion in another forty million years. You really are a *shit*.'

'Why can't you just turn me in?' I asked, helpfully.

'Are you deaf? It's too late. It was too late from the moment you walked out of that cell without authorization. We were both doomed from then on.'

'I don't get it. Why did you follow me then? Why did you save me from Trixie?'

'There's doomed and there's doomed. That idea of yours isn't *completely* crack-brained. As soon as I realized you'd flown, I knew my only chance was to throw my lot in with you. The two of us travelling together' (at this, Scrote looked up from the pool of slime, *my* slime, that he'd been lapping, and whined) '. . . oh, all right, the *three* of us, might just make it to the other side. But I hadn't countered on Trixie being here and now I'm even deeper in the ordure. Thank Satan she was too busy drooling over your innards to notice me or I'd never have got the better of her. She can do terrible things with that tail of hers, you know.'

I did know.

'Are you going to help me get away then? And what do you mean by "the other side"?' I asked. I just couldn't believe my luck.

'I've no choice. We're in this together now. Either we all make it, or we all get shovelled into the Annihilator. You really don't pay attention, do you? I've already told you that Hell is divided into administrative districts. There are two main ones: Sheol and Gehenna. It was decided aeons ago that Hell as a unitary authority had become just too unwieldy – there was a lack of direct accountability, leadership was too remote, complacency had set in. It all worked very well for a while, but things have become a little troubled lately. In theory Sheol and Gehenna are still working in harmony, but the fact is that there's rivalry between the two and a distinct lack of communication. But it's not so bad that anyone wants to go through the trauma of yet another reorganization.

'Each year a league table is prepared, showing which district has the best performance – you know, the best pain yields, the highest anguish ratings. I know it's not much of a league with only two competitors, but it does the trick. Occasionally we get a bit carried away and go to war, but it's all part of the fun and, as you know, war is a very great generator of misery. The point is that your hare-brained plan can only succeed if we find you, and me for that matter, a lair in the other district. That way they'll never track us down and we can spend eternity in some degree of comfort. We're in Sheol, and we need to find someone in Gehenna, so get out of the way and let me get to work.'

Clarence pushed me rudely out of his chair and starting punching keys. He found his way into some horrid-looking pre-Windows database where the screen was all flickering green LEDs and you had to type out commands rather than just click stuff.

'Search criteria,' he mumbled to himself, 'middle-aged to elderly. Likes classical music, drama, nineteenth-century novels, antique-collecting, flower-arranging.' He typed SE (for 'send', I guessed) and sat back. He was still narked, but had calmed down a bit. He seemed to love his job – just gazing at the monitor soothed and relaxed him.

A list of names and details came up on the screen. Clarence went through discarding the candidates as too young, too interesting, too heterosexual, too loutish.

And then: 'Wait a second. Just wait a second,' he murmured in rapt delight. 'Interesting, very interesting. I believe you know this gentleman. Mr Bass, Mr Lionel Bass.'

Chapter 20
Bass

Why hadn't I thought of it? It was so obvious. Bass of the moist lips and the soft, sly, insinuating voice.

Perhaps it's time I told you a bit more about the teachers at my school. After your parents, teachers are the most important adults in your life – the ones you have to spend most time trying to please; the ones you fear the most; the ones from whom you most crave appreciation; the ones you most despise. I haven't exactly hidden the fact that most of the teachers at The Body were crap. Because it was such a hole it became a repository for the worst qualified, most incompetent and, generally speaking, ugliest teachers in the county. True, the odd lunatic would turn up, eyes ablaze with idealism, determined to transform the lives of the wretched and forlorn urchins under their care. We soon saw them off.

But were all the teachers equally bad? Of course not. As in all things there was a spectrum. Mr Rackham, for example, was a poor teacher by almost every conceivable criterion: he was too lazy to mark our homework and so made us swap books around so we could mark each other's; he was horribly under-qualified to teach maths, his supposed subject, as he had only some kind of flimsy certificate in geography; he was as ugly as a gnu and he stank of chip fat. He was at the *good* end of the spectrum.

At the opposite end was Mrs Allworthy. She taught French. She couldn't speak or write French, but she taught it. As we all trooped into her deskless classroom (for some reason hers was the only room equipped not with desks and chairs, but with chairs alone, curiously fitted with a flat writing panel on the right arm – useless, of course, for left-handers), her pale eyes would search through the shuffling lines for a victim. Never the baddest kid in the class, never one of the bullies or braggarts or bastards, although there were always plenty of those. No, she would pick on some pathetic loner, some harmless wisp of a boy, or a shy girl struggling to come to terms with her body, or a fat kid, or one raddled with acne. Having found herself a victim, she would spend the entire 'lesson' mauling him or her with a feline grace it was hard not to admire. And the worst thing was that she would draw the rest of the class into the humiliation process until we all began to loathe the helpless victim. And behind the sarcasm there lurked something altogether more brutal. If anyone struggled to escape the hook, or fought back in any way, or showed any kind of rebellious spirit, she would summon up the unholy spirit of her enforcer, Mr Kerr. Kerr was a batterer of the old school. A man in his fifties, of massive proportions, with great clumsy batterer's hands, he was clearly helplessly in love with Allworthy who was, it's fair to say, possessed of a certain air of decadent sexual allure. He was the Deputy Head, and took care of discipline.

'You're disrupting my class,' she would say to some kid who hadn't reddened or cried or wet himself at her whim. 'Go to Mr Kerr and tell him I sent you.' It all sounded so innocent, but no child ever emerged the same after entering Kerr's chamber. I was only ever sent to him once. He took my face in his big hands and squeezed, his eyes burning into mine. I thought my head was going to burst.

OK, so they weren't all as bad. There was one we all liked – a beanpole called Mr Brightman, who taught chemistry. He did his best to get us through the exams and he tried to make us laugh. True, he did it by insulting us, but there was no malice in it and it was almost a sign of acceptance to get one of his quips:

'Johnson! You're so dense, light bends round you.'

'Conway! If you were any more stupid, you'd have to be watered twice a week.'

'O'Neil! We shouldn't keep you here – it's depriving a village somewhere of an idiot.'

'Brennan! A prime example of a room-temperature IQ.'

And then, one morning, I went into his lab to give him a message from another teacher. He wasn't there so I left the note on his desk. A drawer had been left open and, naturally, I looked in. At the top of a pile of papers was what looked like a couple of pages downloaded from the internet. They contained every joke Brightman had ever cracked. I don't know why I should have found this so disillusioning but I did. I never told anyone, but I stopped laughing. One time Brightman looked into my unsmiling eyes after one of his specials ('Moody! You must have got into the gene pool when the lifeguard wasn't watching') and he knew that I knew. After that he lost most of his spark and sank slowly into the mire.

Back to Bass.

Bass taught music. When I say he taught music, what I mean is that he had us all mess about on glockenspiels and marimbas and xylophones whilst he took one of his favourites into a sound-proofed room for 'special tuition'. I was never gifted enough on any instrument to warrant the status of special pupil. Probably a good thing.

Bass was big and moist and combed the hair from his armpits over his bald patch. He wasn't particularly cruel or much hated but he gave us all the creeps.

'Bass?' I said, back in the office with Clarence.

'Yep, he's our man,' said the devil. 'Highly cultured, refined taste, a lover of quiet contemplation and subtle thought. In other words the antithesis of you. Oh, and gay.'

'Is that why he's damned?'

Clarence looked shocked. 'Conor, yet again you disappoint me. People aren't damned just for being *gay*. The place would be full of Church of England vicars and that would be no good at all. No, he's damned because for the last ten years he's been pilfering from the school music budget.'

'So that's why the orchestra consists of one violin and forty-four wood blocks.'

'If you say so. But gay is useful to us – or you, at least – because of the torment lined up for him, which includes . . . now, let me see . . . yes, regular smothering by voluptuous naked human females.'

So, not the life of Riley, but the life of Bass. I smiled, thinking about the voluptuous naked human females. It was all too perfect. Except . . .

'But Bass isn't dead yet, is he? Or at least he wasn't when I bumped into the ice-cream van.'

'No, not yet, not for another couple of Earth years. That's the only way we can make this work. I just change these records, and Roberto is the sibling of your maternal parent. Got it. According to our records you, Conor O'Neil, are now sentenced to be blasted by raucous, dissonant dance music, surrounded by nubile girls, forced, yes forced, to spend your time playing *Tomb Raider*, *Unreal Tournament* and *Quake*. And Mr Bass will while away eternity listening to classical music and reading Ibsen, with the odd indignity that goes with the territory thrown in just to help him appreciate how lucky he is.'

'So that's all there is to it then?'

'Not quite. As I told you, Bass was destined for Gehenna, and we must make our way there. It is a perilous journey, fraught with danger. There is no guarantee of success and failure means Annihilation. It requires courage and endurance and endeavour. Are you up to it?'

'Probably not. But there is no alternative. How do we get there?'

'There's a map on the wall. I'll show you.' Clarence led me to a huge and detailed map. 'Here's where we are, off the coast on the Islets of Langerhans in the outer circle of Sheol. I should point out that the circles business cuts across both districts, as you can see.'

Now I suppose that you might expect, at this point in a story of this particular kind, a gloriously detailed reproduction of that map, so that you could follow the route we were to take. Two things make that impossible. The first is that the map Clarence showed me had a very curious property. Before my eyes the shapes of the continents and the contours of the land began to move and slide, like a plate of food toyed with by a fussy eater. It seemed that the land itself, like time, was malleable and could not be trusted.

The second is that I can't draw.

Clarence, however, seemed to know what he was doing. He traced a line across the shifting shapes on the map of Hell, saying, 'Well, here *we* are. We can get the underground over to the mainland. From there I'm afraid it's a bit of a schlep through the Hercynian Forest and across the Great Salt Plain. Then we can go by air up into the Golgotha mountains. The Sheol–Gehenna boundary runs through the middle of the range. From there it's all downhill to Bass's quarters down here in Wandsworth.'

'Some of these names sound familiar. Isn't Wandsworth in London? Are the Earth places named after the Hell places or the other way round?'

'A bit of both. We liked what the local council was doing in Wandsworth, and so we named one of our newer suburbs after it. We also have a Westminster and a Brent. But we must crack on. It looks as though Trixie's coming round, and without the element of surprise I don't think I can get the better of her.'

All the while Trixie had been snoring quietly, her head lolling, a thin line of spittle making its way down her lovely chin, but now her eyes were beginning to open, blearily. Clarence printed off a couple of pages and we split. Scrote sprayed Trixie on the way past, and I paused to try to look down her partially unbuttoned blouse. In place of a nipple, a cold eye stared back.

Creepy.

Chapter 21
Going Underground

'For Hell's sake keep up,' urged Clarence as we slipped out into the street. 'Trixie'll have the Malebranche after us in no time.'

The Malebranche. I remembered: Hell's SS.

It was still dark, but the led zeppelin of the skies seemed to be lightening into a deep purple. I wasn't happy about having to put all my trust in Clarence who was, after all, a devil of proven incompetence, but I couldn't see what option I had.

'How can we get through the gate if they know about us? And I don't think Scrote can make it back through the sewer. Can't you fly us out?' I flapped my arms chicken-style to mime a flying devil.

Clarence looked exasperated. 'Even if I could get off the ground,' he said, 'with all that excess baggage it's a bit obvious, don't you think – a devil, a boy and a dog sailing through the air? They'd pick us up on radar and bring us down with surface-to-air rissoles.'

I would have assumed he meant missiles if I hadn't tasted the food here.

'No, I told you we were getting the tube. Our only chance is to make it to the underground and try to pass through with the rush-hour crowds. But I've got to warn you, you may think that you know about public transport down here, but until you've tried our tube system, you really haven't seen what we can do.'

Clarence could not stop himself from smiling as he spoke. Just whose side was this devil on?

The city was now noticeably lighter and the night-shift of secret and shadowy horrors was giving way to the cacophonous frenzy of the day. Doors were thrown open and ragged crowds emerged from their nocturnal torment into a morning that offered no relief or escape from the nightmare. As ever, they were harried and pursued by devils – intent, focused, fervid.

Clarence set off through the mob and we followed. Panic rose in my chest. The city was made for paranoia – new terrors lurked around every corner, quick eyes watched your every move; jabbering, foaming madmen would turn to you and shout, 'They're coming! They're coming! They'll eat you. Run for your lives.' But of course this wasn't paranoia: I was in Hell, and bad, bad devils were after me.

And then, above the background bustle and clamour, a voice cried out, 'Clarence! Stop right there.'

Clarence stopped dead in his tracks, a look of stunned recognition in his weaselly features. It seemed that our great escape was over before it had begun. A smartly dressed devil I recognized from Clarence's office ran up to us, waving. In his tow there followed Olaf, the melancholy Viking. He was wearing a rather pretty red polka-dot summer dress, a pair of fluffy mules and a horned helmet of burnished bronze. He was carrying several large cardboard boxes, which he kept dropping and stumbling over.

'Christ, Clary me old mate, am I glad I've run into you. I've been paged,' the devil said breathlessly. 'There's some sort of a flap on back at the office – no idea what, but I've got to get back there. You can't do me a huge favour, can you?'

'Anything, Col, you know me.' Clarence was obviously relieved. It looked like we were, for the time being, OK.

'Look, I'm stuck with fuckwit Olaf here. You can't look after him for the morning, can you? Just till I get things sorted down at the office? He doesn't need much tormenting – he takes care of that for himself. As you can see, I've got him nicely kitted out.'

'Well, it's a bit tricky at the moment. I've got some big plans for O'Neil,' said Clarence, nodding in my direction.

'Come on, Clary, I'm being shafted here. It's not even meant to be one of my office days. Don't you remember when I lent you my cattle prod after you left yours up that poor bugger's arse? That got you out of all kinds of bother with the supervisors. You owe me.'

Clarence was getting nervous about the time this was taking up. 'All right, all right,' he said, the irritation prickling in his voice.

'Baal bless you, Clarence. You're a fallen angel! I'll tell Trixie you bailed me out – she'll be well impressed. Might even give you one of her specials. And I tell you from first-hand – or should I say first-*mouth* – experience, her specials are *special*.'

With that he raced off in the direction from which we had come, leaving the Viking behind.

'What can we do?' I asked.

'It's no use. We'll have to take him with us. Olaf?'

'Uh?'

'Listen very carefully. I shall say this only once. We are leaving this place. You are coming with us. If we manage to escape, you'll never have to wait on tables, play the violin or wear a dress again. Do you understand?'

'Uh?'

'Oh just follow us, you cretin. And dump those boxes.'

'Uh?'

We plunged back into the crowd and made good progress, flowing with the current towards the underground station.

The steady stream became first a fast-moving river, and then a torrent. I saw in the distance the entrance to the station. In a grim parody of the London Underground logo, a skull and crossbones leered down at us from a tall signpost.

Wherever we'd wanted to go, there was no way now of turning back. The crowd drove us along. At times I was like a moonwalker, taking fifty-metre steps as I was lifted and carried by the mass of dead flesh around me, and more than once I almost fell beneath the trampling feet. And then I felt the grasp of a huge and powerful arm as the massive Olaf picked me up and placed me up on his shoulder, like a toddler. On the other shoulder sat Scrote, grumbling to himself about how everything was rubbish and snapping at ears and necks as we passed.

We forced our way down the stairs and into the gloom and ammoniac stench of the ticket area. The smell was so thick it coated your tongue. Bodies piled up under our feet. Heads were squashed, and popped like bladderwrack. Devils among the crowd tripped and goaded, stabbed and raked, but we were kept safe by Clarence, who hovered above us, giving just the occasional cuff for realism's sake. None of the ticket machines were working, and vicious Bruisers at the barriers would let no one past, increasing the crush. Finally the gates were opened and the compressed mass piled through, leaving more crushed and torn bodies behind.

Somehow we managed to stay together as we tumbled down an escalator and rolled onto the platform. Olaf was magnificent, laying about him with his huge, hammer-like fists to carve a little breathing space. There were thousands of us. I looked up at an electronic sign with moving LED letters. I assumed it would tell us when the next tube was due. It said, 'Anyone reading this sign will receive an electric shock NOW.'

It didn't lie; the crowd fizzed and popped and stank of burning pork.

'Don't get too close to the edge,' shouted Clarence above the snarls and groans. Unfortunately, we were already close enough to see why it wasn't a good idea: the platform edge was greasy with blood. Over the edge, on the rails, we could see bodies, and bits of bodies. And they were moving, like maggots in a bait bucket.

'Once you're down there, that's it, I'm afraid,' added Clarence. 'You just stay there, getting run over ten or twenty times a day. Some try crawling up and down the tunnels, but it's all the same.'

Now as you might guess, this really got to me. I didn't want to be down there with the chopped-up tube people. I didn't want to be down there so much that anywhere else in Hell looked cosy, including – perhaps even especially – my own little cell, with its antimacassars and dusty journals and radio plays about housewives in Hampstead contemplating adultery.

'Any chance of bailing out and going home?' I asked without much confidence.

Clarence went berserk.

'Home? Home? You really are a spineless little nonentity, aren't you? You've wrecked my own *promising* career. You've dragged poor old Olaf along, thereby damning him to the Annihilator . . .'

'Uh?' said Olaf.

'And now you want to' (putting on an annoyingly girlie voice) ' "bail out". Well, boy, you've crossed the what-do-you-call-it, and it's time to stick your courage to the screwing place, or wherever. Right now you've got nothing to gain and everything to lose. I mean the other way round. Anyway, here's the tube train.'

The crowd surged forwards. There was no way of resisting the weight of bodies behind. Those right at the front soon lost their footing and fell, scrambling, scratching and screaming, over the drop and onto the lines. More followed and fell on top of them. There was a great whoosh and a blast of hot air from the tunnel and the tube exploded into view. The front of the engine was an open mouth, like a great white shark's, blood dripping from its teeth. It had come for me. I knew it had. I was mere centimetres away from the edge, and the fall. I could see the terrified figures, some dumbly staring at the horror awaiting them, but most still frantically scratching at the blood-oiled sides of their death pit. My feet were slipping and sliding, and still the pressure from behind urged me on. And then a tenth of a second before I fell, and just as the front of the train screamed past, sucking me under, a strong finger hooked itself under my collar and I was pulled back into the arms of Olaf, who I was growing to love like a brother. The hot metal of the train had kissed my nose, leaving a smudge of soot, which I wiped off with the back of my hand.

The doors sighed open, right in front of us. Inside there were some seats, but they were covered with chewing gum (in every hue and texture from soft pink to tarry black), lazy slug trails of phlegm, smears of shit or chocolate, and pools of taupe vomit. I reached up blindly for a hand strap. I felt something horribly moist. I looked up. A woman's face stared down at me, its eyes full of fear and hate. Her tongue had been pulled and stretched and then tied back to form a loop. There were dozens of these gloomy heads all staring down into the carriage, all with the same knotted tongues.

I looked for something else to hold onto. There was nothing, and the train was already full to bursting with the dead commuters. Soon even the vomitty seats were taken. Outside, devils with whips and tridents forced everyone on the platform into the impossible space. Finally the doors closed, but one man was trapped, one arm and one leg within, his head, and the rest of him without. As the train hurtled towards the tunnel at the platform's end, he began to wail. Thankfully that sound, certainly the most awful I had heard in Hell, lasted only a couple of seconds. With a quick crunch and a splat he was gone, leaving behind that arm and leg. Those inside the carriage barely paused to note this horror, so relieved were they to be 'safely' inside. Although I was sickened, I too felt relief that some other poor sap got the splat. We all had our own crosses to bear, here in Hell.

'Everyone OK?' asked Clarence in scout-leader mode. We were all scrunched up together, hostile alien faces, necks and heads all around us.

'Now look,' said Olaf, 'I don't want to get heavy here, or anything, but can you tell me what's going on? I mean, there I was, out for my usual morning ritual humiliation – by the way, do you like my new dress? Made it myself, you know – when out of the blue I'm handed over to you, Clarence, and the next thing I know I'm on the underground to Odin knows where, on some berserker scheme. You know, if this is some kind of a quest, or a raid or what have you, there should be planning involved. When I was pillaging with Storri 'Bum Face' Storrison, everything was worked out down to the last detail: who was to kill which bishop, who got to castrate the village elders, who had to clean up after the Blood Eagle. If only I'd followed the plan and left the nun to old Bum Face I'd never have got that pike up my jacksie, as it were.'

'Why don't you fill our friend Olaf in on your wonderful plan, Conor? Or shall we ask the dog? He seems to be the one with the brains.'

Clarence could be a bitch when he tried. Somewhere below, Scrote snickered.

'Well, it's quite simple really. You know how we all have punishments that reflect why we're down here, and that are specially designed to maximize our suffering?' I began.

'Er, oh yeah. I hadn't really thought of that,' said Olaf.

'Well I worked out that if I could find some bloke who was gonna be sent down here, and who hated the kind of stuff I like, I could sort of swap with him. We'd both win, you see?'

A look of understanding slowly dawned on Olaf's face.

'Corrrr! Bloody clever. Not even sly old Bum Face himself could have thought that one up.'

'So,' I went on, not unpleased by Olaf's reaction, 'I borrowed Clarence's security pass' (heavy sniff from the lender) 'and sneaked into his office, so I could hack into his computer and find the right man. But I got jumped by one of his colleagues and she turned me inside out. Then Clarence showed up and saved the day. He was gonna be Annihilated for letting me escape, so he decided to help me out. He's found a man who hated girls and loved classical music, but he lives millions of miles away. And then you came along. I suppose I can share with you, if you like. There'll be all kinds of stuff, with nude girls and loud music and video games.'

'Can I hew people with my battle axe?'

'No, it won't be that sort of place. But you can play *Unreal Tournament*, and slaughter millions of aliens.'

'Oh. All right then. But can I still wear this dress, sometimes? It took me long ages to sew.'

'As far as I'm concerned you can wear whatever you like, except for a Man United top.'

'In that case I will cleave to you on this quest, doomed though it may be.'

It sounded brave and noble, but he really didn't have much of a say in the matter. I suppose it's a useful psychological crutch – persuading yourself that you've chosen to do something when you didn't in fact have any freedom of choice at all.

'One thing though, Olaf.'

'Yes?'

'You said "Blood Eagle". Er, what's that?'

It had to be interesting, because it wasn't in any of the books I'd been forced to read.

'The Blood Eagle? The finest work of Viking art.'

'Oh.' I was disappointed, imagining he meant a pretty carving or a nice broach.

'Much skill required,' carried on Olaf, with passion. 'First, you take your captive, usually someone pretty high up, a chief or famous warrior by preference, and then you tie them to a frame. Then comes the tricky bit. You have to cut through the ribs where they join to the spine, without killing the captive. Delicate work. Then you pull his lungs out through the slits in his back. If he's still alive, his breathing makes the lungs inflate like two great wings. Very beautiful. Very profound. A great and fitting tribute to Odin. But usually he dies first, which is a bummer.'

Why did I have to ask?

The tube rumbled, whined and juddered its way on. It stopped a couple of times at stations with strange names like Quetzalcoatl Junction and Balham, but more people always got on than alighted, and so the conditions became ever more constricted and stifling. Finally I could take no more. My arms and legs were splayed out at bizarre angles. Every inch of my body had an inch of somebody else's body pressed against it. Worst of all, I had the vague feeling that some of those other bodies were . . . well, if not enjoying themselves, at least starting to display certain physical manifestations of excitement.

Yes. I was being frotted. The dirty buggers.

'Clarence!' I whispered, hoarsely. 'We've got to get off. I mean *now*.' Clarence was floating above the mêlée, in relative comfort, reading a copy of the *Daily Torturegraph*.

'Well as it happens, ours is the next stop. Gehenna Forest. And here we are.'

The tube rattled out of the tunnel, shushed itself, and spat

139

us out like cherry stones. We found ourselves amidst another surging crowd, on yet another platform, but this time we seemed to be above ground. We were carried out onto a busy provincial high street with buses, taxis, roadworks, shops and people. But the whole thing was devoted not to the stuff of life, but to punishment and misery. The buses were mobile torture chambers; the hammers and drills of the workmen were formed of hot human flesh; the shops sold only pain.

Chapter 22
Into the Forest

'Quickly, this way,' urged Clarence. Beyond the street and the buildings I could see the looming shapes of green trees. In my reading, I had learned that people long ago used to fear the forest, that the woods meant death and doom. The forest harboured monsters, real and imagined: trolls, witches, wolves, men with bad teeth. It was the dark place from which you might never emerge.

For us living now, of course, trees are vaguely benign. Nice bits of greenery in the grey of the city, or pleasant places to walk the dog. Who could be afraid of trees? Who could fear the neat and boring lines of fir and pine, already, even in their spindly youth, more kitchen table than scary Celtic deity or demon? But something about that green-black cloud took me back to the old way of the forest.

Clarence took off down a small side street.

'We've been very lucky so far. You can be sure as anything that the Malebranche are already on our tail. They can sniff out a runaway from fifty kilometres through lead sheeting. Our only hope is to try to lose them in the forest. And I warn you, it isn't pretty in there. There are thousands of trails, most of them false. But I've been on a couple of team-building outward bound courses in there, so I know my way around, up to a point. You must follow me closely, and on no account leave the path or lose sight of the person in front of you. We must all stick together.'

As he spoke, a deafening *whomp, whomp whomp* shook

the air. We looked up to see two helicopters coming in to land in the centre of the town. The helicopters were living creatures: huge dragons, with ragged leathery blades. Four devils rode on each dragon's back, and another was held firmly in each of the four clawed hands. The devils spat and scratched and snarled at each other. One, hanging beneath the helidragon, crapped into his clawed hand and hurled it at another. The beshatted one farted a blast of orange flames, singeing the thick eyebrows of his assailant.

If that was how they treated each other, what would they do to us?

'Oh dear,' squealed Clarence. 'It's the Malebranche. It looks like the whole garrison. And they're pissed off. Quickly, run, *now*. Our only chance is to make it to the trees.'

As we ran, what had appeared to be a narrow lane between two buildings became thickly tangled with briars and ferns, and creepers that clung to our legs like children's hands. There had been no obvious transition between the town and the forest: we had been in the middle of the town and now we were in the midst of the forest.

I looked up. Trees towered above us. No light penetrated the canopy. The trees themselves seemed to have neither a beginning nor an end. We crashed through the undergrowth, following what might have been a trail. Behind us I could hear barbarous yelling and cursing and what sounded like loud rasping farts. Ominously, there was a smell of burning and the gloom of the forest seemed to have taken on an orange glow.

'They've set the forest alight,' shouted Clarence.

'Great, so we're all going to fry,' moaned Olaf.

'And then they pick up our charred remains and Annihilate us,' I added, cheerily.

'No. It's a good sign. It means they've given up on us. The Malebranche hate the forest. They can't use their aerial support. And there are things in here that even they fear. Their only tactic is to flame-fart the whole place. Hardly ecologically friendly. There're all kinds of rare species in here, you know: unicorns, griffins, snark. It really is an outrage. They've got no idea about preserving things for future generations of sufferers. Don't they realize that we don't own the place, that we're only custodians?'

I gave Clarence my *what the Hell are you on about, you raving lunatic* look. 'That's all very well, Clarence, but what about us? How do we get ourselves out of the barbecue?'

'Unless I'm mistaken, this trail leads down to a river. That should act as a natural firebreak. If we can get over that, we should be safe. From the fire at least.'

The raucous jabbering of the devils receded behind us, but the crackle and fizz of the fire was catching up. As well as being behind us, the fire also seemed to be on both sides. The Malebranche must have lit a semi-circle of flames around us.

'Faster, faster,' urged Clarence, but it was all useless. The flames were racing after us, fanned by some unholy, stinking wind. Smoke was in our eyes and our lungs. The brambles and briars clung to us more than ever. Trees were falling on either side, burned to arthritic black skeletons. The very ground beneath our feet was smouldering.

Scrote's paws were badly burned and even Olaf, indefatigable warrior and seamstress, was flagging. His neat polka-dot dress was tattered and torn and his helmet sadly askew. I thought about Francesca. Was this the time to call her for the second time? But it was still so early in our journey, and who knew what trials lay ahead?

And then Clarence, who had scuttled ahead, called out, 'It's here! It's here! The Camelpiss river! It's here!'

We tore ourselves loose from the strong fingers of the undergrowth and burst out onto the banks of a river, a good stone's throw wide. Its thick, yellowy-brown water made me think of the Ouse, or the Humber, or one of our other earthy northern rivers, their banks dotted with pale fisherboys, slow tench and chub flopping in their nets. But not even the Ouse at its worst smelled like this. It seemed that the Camelpiss river was aptly named. Scrote, Olaf and I lay panting by the bank as Clarence ran up and down, panicking. We were all blackened with soot and scorchmarks.

'We've got to get across, we've got to get across,' he jabbered.

'If it's too deep to wade, I can swim,' I said. 'So can Scrote. He often goes after ducks.'

'Dinner,' added Scrote, his first word in some time.

I looked at Olaf.

'Vikings do not swim,' he said with some dignity. 'That is why we have ships. The finest in the world.'

'It's not as easy as that,' panted Clarence. 'There are things in the water. Piranha. Crocodiles. Things that eat piranha and crocodiles. Things that eat the things that eat piranha and crocodiles.'

As he spoke the wind blowing the hot flames came on again, and the trees and bushes along the bank began to crackle and curl with the heat.

'Bugger,' exclaimed Clarence. 'I'm just going to have to fly you over one at a time. I hate this bit.' He unfurled his leathery little wings and fluttered them, like a butterfly on a buddleia. 'You first, Conor,' he said, taking off and hovering just above me. 'Get hold of my legs and don't let go.'

And then we were up and away, skimming over the water. I could see shapes beneath the surface. Some were small and agile, in perpetual motion. Others were large and almost still. In a few, hairy seconds, we were on the other side. Clarence hovered again and I dropped down, straight into a pile of what I assumed was crocodile poo. Clarence flapped back across the river, collected Scrote and dumped him in my arms. But the real challenge was the big Viking.

'Piss,' prophesied Scrote. 'Dinner.'

I could see that Clarence was struggling. He had managed – just – to take off with Olaf hanging like a . . . like a . . . No, I just can't do it. A depressed transvestite Viking dangling beneath a diminutive red devil over a river of piss in the middle of a burning jungle is not like *anything*, except itself.

So, there's Olaf dangling and I have this feeling that they just haven't got enough altitude. They skimmed the waves, Olaf's fluffy mules leaving two lines of paler foam in the green water. He's shouting at Clarence: 'Higher, in the name of Odin, higher.'

'I'm trying, I'm trying,' Clarence shouts back. 'This is way over my maximum payload.'

And then I saw it. Coming at them from behind, at an angle. The water took on a form, swelling and mounting. Olaf sensed that something very nasty was about to happen. He twisted and looked behind him just as the huge jaws broke the surface, lunging towards him. Somehow he managed to pull himself up a little higher and the teeth caught only the flapping skirt between his legs, doing terrible damage to the very nicely finished hem.

Clarence, aware now of what was happening, began to panic and tried to kick Olaf free. I couldn't blame him. The thing, part-shark, part-crocodile, was coming in for another pass. Olaf was doomed, and he seemed to be dragging Clarence down with him, thereby also scuttling *my* chances of salvation. Vikings can be *so* selfish.

Again the monstrous thing cruised and leaped; again Olaf managed to pull away, this time losing one of his mules. It looked as though they were going to make it, after all. But then, with only a metre or so of piss and teeth between them and the safety of the bank, Olaf's grip failed and he splashed down into the river. Clarence, relieved of the 120 kilos of prime Viking beef, shot high into the air, and became entangled in the branches of an overhanging tree.

Bellowing like a bull, Olaf surfaced and attempted to force his way to the bank. About him, the water turned frothy and pink. Fortunately, he was only seconds away from the shore and he soon dragged himself clear, still yelling and hollering. His lower half was alive with fat red-bellied fish and cold-eyed eels.

'Get 'em off me,' he screamed, now rolling around on the muddy bank. 'They're up me dress.'

Scrote and I started pulling at the horrid things. They'd taken big bites out of his bum, but apart from that he seemed to be more or less intact. Clarence fluttered down with twigs and leaves hanging from his horns.

'Ah. All's well that ends well. Looks like we've escaped the flames, and no one is badly hurt. Time to press on.'

'What about my bum?' moaned the big Viking. 'And this dress is ruined, *completely* ruined.'

Clarence ignored him, and set off once more into the undergrowth, to be followed by me, a limping, bloody, grumbling No-laugh Olaf and Scrote, chewing on a fish head that still had, clamped in its toothy jaws, a small piece of hairy Viking buttock.

In the excitement of the chase and the fire, I had not really taken in the full weird creepiness of what Clarence called the Hercynian Forest. For the most part the forest was still and silent: no wind now moved its leaves, no birds flitted through its branches. Only occasionally a distant scream reached us. Or other sounds, stranger still. The undergrowth was thick and brutal and, but for the handy machete attachment on Clarence's trident, it would have caught and held us fast.

There was a terrible thick, wet heat under the dark canopy

and we were all soon running with sweat. Flies and mosquitoes as big as bats fastened to us; tearing them off left deep, jagged punctures. But worst of all were the leeches. I've always feared leeches. They manage to combine two of my – or I suppose I mean humanity's – greatest dreads: things that suck your blood, and things that are soft and squelchy and move by stealth. And now they were all over us: in our ears, up my trousers, feasting at the wounds left on No-laugh's arse. Scrote had a whopper on his tongue. Now anyone knows that the only way to get rid of a leech is to burn it off with a fag. But did we have any? Not so much as a Woodbine tab end. Clarence did his best with the little flame he could conjure up from the end of his right index finger, but soon even the leeches had leeches, sucking the blood down the line.

'Who lives here?' I asked Clarence. 'I mean why did they make this place?'

'Good question. As you know, we've been trying to generate self-regulating and regenerating ecosystems for some time now. Essentially, what we're working towards is a Hell which pretty well runs itself. So we have these, er, I suppose one might call them game reserves, where we can deposit sinners and more or less forget about them. That way we can devote more time to the special cases: the politicians, generals, mass-murderers, tabloid journalists and so forth. Of course the reserves do require quite a lot of management, but it's nothing like as labour-intensive as the manual, talons-on approach. But, you know, for relatively humdrum clients such as yourself, the days of the personal tormentor are almost over. Once I'd cut my spurs on you, I could have looked forward to a really juicy client.'

He smiled wistfully. He seemed to have got over his huge sulk about me screwing up his career. Good to know that he didn't carry a grudge. Not like my sister, who could remember a stolen fruit gum for five years, which is a bit much – even if it was a black one.

'So there are people – I mean dead souls – here?'

'Oh yes. This zone is reserved mainly for greedy city types, fat cats, capitalists in top hats. That sort of chap. You know, it's a jungle out there. But there's also a Roman legion or two, who've been lost in here for donkeys' years. And some loggers.'

But we saw no other sinners to entertain us on our jungle hike. Instead *we* were the entertainment, also providing a five-course banquet for the swarms of biting flies and crawling vermin. I could feel my strength sapping, drawn away by the leeches, the whining, mechanical mosquitoes and the big blue-black flies with piercing stylets and rasping labia.

Chapter 23
Two Boils in the Heart of Darkness

As we trudged through the dense green heat, I focused on Olaf's neck. He was in front of me, directly behind Clarence; Scrote scrambled along behind. Something was happening to it. The neck. It had changed from a pale pink to an angry red. And it was growing, swelling perceptibly as I looked on, fascinated. Olaf kept pulling at his collar and scratching at the lump.

It reminded me of the famous boil on Cathy's bum. It was the only moment of real intimacy we'd ever shared. I'd noticed that she'd been sitting strangely for a couple of days, one buttock raised as if to ease out a fart, a fart that never came. Now, as you've probably been able to work out, me and Cathy were not particularly close siblings. Yep, we hated each other. So you'll be as surprised as I was to hear that later that evening she came a-knocking on my bedroom door.

'Conor?' She stuck her head round the door. I threw a crusty rolled-up sock at her.

'Get out! What do you want?'

'Nothing. Just a little chat.'

'What for?'

'Oh, you know. We should talk sometimes. We are related after all.'

She came in and sat on my bed. I was listening to some grunge shit on my Discman, watching my portable telly and reading a graphic novel about a new plague, all at the same time.

'Cathy. You hate my guts and think I stink, and I think you're boring and ugly, so what's it all about?'

'OK, you evil little turd. I wouldn't ask you, but I'm desperate. Do you swear to God, swear on Mum and Dad's lives, that you won't tell anyone what I'm going to show you?'

This sounded interesting.

'Yeah, sure,' I lied.

And then it all came out in a rush. 'I've got a bit of a spot on my bottom. I can't get at it. It's killing me. I can't sit down. I'm too embarrassed to tell Mum about it. She'll make me go to the health centre, and that Dr Loveage is gorgeous. I'm telling you all this, and I know you're going to destroy me, but I've got to do it. Stop laughing. It's not funny.'

'It is funny.'

'Look.' She was deadly serious. 'Will you squeeze it for me? You're always squeezing your own spots. You seem to love it, no matter how much it hurts, or whether it leaves you looking like a leper. Well, you can squeeze mine, and it won't hurt you but me, and it's my bottom and not your face that will look stupid.'

Put that way, there was no arguing. She lifted her skirt and gingerly pulled down the left knicker cheek, careful to display as little of her precious arse as possible. Thank God. And there it was. Now I've seen some sights in my life and in my death, but that boil was a thing of wonder. It somehow managed to combine the crystalline perfection and regularity of the mineral world with the moist, moving suppleness of the vegetative. A puckering red aureole, a massy medulla and a glistening pearly nipple.

'Wow,' was all I could say – perhaps the only 'wow' I've ever uttered in sincerity.

'Ow!' said Cathy, responding to my first tentative probe.

But did I have the courage, the strength? 'Cathy, I'm sorry. This is an evil too great for my meagre skill. If I grapple with this Balrog I may vanquish it, but it could drag us both with it into the pit.'

'Get on with it, you ponce,' was all she said.

And so I did. I came at it slowly, avoiding the direct gaze of that cold white eye (I mean the boil, not Cathy). Cathy tensed as my fingers travelled lightly over the low foothills. And then I began in tiny degrees to increase the pressure. She straightened, emitted a 'Nngfffck' from between clenched lips and then, losing control, she kicked and bucked like a wild horse, begging me to stop. But we were past the point of no return. I shifted from a finger to a thumb grip, pushing with all my might.

Cathy was now rigid with pain, providing a good, stable foundation for my work. Beads of sweat burst out on my forehead, but this Krakatoa would not erupt. There was nothing for it but to use the blade. I still had my old modelling knife from my carefree Airfix days. Keeping one finger on the monster, I reached over to the shoebox that was home to my bits and bobs: embarrassing badges, rubber bands, football medals, used cotton buds, crumpled tissues. And there she was: my trusty, rusty scalpel. Totally careless of the risk of infection, I used the still-sharp point to prick a tiny point at the epicentre. Cathy let out a sound somewhere between a squeal and a moan. A thin, disappointing line of white goo appeared. But then, with an audible 'pok', she blew, and all Hell broke loose. Pus flew in every direction: it dripped from my eyelids and chin; it clung to the red viscose of her shirt.

'OOOOOOOOOOOO,' she moaned, 'that's good, that's sooooo good.' The operation had been a success, but now the surgeon sickened. I fled to the bog and chucked my guts up. When I returned, she was lying on my bed, flushed, calm. She got unsteadily to her feet and, for the first time ever, we embraced.

Sorry, got a bit carried away there. You want to hear about the thing on Olaf's neck, not the boil on Cathy's bum. It had grown now to the size of a fist.

'Olaf, you've got a Hell of a lump on your neck, you know.'

Clarence stopped in his tracks. 'Let me see.'

Olaf reluctantly submitted to Clarence's examination. Clarence looked closely at the bite, if bite it was. 'Nasty. We're going to have to lance this. Stand back.' With no further ado the devil chopped down on Olaf's neck with his machete. The lump split neatly and out popped an ugly dwarfish little man, who scuttled gleefully off into the undergrowth. There then followed a bat, two toads, a length of barbed wire, a toy fire appliance, a large hairy spider, a cardigan and a packet of vanilla Angel Delight. With each new birth Olaf emitted a resigned 'Oeph'.

'Come on,' said Clarence cheerfully, after he'd made up the Angel Delight with puddle water and offered to share it out. 'It's not far now.'

'Not far to what?' I asked. Given that everything always got worse in Hell, I was more than a little bit concerned about what might be waiting for us beyond the sheltering gloom of the forest.

'The next stage in our journey will take us across the Great Salt Plain.'

'Is it bad?' I asked.

'Oh yes, it's bad.'

Chapter 24
Prey for Us

We trudged on after Clarence: bitten, sucked, chewed, scraped, scratched and tripped up. I felt the presence of other beings hidden in the trees around us, scampering, avoiding our path, but keeping up with us. Whisperings reached us, and cries and moans. We saw the ghostly, tattered remnants of the lost legion of Publius Quinctilius Varus, fleeing wild-eyed through the trees from some terrible ambush, pursued for ever by barbaric, naked spearmen.

'By now,' said Clarence, gathering us together, 'the Malebranche will know that we've escaped the flames. They'll be on our trail again. Once they've got the scent – and they're sure to pick *that* up by the river where Olaf left some flesh behind – they are relentless. We must hasten.'

And it did indeed seem as though somewhere in the dark wood behind us, a trumpet or hunting horn blared.

Eventually, after more scrambling entanglements and moist encounters, I saw that at last we were coming to the edge of the forest. The trees began to thin, and the moans and low cries that had accompanied us grew faint and then ceased. The intense gloom of the world beneath the boughs began to give way to the foul red glimmer of the Great Salt Plain.

The thorns and briars had torn strips of flesh from my arms and legs and I was dumb with fatigue, but we were through the forest. Even Scrote, whose hide was made of some curious weave of asbestos, wire wool and Teflon, designed to shrug off Rottweiler canines and the flailing claws of dying cats, looked in a bad way. Somewhere in the undergrowth he had lost an ear. Olaf looked even worse, like a raddled old slapper at the end of a long Saturday night. But surely now things could only get better? There couldn't be a law, could there, that said that things always had to get worse, not even here in Hell?

'We've made it,' I said, my voice weak and slurred.

'I wouldn't have thought so,' said No-laugh. 'I reckon there's a law in this place that says that everything has to get worse. It's like a bogey stuck to your finger: you keep trying to wipe it off but you just move it from finger to thumb and back again, with it getting blacker and stickier each time.'

'Thanks,' said Clarence, 'for your characteristically life-enhancing contribution.' Coming from a devil, whose sole reason for existence was inflicting pain and misery, that seemed a mite hypocritical. 'But, as it happens,' he went on, 'you're not far off the truth. I'm afraid the next bit isn't much fun. If you look over there you'll see what I mean.'

We all looked in the direction he was pointing. Beyond the last of the trees a lone and level plain stretched out as far as the eye could see. It seemed at first that there was nothing on its barren expanse, but then I noticed some tiny shapes moving towards us. As they came closer, I saw that they were people – naked men and women. They were running, stumbling, crawling across the plain, in a raggedy but still coherent group. And they were not alone. At their heels, snapping, biting, clawing, were what seemed to be sabre-toothed tigers, huge wolves, lions and creatures like nothing on earth – hybrid brutes dreamed up by some mad scientist to haunt our dreams. They were the beasts that had lived in my wardrobe when I was a kid, shrouded but for the gleam of a tooth or a talon by gloom and shadow.

Monsters.

The hunting pack pursued the naked prey. The spectacle was horrific, but fascinating. I thought at first that the people might be helping each other, the men protecting the women. But they were not; they fought amongst themselves, tripping and laming each other. Each person was trying to save him- or herself by sacrificing someone weaker. And always the frantic motion; if any flagged or paused for a moment, they were instantly set upon by the pack.

One old man, limping, weeping, his eyes searching for a woman or a child to cast down to buy himself some time, finally fell to his knees. A dozen pursuers broke off from the chase and surrounded him silently. Tongues lolled and yellow eyes gleamed in the red light. The old man called for help, but the herd had already moved on. And then there was only a flurry of gnashing teeth and tearing claws and blood and bowels. The pack rooted in his soft parts, chewed and champed at his limbs. And all the time his eyes were open, and alert: he watched his own dismemberment, a scream frozen in his mouth. Munch. Bosch. Bad things.

Another younger, fitter man had been cut off from the herd. I need a better word than herd, which conjures up a pleasant pastoral scene with milkmaids and passive, long-lashed Friesians. What is the collective noun for a load of naked, damned people running away from monsters? A panic? A rout? No, no, a viscera. So this one bloke, power-fully built, hairy-arsed, had separated from the *viscera*. Was he trying to slip away unnoticed, to escape into the forest? Or was he just an amusing challenge for the blood-keen beasts, bored with gnawing the dry bones of old women? But he moves quickly, this lean and muscular man. It seems that he might reach the shelter of the trees and, bad though the forest had been, it was better than the carnage on the plains. Fast, but not as fleet as the leading wolf. Miles from the first low thorn bushes, it caught the man and bit through his Achilles tendon. He writhed and flailed on the brown earth, bellowing. In a second the whole savage pack was upon him. He fought and pushed at the beasts, but it only extended his agony. His cries ended only when a sabretooth plunged its thirty-centimetre teeth into his neck.

I felt sick. I *was* sick. Even No-laugh, who'd seen his fair share of this sort of thing before, turned pale. But Scrote licked his lips and Clarence was smiling.

'Nice work,' he said quietly to himself.

'You seem to be enjoying this,' I said.

'Oh, years of training, you know. Can't teach an old dog new tricks.'

Scrote wagged his stumpy tail. He'd never learned any tricks at all.

'How are we going to get past those fell creatures of the plain?' asked No-laugh.

It was a good question. My cosy little cell was again growing more attractive. I was even starting to miss the opera music and the books that smelled like an old librarian's vest.

'Fear not, I have a plan. You know, I am *technically* senior to those chaps over there. I am an *Executive* Devil after all. I passed my exams. Unless they've been told about us they should let us through without too much bother. But we have to make it look convincing. Same routine – I'm afraid I'll have to use a little chastisement on you – just for the sake of, er, veracity.'

'So we're just going to walk past them?' asked No-laugh, incredulously.

'Well, run actually. Nobody walks out there. We just jog along with, as I say, a few flourishes for form's sake.'

I was starting to worry about those flourishes. I worried even more when I saw the whip that Clarence pulled out of his deep trouser pocket (by way of the comb, elastoplast, thermos flask and asthma inhaler).

'Off we go then,' he said chirpily and cracked the whip a centimetre from my ear.

We started to run, heading for the distant peaks. Except for Scrote. He wasn't shifting. Clarence, after a couple of 'here, boy's and a vicious but futile stroke across the dog's buttocks with his whip, asked him what was up.

'Piss?' was the reply, Scrote gazing out at the tree-less, lamppost-less wasteland ahead of us.

Typical. Here we were, in Hell, with a very real chance of being torn to pieces by ravening beasts, hunted by the relentless Malebranche. Our one hope of salvation lay on the far side of this bleached and barren plain, and all Scrote could think about was where he was going to piss. Dogs!

'You can do your business,' said Clarence, primly, 'on Conor's leg.'

I couldn't really argue. Scrote tested out the solution, and found it satisfactory. We were off. No-laugh set a fast pace – he was after all a Viking warrior, and in pretty good shape. All that rowing while he had been alive and, of course, since death, as any waitress can tell you, being on your feet all day is as good as a gym work-out. Scrote had chased enough cats and small children to stay in reasonable trim. But right from the beginning I suffered. Most of my ingenuity in school had gone into forging notes to get me off cross-country. Time and again I felt Clarence's whip play like electricity across my back.

Within a few minutes we attracted the attention of the hunters of the plain. The sabretooth, muscles bunched on its shoulders, dripping teeth curving down like an assassin's daggers, broke away from the pack and trotted towards us. It was followed by a creature with the body of a tiger, but the head and bare neck of a vulture.

'Whatever you do, don't stop, not for a second,' urged Clarence. 'These fellows are conditioned to rip into anything vulnerable.'

The sabretooth and the other thing pounded along beside us, uncertain whether or not to attack. Clarence lashed out with his whip, the stroke simultaneously catching me, Scrote and Olaf. Nice shot!

'These are mine. You clear off,' he barked.

'We rule the plain. Leave them to us,' hissed the vulture-head.

'You don't rule your own arse, you cock-headed shitehawk.' This was a side to Clarence hitherto unseen.

The sabretooth joined in: 'Why should we give up our prey to you, *little* devil? We have the might to take them.'

'You know my rank. I can have you assigned to sentry duty in the north. No flesh there. No blood. Just the cold wind to blunt your teeth, and ice to fill your guts.'

The predators winced at the thought.

'Where do you take this meat?' asked the vulture.

'War zone. Cannon fodder.' And then a twinkle came into Clarence's black eye. 'And we carry a message. Behind us there is a company of Malebranche who are defecting to the other side. I must warn our High Command. If you would curry favour, you should harry them. The Malebranche are well fed, and plump.'

The two hunters conferred for a moment and then turned back towards their comrades.

'That was pretty clever, even if I say so myself: it should earn us some breathing space,' said Clarence.

'But will these beasts really attack their own kind – your kind?' asked Olaf.

'They're not the brightest bunch. Specially trained and bred to bite before they think. And the Malebranche aren't known for their silken tongues, so there's a good chance that there'll be a bit of rough and tumble. Shame we can't hang around to watch. But we can't so, er, get moving, eh?' And with that he whipped me again on the arse, which was totally unnecessary.

Chapter 25
The Peripatetic School

And so our marathon across the plain continued, with No-laugh Olaf ever at the fore and me shailing and wambling at the back, goaded and chided by Clarence. Clarence had it easy. After jogging with us for a short time, he somehow produced a bike, and cycled along quite merrily on the hard, flat, salty plain, steadfastly refusing all entreaties for croggies and backies.

The searing heat and the bitter, alkaline saltiness of the plain gave me a raging thirst and a mouth like a camel's snatch. To take my mind from the misery I tried chatting with Scrote. It wasn't much use, although he *had* learned a new word: *arsecheese*.

Olaf was better value, but even his best friends back on the longship wouldn't claim him as a natural conversationalist. His small talk was limited to rowing tips (pig fat on the hands prevents chapping), tales of monk-slaughtering (heard one, heard 'em all), and an obsessive mulling over exactly what was happening with hemlines this season.

But at least he was human, and there was much about him to admire. He spoke lovingly of his old comrades, and I could see that there was no natural malice in him: his crimes were the crimes of his culture, his sins the sins of his fathers, and when it looked as though I couldn't carry on he pulled me onto his shoulders and allowed me to rest. But soon even his strength was sapped by the plain and he set me gently back on my feet. And so the grim journey continued.

Later I found that Clarence was cycling beside me. By now my tongue was so fat and knobbly and foul I felt as though I were running with a toad in my mouth. But there were some things that had been seriously bugging me since I'd got damned, and so I made myself speak.

'Clarence,' I began, 'there's still some stuff I can't get my head round. Stuff the judge talked about.'

'Go on,' said Clarence. 'I'll try to enlighten you.'

'I still feel really narked about being here – even if this all works out, and I don't get Annihilated. I just wasn't *that* bad, apart from the lying and the thieving and the, er, "murder" business. I mean, just what should I have done? How could I have lived a good life?'

Clarence didn't answer for a couple of minutes, and I thought he'd chosen to ignore the question, but then he said: 'The nature of the good life has interested philosophers from the beginning. The Sophists, Socrates, Plato and Aristotle, the Epicureans, Stoics . . . they all had a go. Is it living your life in tune with the wishes of the gods, whatever those wishes might be? Is it moderation in all things? Is it acting always in accordance with some rule that you've decided on for yourself? Is it living a life appropriate to the kind of being that we – I mean you, humans are?

'Thomas Hobbes, who I should say is a favourite of ours down here, wrote that . . .' There followed a fumbling for the good old *Infernal Encyclopaedia*, during the course of which Clarence fell off his bike. 'He wrote that, "Whatsoever is the object of any man's appetite or desire; that is which he for his part calleth good." So is good just a smokescreen for our desires? I suppose Nietzsche was the ultimate exponent of that line of reasoning.'

'I've heard of Nietzsche. He's big in Death Metal circles.'

'Really? Oh, that's nice. Well he argued that the whole Christian ethic was a slave morality – a system designed by the weak to keep the strong in check. You know, all the usual business about being kind and turning the other cheek, and the meek inheriting the Earth . . .'

'And blessed be the cheesemakers,' I added.

'Eh? Whatever. In place of this slave morality, Nietzsche claimed that we, or rather an elite of supermen . . .'

'Faster than a speeding bullet . . .'

'*Supermen*, should make their own morality, celebrate their own power, their own will, shunning convention, rising above humdrum passions, trampling those who stand in their way or who try to shackle their freedom. All good stuff.'

'Small man, was he, Nietzsche?'

'Small perhaps in stature, but great in heart. Wonderful moustache. Wish I could grow one like it.'

'Yeah, so the point is that there're loads of theories about what we should do. How can we decide which is the right one? I'm a teenager – how can I be responsible? Is it enough just to go to church, just to believe in God? But it can't be, because I saw a telly programme about it. The Inquisition; the Crusades; burning witches.'

'Yes, well, it's a tricky subject. Now I'm the last one to try to justify the Church – that can get you into *serious* trouble down here, let me tell you – but I think if you balance all the good things the Church has done against the bad things, it *just about* comes down on the side of good. And there aren't many institutions about which even that much can be said. Throughout most of human history there has been a choice between naked power – the power of the state, or of various strong men – and another form of power which, however corrupt and fallible, at least had an *ethic*. The alternative to the Church wasn't some form of enlightened rationalism, no, it was men with swords, with one eye on your sheep and the other on your daughters. And I'm told that even the

Inquisition wasn't quite as bad as it's made out to be – they had the most comfortable jails in Spain.'

'I'm still lost. What could I have done to stay out of Hell? Was it all really predestined, like you said before? That would make everything you've said just now redundant.'

'Well, I've got a bit of a confession to make there. We tell all of our new entrants that stuff about predestination. Helps to get them off on the right foot, you know: bitter, resentful, cursing God and the universe, railing against fate and yet beaten down with the futility of it all.'

'So you mean it isn't true – there's a place for free will and making the right choices, and we're not all just screwed from the day we're born?'

'Yes, I suppose that's one way of putting it.'

'So, about ten K back, when you began talking about the good life, and the right stuff to do, what's the answer then? What's the secret of leading a just life and not having to spend eternity in this crap-hole?'

'You know I'm really not supposed to let you in on that kind of information. We'd be in deep do-do down here if word leaked out.'

'Come on, you owe me, after all we've been through together. And anyway, I'm hardly going to get out and tell anyone, am I?'

'No, that's true. So, you want the secret of virtue, the holy grail sought by the greatest minds your species has produced in the four thousand years since the first inklings of civilization?'

'If it's not too much trouble.'

'Be nice.'

'I am being nice. I've listened politely to everything you've said, even though most of it sounded like gibberish.'

'No, I don't mean be nice, I mean *being nice*, that's it, that's the secret.'

'BEING NICE? Are you taking the piss? That's so banal. Is that really the best you can come up with?'

'I don't like your tone, Conor,' said Clarence, obviously nettled by my less than rapturous response. 'What's banal about being nice? About offering up the everyday pleasantries, and not telling big stupid lies, and not hurting people's feelings, and remembering birthdays and getting your round in at the pub, eh? What's wrong with telling people that they're looking great, and not beating up weaker kids, and not putting your chewing gum under the desk where you know it's going to stick to someone's knee?'

'But that's all too easy!'

'Easy? Well how come nobody does it? Why are you all so horrid to each other? I admit that it's simple, but that doesn't make it easy. If it was easy, I'd be out of a job. The beauty of nice, from our point of view, is that nobody, or rather hardly anybody, bothers with it. Godly or ungodly, rich banker, poor labourer – nastiness is evenly distributed.'

'This is a wind-up. My dad always said that things like good manners and conventional morality – the lying stuff – were just a way of keeping things as they are, just the elite's way of making sure the elite stayed elite. Or something like that. I wish I'd listened to him. "Nice" isn't enough. "Nice" *can't* be enough.'

The whole debate – OK, not debate, lecture – had got me down. Here I was being sermonized at by a devil. I'd almost come to see Clarence as a friend – after all, he seemed to be trying to help me, even if it was just for his own sake. But did that mean that I could trust him? Can you ever be sure that when someone tells you what the right thing is, that they're not just telling you what the right thing is for *them*? My pre-mad dad criticized the way things were in our society, but he thought he knew the way things *should* be. Was his way better? How could it all just come down to being nice? It was all too much. Here was I – a teenager, a scabby, lonely kid, my mind frazzled by computer games and drum machines – having to deal with the heaviest stuff in the universe, heavier than osmium, heavier than kryptonite. An expression I'd picked up from somewhere came into my head: existential angst. That was it, that's what I had: I was suffering from existential angst. Was this just the latest punishment Hell had devised for me?

Chapter 26
A Flight and a Fall

All the way through this brain-bashing, we had been pounding along across the plain, salty dust in our eyes, a burning heat on our backs. The sky was the colour of a slaughterhouse floor: sunless, but with patches of red intensity. The only relief from the dull monotony of the baked earth came with the broken towers and battlements of four ruined cities: Gomorrah, Sodom, Admah and Zeboiim, the sad histories of which were told to us by Clarence. Attempted sexual interference with angels is not, apparently, to be recommended.

As we ran I looked up occasionally to the horizon, and towards the blue-black mountains. They never seemed any closer; if anything they seemed to be drifting away from us. And then, as my will began to break, bruised and battered as it had been by Clarence's discourse, the mountains suddenly reared up before us like a breaching whale.

'Nearly there,' said Clarence, climbing off his bike, which he folded away into a matchbox. 'We've made good time.' Then, gazing back across the burning plain, his face clouded. 'So have they, by the look of things.' He pulled out a brass telescope (after the usual fumbling preliminaries which brought forth a fishing rod, a pouffe, a can of baked beans and a rectal thermometer) and put it to his eye. He then passed it to me, saying, 'Appears as though they've had a hard time of it too.' He pointed in the direction of a distant dust cloud.

I peered through the telescope and found myself in the

middle of a cursing, grumbling, all-too-familiar troupe of devils. They did look in a bad way, with bitemarks tearing through their leathery skin and the odd stump where a limb should have been. There were twelve of them, pounding relentlessly across the plain. Every few moments one would leap into the air, and shoot forwards like the Batmobile, propelled by a turbocharged flaming fart. One of them carried a trident on which were stuck two heads: a vulture and a sabre-toothed cat. The severed heads hissed and bit at each other like an old married couple.

'Rubicante, Barbariccia, our old friend Draghignazzo, Cagnazzo, Farfarello, Alichino, Calcabrina, Libicocco, Ciriatto, Graffiacane, Scarmiglione, and Malacoda – their leader,' intoned Clarence. 'The A-team. We're lucky we've got this far. Thank Satan we're near the Geryondrome. We might just make it yet. We simply follow the line of the mountains round to the left for a couple of—'

We pushed on, fear now overcoming our exhaustion. The dark rock of the mountain loomed up on our right. Although it seemed to be made of hard granite, it acted like a malevolent, breathing entity. A leg would shoot out to trip me, or a stony hand reach up from the earth to grasp an unwary ankle. And as we ran, I was aware that the cloud behind us was getting ever closer, like a coming storm.

But soon I saw our destination: a collection of low concrete buildings, a forlorn windsock, and a *thing*. A *thing*? Well, what would you call a beast the size of a bus, with a human-like face, a body covered in really rather pretty, paisley-pattern scales, and with the tail and barbed sting of a scorpion? It was standing on a wooden perch like Edgar Allan Poe's pet budgie. Well, I soon found out what you'd call it.

'Ah good, there's a geryon in. I'll get some tickets. Hope they take plastic,' said Clarence.

He went off towards one of the low buildings while the

three of us stood around trying not to look scared. No-laugh was living up to his name big style, and was mumbling and moaning to himself. Scrote was all skin and bone, his tongue lolling out like a piece of his own guts he'd coughed up.

Clarence came running back. 'We're OK. They're a bit pissed off that you haven't got any luggage to lose, so they've radioed the geryon to give you a hard time, but apart from that things are looking good. We take off in five minutes, as soon as they've refuelled. And what's more there's not another one due for decades.'

We followed Clarence over to the geryon. A couple of skinny devils in overalls attached a large bag around its head, above which only the creature's mild blue eyes were visible. It was eating. Muffled cries and screams came from the bag, which squirmed as if it were full of puppies destined for the canal.

'All aboard,' said Clarence cheerfully.

There was a rope ladder leading from the geryon's scaly legs up to its iridescent shoulders. I scrambled up first. Olaf passed Scrote to me, then I held out my hand and Olaf took it and I helped him up too. He nodded at me and smiled a quick Viking smile, and for a few moments I felt as though I had taken on some of his strength, some of his courage.

I needed it. From the towering height of the geryon's back I had the perfect view of our pursuers. Figures were now distinct within the cloud even without the telescope.

'Clarence, we've gotta get out of here. Those bastards are getting close.'

'Quite agree,' replied Clarence.

Just then the geryon shook loose the feeding bag and licked the gore from its face with a long, thin tongue. It smiled, but made no sound. Clarence took out his trident and gently prodded the beast's side.

I'd been wondering how the thing would get off the

ground: there were no wings visible. The answer came as the geryon whipped its long, cruel tail backwards and forwards, faster and faster. We took off and began to spiral upwards. When we were a hundred metres or so up, the Malebranche came steaming into the Geryondrome.

'Can these devils fly?' asked Olaf; the same question was on the tip of my tongue.

'Of course. All devils can fly. But they are so heavily armoured they haven't got much manoeuvrability or speed. And their ceiling's very low. We should be OK.'

Below, I could see the Malebranche running around flapping their wings, trying to build up enough speed to get airborne. They looked like albatrosses. One by one they lumbered into the air, but even their afterburners seemed practically spent, just emitting the odd, puttering spark.

Their leader, the one called Malacoda, shook his fist, and we could just catch his bellowed curses.

'Slawkenbergius, you runt! You're effing dead, *dead*! You're for the effing Annihilator, you bastard renegade, you and that Viking poof, and that little wanker.'

With one final, momentous effort, the chief of the much-feared Malebranche hurled his great trident, its shaft as thick as a wrestler's arm and as long as a wet weekend. It came at us as straight and true as an Exocet missile. We were still accelerating upwards; the missile had almost died its death when it clattered into Olaf's helmet, but it still had just enough force to knock the beautifully burnished iron helm from his head. Olaf, anxious to cling onto this last vestige of his proud Viking heritage – albeit a bastardized one, with its fake horns and satin lining – made a desperate lunge. He managed to catch the tip of one horn in his outstretched fingers, but he had overreached himself. With an almost whispered, 'By Odin, no,' my friend the melancholy Viking fell from the back of the giant geryon.

There was nothing we could do. I watched in stunned horror as Olaf drifted slowly down, almost peacefully, into the clutches of the circling devils. I watched as he struggled with those heartless fiends, punching and kicking at them as they swooped and cackled, like crows on a carcass. It was magnificent and it was futile. His dismemberment began before he reached the ground. I covered my eyes, unwilling to be a witness to this obscenity.

'What will happen to him, Clarence?' I asked.

'If he's lucky, it will mean Annihilation. But first they will have their sport. He will pay the price for our escape.'

I replayed all my memories of Olaf, from our very first meeting in the Valhalla Café. I thought of the times he had saved me, his strong arms lifting me above the horror of Hell up onto his broad shoulders. He had his faults: he'd murdered and ravished, but there was still more nobility in the tip of one of his fake Viking horns than in the rest of Hell put together. I found that I was weeping.

Even Scrote looked sad. It may just have been a selfish response to the thought that now he had only Clarence and me to help him out. Or perhaps the ugly mutt was beginning to have some feelings other than greed and anger. Maybe that was part of *his* punishment.

And all the while we sailed upwards, through choking sulphurous clouds and past the jagged, glowering peaks.

Shit.

I went and said it.

Peaks.

Part Three
The Idiot

Chapter 27
Peaks and Troughs

Peaks. God, I hate language sometimes. Some little accident of sound and suddenly a memory hits you like a diagnosis of cancer. Peaks. Sara Peaks. Even now I cannot utter or even think those phonemes without feeling sick. Sara was my first ever girlfriend: the first girl who I had kissed with my mouth open; the first girl to let me touch her; the first girl to break my heart. You might think that it's stupid to talk about breaking hearts when you're only twelve, but I can tell you now that it can happen. Sara was tall and lithe and had the most perfect German helmet haircut you ever saw.

I first noticed her in the playground, eating an apple with her friend, Trudy Trebble, who was also tall but lacked Sara's astonishing elegance, poise and serenity. At the breaks, the boys all used to play football while the girls stood in groups, talking about whatever it is that girls stand in groups talking about (International cheese prices? The best way to eradicate squirrels? The relative merits of Napoleon's generals at the battle of Austerlitz?). But for some reason that summer a weird hybrid game took possession of us, girls and boys both – a cross between netball, basketball, football, and heavy petting. No one really knew the rules, but we all understood when they were broken. It was a magical time. Even the psychos and killers recognized that something strange was happening with the game and, after a couple of beatings, ball slashings and shit-stick forays, left us to our arcane and elaborate dance.

Sara was the acknowledged star among the girls. She was in the school netball team, playing goal attack, which I suppose gave her an advantage, but with her it was more a natural grace thing. I was the tallest of the boys who played, and so it fell to me to 'mark' her. We would leap together in the air, perfectly matched, synchronized like dolphins. She had the coolest pair of green suede Golas. We never spoke – both too shy – but began to exchange little smiles. Once we fell over together and I gave her my hand to help her up. Our duel, restrained, understated, courteous, but urgent, became the most important thing in my life.

And then, oh the joy! Trudy used to get the bus with my mate Fingers Fairs (although he wasn't known as Fingers then, it was well before the Angels were on the scene) and she asked him if I liked Sara. With much sneering, pushing, goading and general piss-taking, Fingers passed the message, for message surely it was, back to me.

I was in.

In, but not in. I'd never asked a girl to go out with me before. What did you say? What if I was wrong and she said no? What if it was all an elaborate plot to make me look like a tit? What if an overflying vulture dropped a rock and hit me on the head?

I needed reassurance. I needed reassurance *bad*. I had to do it through Fairs and Trudy.

'What would Sara say if I asked her to go out with me?' I got Fairs to repeat it three times, before I sent him off to put it to Trudy.

A day later came back the reply: 'Why don't you ask her and find out?'

It was too, too cruel. But there was nothing for it. And so, that same afternoon, I approached her in the covered way (a sheltered area in between two of the school buildings, always bitterly cold, even in summer), my body and soul trembling in fear and horror at the prospect of having to talk to the object of my desire.

'Sara Peaks,' I said.

'Hello,' she replied. These were the first words we had uttered to each other, despite our tussles and hard caresses over the ball in the game. It was a promising start.

'What would you say if I asked you to go out with me?'

I thought this was very cunning – if she told me that she'd say 'no', I wouldn't ask her – face saved!

'Why don't you ask me and find out?' she replied.

Doh!

'Will you go out with me, Sara Peaks?'

'OK then. Where shall we go?'

Mmm. Hadn't really thought about it. Where do you go with girls? What do you *do* with girls? You have to remember that my experience was limited at that tender age to punching Cathy.

'Fishing,' I said.

Why? I swear to God I have no idea. I'd never been fishing in my life. It looked like a boring, pointless, joyless thing to do. I didn't have a rod. I didn't even have a long stick.

'Fishing?' she said, clearly perplexed.

'Yeah, it's great,' I said, with all the enthusiasm I could summon, set now upon this road. This was turning into a nightmare. 'We'll go to the Bacon Pond. There's massive pike. They eat babies.'

'Is that what you use for bait then?'

She looked innocently at me. I was being mocked, and quite rightly. Why hadn't I said 'Let's go to the pictures' or 'What about my granddad's shed?' or 'Beyond the realm of ecstasy into a new dimension of pleasure'? But no, I had to say 'fishing', like a stalker or a bus enthusiast. And it was too late to go back. We fixed on the following Saturday. My mate Chris Rushby lent me his rod, and wrote out some instructions in a little notebook, which was pretty decent of him, and completely out of character.

The Bacon Pond took its name from the fact that it lay in the shadow of a huge meat processing plant, the biggest employer in the area once the pits had gone. It really was famous for its huge, cannibalistic pike, and its banks were always dotted with eager pikemen. A day's fishing cost ten pounds, which was exactly twice my pocket money. I did briefly think about asking Sara for half the money, before sanity was restored.

The worst thing about the whole business was that word of my date had leaked out. I could take it from my friends – what are friends for, after all, if not to taunt and humiliate you when you're in trouble? But inevitably, Cathy picked up on it through her infallible network of informers. She was only nine at the time, but she somehow realized, with that uncanny ability she always had for locating the soft under-belly, that I was vulnerable.

'Mum,' she announced at Friday teatime, 'Conor's got a girlfriend and he's taking her to the Bacon Pond so he can kiss her.'

'Liar,' I screamed, and threw a Scotch egg at her. It missed, and Scrote – a mere pup back then – picked up the rebound off the wall. Mum and Dad looked at each other, smiling. Now *that* didn't happen very often.

'Now, Cathy,' said Mum, smiling the sort of smile you want to hit with a hammer, 'just be quiet and leave Conor alone. He's going through puberty at the moment and it's a very difficult time for him. I think it's nice he's got a little girlfriend.'

Cathy was helpful in one way: I stole a copy of *J17* from her bedroom and mined it for useful information. Much of it was incomprehensible stuff about eyeliner, blusher and vaginal discharges, and it confirmed my view that girls can't be trusted on the subject of pop music, but I did at least gather that it was important for a boyfriend to drive the girl back after a date in his Porsche Boxster or 4x4 off-road vehicle. Translated into my terms its meaning was clear: I must give Sara her bus fare home.

I waited for Sara at the shed where you bought the fishing permit. The sky was the colour of old zinc, and an evil wind whipped the rain into my eyes. Under my parka I was wearing my best jeans, neatly pressed by Mum, and my favourite jumper, bedecked with farmyard scenes. I was a crucial, and tragic, six months away from the dawning of style consciousness. Sara was way ahead of me. She was covered in names that I'd never heard of, but I knew she looked superb.

'Hello,' she said, smiling, and kissed me on the cheek, the very last thing I was expecting. I glowed a luminous red and mumbled something about assembling the rod. I was so innocent I had no idea of the potential for saucy double-entendre-ing. We walked along the bank to try to find a good spot. I had no idea what a good spot might be. Was it shady and overhung, or open and airy? We ended up on a shingly bank, woefully exposed to the rain and bluster. I had a plastic bag with the rod, reel and bait, and a Tupperware box of sandwiches made by Mum. She'd put in two Wagonwheels, which I was simultaneously pleased by and uneasy about.

I had absolutely no small talk. I tried one or two gambits, but when it became clear that she had no interest in football, Airfix models or skimming stones, I realized that my only hope of impressing her was with my skill as an angler. The first task was to assemble the rod.

Easy!

The three bits slotted together. Sara looked on approvingly. But then there was the reel. Where did that go? There seemed to be some sort of clasping mechanism. It was in! This was a piece of cake (which, by the way, makes very good

177

bait for carp, I can now tell you). And then it all started to go wrong.

The string stuff.

I had a vague notion that it had to be threaded through the eyes that lined the rod, but it had all become horribly tangled. I started to sweat, despite the chill. I pulled out the notebook that Chris had so kindly filled with tips. He'd written on the front:

The Roodiments of Fishing
by
Christopher B. Rushby

It looked at first to be full of handy hints: fish, it claimed, could not see the colour pink, and so you should always wear pink while angling, thus rendering yourself invisible. But on closer inspection it became clear that Chris was a shit and had stitched me up tighter than the ball of line he had planted. The following example was from the chapter entitled *Notts*:

Sara laughed. It was plain to her that no fish would be caught on this expedition. But she didn't seem to mind. She appeared to be quite happy just sitting with me on the bank.

We opened the tin of maggots and watched them wriggle as we ate the sandwiches and the Wagonwheels.

'Do you like me then?' she said, more or less out of the blue.

'Yeah, you're all right,' I replied, but squeezed a little closer to her, to show that I meant a bit more than that.

Then the rain began to come down more heavily, and we ran to the bus stop. She lived in the opposite direction to me. I waited until her bus came and then forced forty-two pence into her hand.

Of course all our year knew about it on Monday. The boys took the piss, but I knew they were jealous, at least the ones with fully descended testicles. And the girls looked at me with a new respect. Obviously Sara hadn't blabbed about the fishing fiasco.

Our second date was a double with a kid called Sean Reardon and his girlfriend, Catriona Essen, who played wing defence in the netball team. We went to see a Disney film that I'm too embarrassed to name at the multiplex. But near the end I slipped my arm around Sara's shoulders and we cuddled up. It was great. But my arm went to sleep and I had to move it after ten minutes. I could see that Sean and Catriona were snogging like mad. I wished they weren't: it put all the pressure on me, and I didn't have a clue how to do it.

The bus fare back from the multiplex was £1.60.

Our third date was at Catriona's thirteenth birthday party. Her parents went out until ten o'clock, which was bloody decent of them. I drank a can of Kestrel lager and got drunk for the first time. Sara and me were sitting on the settee. It was dark and someone had put on 'Love Will Tear Us Apart' by Joy Division. It must have belonged to Catriona's older brother, who was a student in Sheffield, where that was all you were allowed to listen to. Sara put her face in front of mine. I tried to think of how I'd seen people kiss in films. I shut my eyes and made a crash landing. I moved my lips around and sucked. About five minutes later I realized that I was kissing her chin. I moved up and found her lips, and with them, Heaven.

I spent the night at Chris's house, in his top bunk. We talked until morning about how brilliant girls are, and about the best bits of our chosen loves – his: nice tits, nice arse er . . . ; mine: the smell of violets, the perfect little mole on the end of her button nose, the infinite melancholy of her dark eyes, the endless fascination of her black, black hair.

It was, of course, doomed. She was too pretty and I was too much of a chump. It all fell apart in, of all places, Venice. The school organized a skiing trip that January. I only wanted to go because Sara was going. It was quite cheap, for a skiing holiday, but my parents could still barely afford it (it was before Mum's career really took off). What they certainly couldn't afford was the right gear. Granddad lent me a pair of, I kid you not, motorcycle goggles. Granny knitted me an earthenware jumper, which even I could recognize as an affront to decency. And I can still hear, in my nightmares, the sound of my flared jeans flapping behind me as I hurtled out of control down the nursery slopes.

The long and short of it is that I looked like a loser, and Sara was simply embarrassed to be seen hanging out with me. We had one evening in Venice on the way home. The trip had been a personal disaster. I couldn't ski, I looked like a buffoon, and Sara had barely spoken to me. Venice, glimmering through the mist, was the most stunning thing I had ever seen. There were hardly any tourists and you would have to have been dimmer even than me not to be moved by the dark silent beauty of it. I managed to cut off Sara from her friends. I tried to kiss her against the curved wall of a bridge.

'Don't,' she said. It was like a hard slap. And then when I

tried some more, she really did give me a hard slap. 'I said, don't. Are you deaf?'

'What is it?' I said, but I knew.

'I'm sorry, but I just don't want to go out with you any more.'

'Please. I'll get some new clothes. It's my birthday soon.'

'It isn't that.'

'What is it then?'

'I don't know. You're nice. But you're just a bit. You know. Boring.'

So, that was it. Time for one last, hopeless gesture. I leaped onto the wall. I looked down into the cold water, flickering with starlight.

'If you don't go out with me I'll jump in,' I said.

Was I joking? That's what I told my friends afterwards. 'I was having a laugh. Don't fancy her anyway. She's a slag.' But no, I wasn't joking. I meant it. I just didn't quite have the guts to do it.

But it changed me. I'd been chucked because I was too boring. What could be worse than that? I resolved that it would never happen again. People could call me whatever they wanted to in the future: obnoxious, loud, foul-mouthed, a troublemaker, an idiot, a vain, prancing poser. Anything. But they wouldn't call me boring. Well, that was my aim. Sorry if you think I screwed that one up too.

Chapter 28
Golgotha Heights

Glad I got that out of my system.

Thinking about Sara was bad for two reasons. Firstly, it just made me sad and, worse than sad, humiliated. I kept playing the old memory tapes, trying to find something good, but all I came up with were close-ups of particularly excruciating moments – the look on her face when I said I liked Elton John (remember, I was a *baby*); the time I choked on a midget gem and snotted-up on my trousers.

The second bad thing was that it made me feel as though I had betrayed Francesca, my new love, and my only hope. It was the thought of her – and only that – that had kept me going through the forest and across the plain. And so I concentrated on her now, using her beauty as a broom to sweep away the thoughts of the failed childhood romance.

The geryon flew higher. It was getting cold. The burnt earth of the plain below us disappeared, sheathed by clouds, leaving only the black basalt of the rocks, which rose ever upwards. Even the mighty geryon seemed to be flagging. Its nostrils flared wide and a film of sweat covered its glistening scales, adding to their icy, iridescent glamour.

And then, with a last whipping of its tail, the geryon carried us clear of the summit and we could look, for the first time, down on the Golgotha mountains in all their horrid splendour. Snow-covered peaks reared before us, filling the world like an endless, agitated ocean. I couldn't see anything that looked remotely like a landing site.

'Where are we going to come

$\qquad$ d

$\qquad\qquad$ o

$\qquad\qquad\qquad$ w

$\qquad\qquad\qquad\qquad$ n,

$\qquad\qquad\qquad\qquad\qquad\qquad$?' I asked, falling.

The geryon had just flipped itself over in a tricky aerobatic manoeuvre I couldn't help but admire, and out we fell. But I was fortunate – the ground broke my fall. I landed headfirst in a pile of snow and heard Scrote plop down next to me.

'My luck must be changing,' I said as I pulled myself out of the drift, shaking the snow from my hair. Just then a great load of what I immediately surmised to be geryon crap (texture of fresh cow flop, but with bones in it) landed on my head.

'Sorry, should have warned you about that,' said Clarence, making his own soft landing. 'Standard procedure. All OK?'

'Think so,' I said, wiping gluck from my eyes.

'Rough,' said Scrote.

'We've done well to make it to here. The worst is behind us. All we need to do now is to ramble through these hills, cross over no man's land into Gehenna, take the lift down the other side and it's a new start for both of us.'

'Sounds easy,' I said, loading it with all the sarcasm and bitterness I could muster with a mouth full of geryon poop. 'But I'm not exactly equipped for alpine exploration.'

I held out the rags that still clung to me. I looked like I'd been put through the office shredder. I was also shaking like a junkie. It was cold enough to freeze the spit in your mouth.

'Mmm. Perhaps I can help you there,' replied Clarence. He took out a large suitcase from his inside pocket and fiddled with the combination. 'That's it,' he murmured, 'six six six, and bingo.' The case sprang open.

It was neatly packed with socks (tasteless novelty jobs with crazy cartoon characters, like Archie the Axeman and Lettie the Leper), underpants (self-aggrandizing, with sharks, grizzly bears and pythons), and vests (thick and woolly). There was also a spare red suit of stretchy fabric, with a hood and built-in horns. 'Try this on for size,' he said, tossing it over.'

'But I'll look like a tit, a big red tit!' I whined.

'Well, you were the one who was complaining. Would you rather spend eternity frozen into a block of ice? Yet again your ingratitude astounds me. That's my only spare. What if I get a ladder? Did I worry about that? No! I was just concerned for your welfare.'

'OK. Sorry. I'll give it a go.'

I slipped out of my filthy rags. They crawled off to die in peace. The new suit fitted rather well. It had been darned more than once. Scrote snickered so much he made a yellowy hole in the snow.

'I believe I have something in here for you as well, Scrote.' This could be fun. 'This should keep the chill out,' Clarence said, stroking a tartan devil-doggy outfit. In a moment Scrote, his will broken, was squeezed into his own little suit, horns where battered ears had been. Scrote used to eat the kind of dogs that wore coats. This was a top moment.

'Bum,' was all he said.

My mind was flung back, by contrast, to what I always thought of (well at least after I was forced to learn the word) as the quintessential Scrote moment. It was a filthy January evening. I had Scrote out on a lead so I wouldn't have to spend all night looking for him. I just wanted him to get his business out of the way so I could get home to my tea and *Top of the Pops*. As usual, when time was an issue, I took him four houses down to Mrs Sheperton's, the local witch. She used to confiscate any ball that went into her garden and she once tried to chop up a football in front of us with an axe as some kind of lesson. But the blade wasn't sharp enough and it just bounced off. We all very much enjoyed watching the old hag dance around taking great futile swings at the ball. It was a good time, but we never got the ball back.

I opened her gate, nudged Scrote through and stood outside, still holding his lead. But something was amiss. Rather than the silent vehemence of his customary excretion, there followed an agitated snuffling. Scrote was straining at the lead, his paws scraping at Mrs Sheperton's crazy paving.

'What is it, you great get?' I cursed.

I tried to drag him out, but he just strained all the harder. I looked through to see what the matter was. Scrote was nosing and nuzzling a naked black bin liner. I'd never seen him so excited. He used the slack created as I came nearer to lunge at the sack. He now began to bite and chew at the plastic. In a second he was in. He growled and champed: '*Hrurr, hrurrr, hrurrrr.*'

I tried to pull him off. 'Get away, Scrote, you'll get us turned into sausages by the old witch.'

By now the dog was in a frenzy. And he'd got hold of something. Something long and quite thin. It was a soft plastic tube of some sort. It contained a loose, brown sludge. What the—? Scrote was in ecstasy, shaking his head violently, growling, chewing all the time. I wanted to get out, fast. I leaned over to pull the thing from his mouth.

And then it burst.

In an instant I realized what it was. That realization struck just as the contents of the tube hit me.

It was a colostomy bag.

Mrs Sheperton shat in a bag, and now it was all over me. And I mean *all over*. Scrote was still shaking the thing, spraying the remnants everywhere. His eyes glowed through the brown icing. My God the stink! I kicked Scrote in the guts so hard even he had to let go of the bag, and I dragged him home. My mum hosed me down on the steps. Scrote had already licked himself clean.

Of course Cathy told everyone at school, and for a while I was the 'Shitbag Boy', but I managed to make a pretty good story out of it, and probably came out of it with a mildly enhanced reputation.

And so we trudged off through the deep drifts and blasting wind, a little snugger than we might have been, but looking about as silly as it's possible to look without actually being a Morris dancer.

Did I mention that it was cold? I knew all about cold. When I was little we didn't have central heating. My dad thought it was unhealthy. The only heating in the house came from the gas fire in the living room. Me and Cathy'd lie with our feet on the cream metal plates around the grille. I remember melting through two pairs of nylon socks one evening. The only time the house ever got remotely warm in winter was when Dad made a cup of tea and left the ring on. The bedrooms were the worst. Each morning we'd wake up (this was back when me and Cathy were young enough to share a bedroom) and our breath would be frozen on the inside of the window. For some other mad reason of my dad's, we didn't even have real hot-water bottles. No, in our house it was old pop bottles filled with lukewarm water, but only when the grass crackled like distant fireworks. Hey Brothers or Citra were the pop bottles of choice. Citra were best, as the glass was thicker and less likely to shatter into tendon-severing blades. We must have been just about the last kids in England to be cold but not poor.

But cold though I was throughout those perpetual child-hood winters, it was nothing like this. The wind was strong, but also clever. It found its way through your clothes like a pickpocket, stealing warmth. It drove ice crystals hard into your eyes. It sent its fingers down into your lungs, feeling along veins and arteries, slowing, stopping, freezing everything that had been warm and quick.

The snow lay thinly on the cutting rocks, but every so often a foot, followed by a leg, followed by everything else, would sink into a deep drift.

I was getting desperate. 'Clarence,' I yelled into the wind, 'I can't go on like this. It's so cold. My legs won't work any more.'

'There's a path down into the lowlands somewhere around here. We just have to find it. You have to keep moving.'

The little devil sounded almost sympathetic. He was suffering too: he was obviously designed for tormenting in warmer climes.

But it was no use. I could go no further.

'I'm sorry, I just can't take any more of this wandering aimlessly about,' I cried out eventually. 'Can't you find the path and we'll just scrunch here until you come to get us?'

I'd found a place under an overhanging rock. It gave just enough shelter to take the edge off the wind.

'Have it your way. But do you know what it feels like to quite literally freeze solid? All of the water in your body turns to ice. When water freezes it expands. So all of your cells burst. It's an all-over agony rush. And you'll be awake through all of it – no dropping off, or dying or anything easy like that. You'll wish you'd stayed the course.'

With that he stomped off into the swirling blizzard, muttering and gesticulating to himself.

That just left me and Scrote. I hunched down. Scrote jumped onto my knees and tried to force his nose into my armpit. It grew darker. There was nothing here except ice and rock and black space and bitter cold. A tingling began in my fingers and at the tip of my nose. The tingling turned into a sharp pricking, and the pricking into a burning. This was like the first knowledge of pain, from my early time in Hell. I writhed and churned with the agony. Scrote was going through the same pain, and kept saying 'Rubbish!' over and over.

I became paranoid and delirious, raving and ranting. Clarence was never going to come back. Why should he? He was a blasted devil, after all. I'd fooled myself into thinking that he was some sort of friend. But his job had been to torture me, and now he'd shagged off and left me to become one with the shagging glacier. All the time the pain was becoming more intense. I had a vision in which I was made up of billions of stars, but they had all gone supernova, exploding with impossible brightness. So it was to end here, on this mountainside. No, not end, but be. Just this, just this pain, for ever.

The terrible beauty of the supernova reminded me of something. Or of someone. I tried to see through the shimmering, shattering agony. A figure began to form. What was its name? Something to do with beauty. I was thinking of beauty. I was thinking of her.

Francesca.

Francesca.

Francesca.

'Conor.'

Her voice was like the sun, and I bathed in its warmth. I could swear that I had only thought her name: my teeth had been clamped together, my whole head as solid and immobile as a turnip. I still could not speak, but my eyes must have been eloquent. She was as beautiful as ever. My lips craved the heat of her perfect skin.

She bent down and gently picked up Scrote, who was as stiff as a dead dog in a cheap butcher's freezer. She breathed into his face. He stirred and whimpered. She put him down and came closer to me. She put her arms around me, and kissed my forehead. And then she did something astounding, something I would never tell you about, had it not been for what was to follow, much later. What she did was to loosen the exquisite cloth, silk, or damask, or God knows what, from around her throat and breasts. And then she took my face in her hands, and put my lips to one breast. And from her breast there flowed life.

I can say nothing more about it, except that I was saved. The agony of the ice in my blood was soothed away, and my mind became clear.

'Thank you,' I stammered.

'You needed me, that is my thanks. But you know that this is the last time I can come to you. You must make the most of this, our final meeting. Ask me anything and I will answer all of your questions.'

I thought for a bit. 'You know that I am with my devil, Clarence?'

'Yes, I have been following your progress.'

'Can I trust him?'

'You can trust him for as long as your interests lie together.'

'What is the best way to get to my destination?'

'You are now lost on the high rim of the Golgotha mountains. There is a path down into the broad valley at the heart of the range. As you know, the rival empires – for so they have become – meet there, and perpetual warfare rages. You must find a way through the war zone. At the far side of the valley there is an easy path down to the Gehenna heartland, where you will find your final refuge. Your devil should be able to guide you through, but he now needs your help. Let me take you.'

Francesca took my hand with her long, pale fingers and led me through the icy winds. Somehow her warmth still coursed through me, flowing down through my body and into Scrote, too, who clung to my leg, absorbing the heat. We seemed to be on a narrow path which wound down between a sheer rock face on one side and a dizzying drop on the other. I hate heights, and I felt sick and drunk.

I was still dimly aware of Francesca's magical presence before me. And then, somehow, I wasn't. She was gone. Immediately I felt lost again, and cold. She had gone out like a candle, leaving me alone in this wilderness. And then I felt again the snuffle of Scrote at my ankle and at the same time I heard a muffled shouting from the path ahead. I hurried on, almost falling headlong into a great crack – a crevasse in the icy path.

The shouting was coming from the crevasse – angry curses interspersed with self-pitying wailing. I peered in, knowing what to expect.

'Hello, Clarence.'

My friend was in a pickle. The crevasse was too narrow for him to properly open his wings, pathetically small though they were. He was half fluttering, half scrabbling at the slippery walls. His little claws would reach almost to the lip of the crevasse before he slithered back down into its depths.

'Where the Hell have you been?' yelled Clarence ungraciously. 'All the help I've given you, and then you leave me down in this . . . this . . .'

'Crevasse.'

'Yes, this crevasse, to freeze my balls off. I thought we had a *relationship*.'

'Well, I'm here now. What should I do?'

'Just lean down and help me out, I'm almost there.'

I crouched by the edge and leaned over. Clarence fluttered and scrambled some more, but he seemed to be tiring, and just could not reach my outstretched arm.

'Oh arse!' he exclaimed. 'This is no good. You'll have to find something to lower down to me.'

'Clarence, we're in the middle of a blizzard in a mountain range in Hell. What am I likely to find? A ladder?'

'You're supposed to be clever. Just use your initiative and get me out of here. Weren't you in the Scouts?'

'No, as it happens. They banned me.'

Oh. A problem. Who do I leave dangling – Clarence down the crevasse or you, desperate to know why I was banned from the Scouts? Sorry, Clarence, Scouts it is, but I'll be quick.

As you can probably guess, it was all Scrote's fault. Next-door-but-two lived Terence Cumberland. His dad, Mr Cumberland, was the scoutmaster. A lot of my friends were in the Cubs. There wasn't much else to do, apart from glue-sniffing and shoplifting. I was getting round to joining, but even at the age of nine I knew that there was something evil and deeply uncool about them. Scoutmasters come in two flavours: the paedophile and the Nazi. Or I suppose three kinds, if you include the Nazi paedophile. Mr Cumberland was a Nazi, plain and simple. He liked the idea of being at the head of a well-drilled army of Aryan boys, ready to kill, die and tie really complicated knots for the Fatherland. He loved uniforms and had one made for himself with so much gold braid a Nigerian general would have thought it tacky. Naturally enough, he favoured jackboots, when he wasn't in his grey plastic slip-ons.

The day before my swearing-in, which in our troop took the form of an elaborate ritual involving the blood of a freshly slaughtered cockerel and a lot of standing around on one leg, I was playing footie down in the rec with the other kids. Terence was there, and we were using his prized leather football. Now this venerable piece of equipment had belonged to his dad, and quite possibly his dad before him. It was of an ancient design, involving intricate lacing, and was made of a special absorbent suede, giving it the quality of a Christmas pudding when wet.

On this particular day, the score had reached 17–19 (I'd scored six myself, playing in goal: it was that kind of match) when some of the frayed stitching gave way and a few centimetres of red bladder peeped out from between the armour plating. Scrote had been watching the game with his usual keen interest, and the sight of the vulnerable bladder was too much for him. He raced like a greyhound onto the pitch and, with unerring accuracy, bit the bladder, thus bursting the football.

I knew this spelled trouble. Terence was a big bastard for his age, and a notorious bully. Scrote had shot off as quickly as he had come, thereby avoiding any retribution from Terence, although Scrote's fearful reputation, and Terence's typical bully's cowardice, would probably have saved him anyway. But that left just me.

Red-faced and bellowing, Terence came for me. Now, as you'll have picked up, I'm no kind of fighter, but here I had no choice. I was also pretty sure that I could take Terence. He had the look of a blubberer, if only I could land a punch before his bulk pinned me down and his own fat fists could get to work. As he charged towards me, I feinted right, and slipped left, leaving my knee out to catch him. He went down like a sack of shit and I was on him. I gave him one punch in the guts and, as I suspected, he started to cry, yelling out, 'Lay off, lay off, leave us alone.'

I was about to get off the big girl when I felt a hand on my collar, and I was pulled up by Mr Cumberland, as red-faced and ugly as his son.

I thought I was in for a battering. Cumberland took off his belt and raised it over his head. The blow, however, fell on the hapless Terence.

'That'll teach yer fer crying, tha young pup.'

Terence squealed all the more loudly, but got up and ran for it. His dad chased him home, flailing about with the belt. Unfortunately he wasn't able to catch Terence as his unsupported pants kept slipping down.

The rest of us were, of course, rolling around on the grass by that stage, and we were still retelling the story, suitably elaborated, for years afterwards. The only down side was that Cumberland wouldn't let me join his troop. I wasn't heartbroken, but it was a bit of a nark, because it meant I had nothing to do on Tuesday evenings when all my friends were up at the hut, learning how to march in step, use a bayonet, and tell a FW190 from an ME109 by its silhouette alone.

I took to hanging around outside the rotting ramshackle scout hut with a couple of other drongos who weren't allowed in: one because he was Welsh and the other because he always had scabs around his nose and mouth. We used to sit on the grass at the back of the hut, stripping the bark off saplings and engaging in other quasi-scouting activities (high-arc peeing, long-distance goffing, etc.), none of them much use when it came to rescuing devils from crevasses.

Clarence, back to you.

'What the flip are you doing?' he said, his voice hissing like piss hitting the barbecue.

'Sorry. Just a quick epiphany. I'm on the case.'

I looked around. There was, of course, nothing: not a tree, or a bush, or a rope ladder. Just snow and ice and rock. And then I noticed Scrote, who'd screwed himself into a ball and gone to sleep. He was already half covered by an igloo of newfallen snow. Without asking, I just grabbed him by his front paws and dangled him over the edge of the crevasse. The length of a dog, even a squat, stumpy-legged brute like Scrote, was enough to make the difference, and Clarence managed to scramble out just as Scrote was waking. Luckily, as the cold had numbed his body and primitive brain, his lunge at Clarence's skinny bottom was seconds late, and he snapped at thin air.

Oh how are the mighty fallen! In his prime Scrote could stalk birds like a cat and leap as they took off, to pluck them from the sky. He had a fondness for finches and would eat them whole, legs and all.

Clarence brushed himself down and set off along the steep and winding path.

'I was just coming back for you, once I'd made sure of the way,' he said, but without real conviction, and I had the definite feeling that he had planned to leave us behind. Perhaps I was doing him an injustice.

Despite the continuing flurries of snow and vicious wind, the going was a little easier now – isn't it always when you know where you're going? The worst thing was the fear of slipping on the sheet ice beneath our feet and flying off the path and into the deeps below. We came across a couple more crevasses, but we managed to jump them without too much trouble, ending in a slithering heap on the far side.

Chapter 29
Into Battle

After a while I began to make out a distant booming. 'What's that noise?' I asked.

'Oh, just the artillery.'

'What artillery?'

'Sounds like a mixed bombardment of trench mortars, howitzers and light field guns. Lively stuff.'

'But how come? Who's getting bombarded?'

'The damned, of course. Who else? You know that the front line passes through the valley below. Both Sheol and Gehenna have armies of lost souls down there, slugging it out. It suits everyone. The leaders get to sort out their little differences, and the damned get blown to bits, chopped up, macerated and so on and so forth.'

'So how do we get through – I mean, they're not just going to let us walk through the lines, are they?'

'No. I've been thinking about this. Our best hope . . . OK, our *only* hope, is to join one of the big pushes from the Sheol side – they happen all the time. The noise down there suggests there's one imminent. We storm the Gehenna trenches, and then wait until they take them back again. With any luck we'll then find ourselves behind their front line, and we can just stroll off into the sunset.'

'But how do you know the Gehenna lot will take back their trenches? What if Sheol win?'

'Come on, Conor – this is trench warfare. No one ever wins.'

'It all sounds a bit . . . futile.'

'Of course it's *futile*. It's *supposed* to be futile, in the sense of not having any real higher goal or purpose. You have to remember that war is an industrial process. All it needs is enough of the raw materials – iron and blood – and it'll turn out the end products: pain and death. It's really very efficient in that sense. It's like life itself – efficient, but pointless. Or rather it serves as its own justification.'

I remembered something I'd read.

'I thought war was the continuation of politics by other means? You know, one country wants something, or thinks it needs it, and it tries to get it by talking, and if the talking doesn't work, they try threatening, and if the threatening doesn't work, they try fighting.'

'I see you did take in some of the educational material back in your cell. But you mustn't confuse the theoretical speculations of eighteenth-century theorists with things as they are. Clausewitz looked on war as chess with real armies. That's the problem with all Enlightenment thinkers: they forget that the mainsprings of human actions are deep, irrational forces and urges – the desire to murder, to rape, to defeat one's enemy and then, after his defeat, to crush and humiliate him.'

Clarence's eyes glowed red through the falling snow.

'I don't believe that.'

'Really? And why not? An expert on human nature now, are we?'

'No need to take the piss. Anyway, after all that boring stuff I was forced to read and listen to back in the cave, there's no end to the things I know.'

'Knowledge and understanding are two quite different concepts,' said Clarence patronizingly.

That was true enough. I'd left the cave filled full of learning, although I was still a child in understanding. But

Clarence was wrong in thinking that that's how I stayed. The horrors of the journey had begun to work a change in me. I certainly wasn't going to let the point drop.

'But I just think that stuff you said about irrational urges and all that is a way of hiding the fact that there is a *good* reason for war. I don't mean that war is good, I just mean that some people always do well out of war, and for them war is good. If you make guns, or sell them to other countries, the last thing you want is peace. If you say war will always be there because it's deep in the human soul, then you're really saying, let's just get on with it and make some money. There's no point trying to stop it any more than there's a point in try-ing to stop blokes from fancying girls or vice versa. But if you see war as some kind of conspiracy, then there might be a way of doing something about it.'

'Oh dear, Conor. You did learn more from a particular nineteenth-century economist than we thought. Perhaps our syllabus needs a little tweaking – it certainly wasn't meant to stimulate you. But, much though I'd like to continue the dis-cussion, we have more important things to think about.'

We had been descending steadily. The ice underfoot became slush, and the slush mud. The snow turned to sleet, and then a steady, drenching rain. The noise of the guns grew louder, and a foul, burning, acrid stench filled the air. The sky flashed red and yellow, strangely out of synch with the rolling thunder of the guns.

'Nothing like a whiff of cordite to clear the sinuses,' enthused Clarence, taking a long, deep sniff, like fat Phil at the fissure of a broken pie crust.

The narrow path had widened into a mud road, and I soon saw the first signs of what guns could do. Horses, dead and dying, lay on the roadsides, eyes wild and imploring in death. Most seemed to have been unzipped, and blue-grey guts coiled from their bellies and sloshed under our feet.

What is it about horses? Why do we love them more than other big, stupid grass-eaters? Why do we feel such anguish when we see them in pain? Why does the idea of eating ponies make us angry, but not helpless lambs? Beauty, grace, I suppose. But that only begs another question: why should we find horses more beautiful than cows? Maybe it's something to do with having long legs. I remember Dad taking me and Cathy on Sunday walks to feed the two scruffy old horses that lived in a field a couple of kilometres away. We'd bring stale bread and Dad would show us how to offer the slices on the flat of your hand, so you kept all your fingers, and we'd squeal at the excitement and wipe the slobber on each other.

But these horses were beyond bread.

And soon the first human casualties. The men were completely silent and half-lost in the shadows by the side of the road, which was why I only noticed them when we were already among them. I recognized the uniforms from school books: English Tommies in khaki, with wide, soup-bowl helmets that seemed designed to cover as little of the head as possible. They were caked in filth and blood. Their eyes followed us as we passed. With astonishment, I saw that they were terrified of us. I looked at Clarence.

'You're a devil,' he said.

Of course. We were all wearing red devil costumes. To these men I was a tormentor, and it was right that they should fear me.

'Where are we going?' I asked.

'This road will take us down to the first of the reserve trenches. Then it's duckboards and, if we're lucky, communication trenches up to the front line. Then we go over the top and get blown to bits like everyone else.'

'But won't we be challenged or something? Who's in charge here?'

'All the top brass are miles away. This is the worst posting for any devil; and only the lower grades ever get sent here, and even then only if you make a real mess of a straight-forward tormenting post. Everyone'll just assume we're a couple of chumps looking for some platoon of the damned to take it out on. Just keep on looking mean.'

Looking mean was difficult. As we got nearer the front the road became a quagmire and we crept along wooden planks that floated uncertainly above the thick slop. I could see half submerged bodies, and hands that reached out from beneath the surface, the fingers still moving.

We ducked into one of the communications trenches – I half remembered that these ran at ninety degrees to the main fighting trenches, and were supposed to cover troops and supplies moving up to the front. But this one seemed horribly shallow and the mud walls had slithered and slopped so much in the incessant rain that the trench was being absorbed back into the surrounding earth. We were stepping over decaying, but still-breathing corpses; rats ran through eye sockets, to be brushed away by half-fleshed hands.

Here, more than anywhere else on Hell, I faced the horror of the dead who cannot die again but must undergo decay and regeneration in endless cycles.

And all the time, the shelling. Hell could be a noisy place: a place of screaming and crying and harsh shouts, a place of undiscoverable mechanical noises, drills and engines boring into your brain. My cell was one of the few quiet places in Hell, though that was a quiet to chill the soul. Nothing, how-ever, had come close to the noise of those guns: first the dull booms from the batteries ranged against us, and then, a second later, the scream of the shells falling and the roar as they detonated.

Even louder were the juddering blasts from 'our' guns. Fists of noise thumped at us from every direction. If it had only been the noise it would have been bad enough, but these were bombs. They blew people into little pieces. I could not shake the conviction that each shell had been aimed with malice at my head. I found myself wincing, cringing, sobbing at each new barrage. I cried and wet myself, and then cried and wet myself some more.

We reached the front-line trench. There were hundreds of terrified troops in there, heads bowed, silent. Muddy water came up to their knees. The walls of the trench were lined with rubbish, and bones and bits of bodies. The stench, a sort of thick paste made from shit and blood and vomit and fear, was truly terrible. As we came amongst them, the soldiers cringed away from us.

A Bruiser was making his way along the trench in our direction, kicking and jabbing at the raggedy troops as he passed. The noise of the barrage had suddenly, ominously, ended.

'Just keep quiet and look as if you know what you're doing,' whispered Clarence out of the side of his mouth. 'I'll take care of this.'

The monster noticed us for the first time, and stiffened suspiciously.

'Help you, sir?' he grunted.

'We're just up from GHQ to have a shufti.'

'No one told me.'

'Precisely. Word has got back that you've gone a bit soft in this sector. We've been monitoring fear and pain levels. There's been a four per cent drop in fear and a six per cent drop in pain over the past month. And there's been talk of fraternizing with the enemy. Singing carols, that sort of thing. You know it's your job to make sure morale stays down. Won't do, you know.'

The Bruiser started to look worried.

'Well, sir, we've been saving it up for the big push, sir. Calm before the storm, sir. We'll give it to 'em now, sir, you see if we don't.'

'That's the spirit.'

'You know we're about to go over, sir? Best if you drop back a bit, sir. Going to get a bit lively.'

'That's what were here for. Want to see the effects on the men at close range. Carry on.'

The Bruiser stomped off down the line, personally stemming the decline in fear and pain figures.

'You're good at this, aren't you?' I said to Clarence with genuine admiration.

'What?'

'Lying.'

'Why, thank you. It's a tribute to one's training. There was a three-day course, er . . . a "dissimulation workshop", I think they called it. We all had to find the liar within us. There was a lot of group hugging and backstabbing.'

The troops were by now huddled around ladders leading up from the trench. Their faces were haggard and grey. They knew what was coming. How many times had they done this before? Thousands? Millions? Pain is always at its most acute in anticipation. No, that's not right. Pain is, of course, at its worst when you feel it. But anticipating it is also very, very bad.

And then whistles started to blow and all Hell broke loose. The men scrambled over the top. Several were hit before they took their first steps and were thrown back down into the trench, bleeding from their throats or with the backs of their heads blasted out.

'Here we go then,' said Clarence, nervously, as he clambered up the rickety wooden ladder.

I picked up Scrote, who'd been standing sullenly in the trench slime, and followed him. My first good look at no man's land was dispiriting. There was about a hundred metres in between the trenches, but hardly an inch of level ground. The surface was pitted with thousands of shell craters and the only straight things in this world were the lines of barbed wire, untouched by the bombardment. Already I could see some of our troops hanging on the wire, their bodies dancing a jig to the rhythm of machine guns. More shells were falling on no man's land, both theirs and ours. Bullets fizzed past my ears, and bodies fell around me, groans and screams lost in the machine cacophony of war.

I put Scrote down and ran as fast as I could after Clarence. He was darting from crater to crater, like a lizard. Ahead it seemed that, miraculously, a few of our troops had reached and taken the first line of enemy trenches. The machine-gun and rifle fire trailed off, but shells continued to rain down. We were almost at the relative safety of the trench when a shell exploded over my head and I was thrown into a deep crater. The blast left me dazed, my head spinning, blood coming out of my ears. The bottom of the shell hole was full of freezing, oily water which reached up to my waist, but beneath the water there lurked something worse: mud – deep, sucking, sinking mud. I could feel it dragging me down. I screamed out to Clarence, and to Scrote. But they could not hear. I could not hear my own shouts. I started to cry. This was rubbish. In a few moments I was up to my neck in the mud and water. And then the water reached my mouth, and then my nose. My screams became bubbles. I reached up, despairingly, my hand clenched into a fist, a fist shaking in futile rage at Fate, and God and the Devil, and death and pain and punishment, and the unfairness of everything.

And then a miracle.

I felt the clasp of another hand around my wrist, and I was pulled from the mud. I lay gasping for breath, face down on the side of the crater. I didn't realize that Clarence had such strength. But as I looked around, I saw only the dim form of a huge soldier disappearing out of the hole. I was still stunned by the explosion and choked by the water, and I might have been dreaming, but I could have sworn that I glimpsed, under my saviour's heavy pack and khaki coat, a flash of polka dots.

I scrambled out of the hole. I just caught sight of Clarence and Scrote jumping down into the enemy trench. I picked my way over to them, between the corpses and bits of corpses. The trench was full of dead boys in grey uniforms. Dead boys who looked back at us as we stared. Most had been bayoneted; one held his guts in his arms, like a baby.

'What kept you?' asked Clarence. He seemed excited by the foul business.

'I thought I saw . . . Never mind. What next?'

'Easy enough from here. There'll be a counter-attack soon.'

He was right. The few troops who'd made it through the wire and bullets and bombs and bayonets were soon under heavy fire. The enemy came in from the rear, and along the trench from left and right. We had no chance.

'Time to hide,' said Clarence, slipping down beneath the bodies that lined the bottom of the trench.

I followed. It wasn't nice. Only Scrote seemed content, licking away at the blood and yellow bile that oozed from the bodies. My face was pressed against the face of a boy hardly older than me. Terrible things had happened to him. You could tell from his eyes. Like the other 'dead' in the trench, he was so cut, blasted and torn that he could not move. But slowly, I could feel him regenerating, coming back together: a canvas cleaning itself, ready for a new painting of pain. He looked at me, as if to ask some question, but his scum-encrusted lips did not move. Then I felt, rather than heard, him speak:

'I am the enemy you killed, my friend. I knew you in this dark; for so you frowned yesterday through me as you jabbed and killed. I parried; but my hands were loath and cold. Let us sleep now.'

I didn't know what he was on about. There were shots, shouts and screams as the battle passed over and around us. And then silence.

'Time to get the Hell out, I suggest,' said Clarence, flicking fastidiously at the filth begriming his red suit. Again we were off. The landscape mirrored that on the other side: mud, dead horses, the stink of old gas and new corruption. Again we passed groups of exhausted soldiers, being yelled at or whipped, or mocked by Bruisers.

'Can we just walk through here like this?' I asked. 'Why don't they stop us?'

'Oh, you know, we're officer class. Sheol, Gehenna, all the same really. No, no, it's all plain sailing from here. Or should be.'

Well, *that* one he got wrong. Almost as soon as he had finished speaking, the world around us began to change. The mud and slime became dust; the purple-black of the sky turned to a burning orange. And the people around us changed also. Heavy chain-mail and plate armour took over from field-grey uniforms; swords and spears replaced rifles and machine guns. And before I could think or ask questions, we were being harried and driven by scimitar-wielding horsemen.

'Ah,' sighed Clarence. 'This is all new. Looks like they've gone for a full, multi-media, all-the-worst-wars-there's-ever-been experience. We've just had Passchendaele, and now this would seem to be the Horns of Hattin.'

'What happened there?'

'Crusaders massacred by Saracens. Spelled the end of Crusader rule in the Holy Land. Top battle!'

For the next I don't know how long we slipped from war zone to war zone, and we were always on the wrong side: with Antony at Actium; with the butchered Byzantines at

Manzikert; with dim Darius at Gaugamela; and hapless Harold at Hastings. We were on the beach at Suvla. And always we ran away, and somehow we managed to avoid being chopped to pieces, or blown to bits, or speared, or sabre-slashed, or mutilated by bagpipes. If my tone sounds flippant, it is only to hide the horror.

You see I found something out. It is the same thing I saw in the eyes of the boy in the trench. You could read it in my eyes now:

Hell is war.

Chapter 30
Blighty

I was beginning to think that we were never going to escape from the pointless bloody cycle of battle. I'd become as jumpy as a flea on a kangaroo. I never knew who was going to chase me next, or whether they'd come at me with a bazooka or a bolas. But always it seemed that Clarence was confident of getting us through, and he somehow retained his cheeriness and his focus.

And, despite minor setbacks (Scrote losing his third nose sniffing at a hand grenade, my brush with anthrax), the day dawned when Clarence declared: 'Blighty,' and pointed through the green fug of war to a tall, skeletal structure like an electricity pylon, but topped by a massive wheel.

'Isn't that the most beautiful thing you've ever seen,' smiled Clarence.

I thought about Francesca's breast, and declined to answer.

Clarence went on: 'That, my young friend, is our way out of here. Our luck has changed.'

'What is it?'

'It's a lift. We take it from this . . . place of strife, down to the lovely lowlands of Gehenna, a land flowing in milk and honey.'

'Doesn't sound much like Hell.'

'Well, perhaps I was exaggerating about the milk and honey. And the lovely. But it's got to beat the buggery out of here.'

'Hrrrff,' yessed Scrote.

We slunk off towards the black tower. As we crept along I picked up the sound of laughter. A group of youngish devils were moving in a straggle in the same direction as us. I pointed them out to Clarence.

'More good luck. It's a bunch of cadets on their way back from a training mission. Follow me.'

Clarence led us to the group, and we slipped in behind them. They were acting like a scout troop on the way back from a weekend's camping: tired but exhilarated, breathlessly joshing amongst themselves about their adventures.

'Did you see it when Ashley got that old git's eyeball on the end of a stick and bunged it out into no man's land, and he had to crawl out after it with all kinds of shit flying around?'

'Yeah, and did you see it when Nige put that hand grenade down that bloke's trousers and blew his arse off? You're mad, Nige! You're a crazy imp!'

'Yeah, cheers. But did you see it when poor old bollock-brains himself, yes the one and only . . .' And so it went on. They stiffened a little when they realized that strangers were among them.

'Who's in charge here?' barked Clarence, playing the officer again.

One spindly devil with buck teeth and erupting acne replied: 'Er . . . no one really. An officer took us out for our first mission, just to give us a taster, but we got caught up in a skirmish. He had to stay behind to sort things out, and he sent us on ahead. We're just off back to barracks. Sir.'

'Well that's no excuse for this ill-discipline. Don't you realize there's a war on? Don't you understand that there are souls out there not being tormented because idle devils like you aren't doing their job properly?'

They moped about, staring at their muddy, cloven feet.

'Get on with it then,' Clarence continued. 'On your way. I'll let it pass this time, but I'll keep my eye on you.' Clarence emphasized the point by stretching out his head grotesquely, looming with one huge eye over the group. Nice trick.

They sloped off towards the tower. We followed. As we came closer I noticed a doorway guarded by two lazy Bruisers. Clarence nudged us towards the group of Gehenna trainees, who made room for us in their midst. The guards, busy with some game of chance played with what appeared to be human knucklebones, barely acknowledged the familiar and despised cadets as they passed through the doorway. Inside we found a large, grimy room full of the noise of machinery: iron and steel grinding and juddering, wheels whirring, pistons pumping. There was a wire cage suspended from a thick cable in the centre of the room. The cadets clustered around the cage, jostling and barging their way in through a gate.

'We'll let this lot go down first and take the next lift,' said Clarence out of the corner of his mouth. 'No point pushing it.'

The cadets appeared pleased to be free from us, and began again to laugh and banter before, with a clatter, the cage dropped into a gaping hole in the floor.

'Looks like fun,' I gulped. Call me a wimp, but I'd never much liked the death-drop school of fairground attractions. Give me candyfloss and a goldfish in a bag any day.

'Means to an end, Conor, means to an end. And that end is well and truly in sight.'

'All I can see is a big hole.'

'You really are a glass-is-half-empty boy, aren't you, Conor?'

'Hell does that to you. And sisters.'

As we chatted, an empty cage emerged from the hole. We stepped in and, before I'd had time to steady myself, the cage moved down into Hell's own underworld. The cage was lit by a solitary red bulb, giving it the feel of a submarine trapped on the ocean floor by circling destroyers. It took a few seconds for my eyes to become accustomed to the gloom. Peering through the bars of the cage I could just make out strange shapes in the wall of the shaft as it sped by. I moved my face closer to the bars. And then I moved back, very quickly.

'What the shag is that?' I yelled, pointing at the wall flying past us.

The wall itself seemed to be alive. Faces, squashed almost beyond recognition, bodies, arms and legs tangled and contorted. Have you ever seen Pete Marsh – you know, the bloke they dug out of a bog in Derbyshire or somewhere? From the Bronze Age, or some other age. All brown and squashed and leathery. Well these were like that, but gone a stage further. They had become, it seemed, *mineralized*.

'Oh, of course, I should have explained it to you. I was lost in my thoughts. Yes, you wouldn't have seen this before, would you? It's soul coal.'

'*Soul coal?*'

I had a serious dose of the creeps and I was an inch away from losing my cool, big style.

Clarence looked almost embarrassed.

'Well, you see, we can't stick too many souls in the Annihilator – as I've said before, it's a terrible waste and completely non-renewable. But we have to get power from somewhere. This is the modern world, and modernity means energy. So we use soul coal.'

'But that still doesn't tell me what it is.'

'Well basically it's people. Souls, I mean. We lay them down in strata, let natural geological forces get to work, and then we mine them.'

'And then what?'

'Then we burn them.'

Clarence looked at my shocked expression. 'Conor, have you learned nothing? This is Hell. Bad things happen to bad people. That's why we're here. Soul coal fulfils two perfectly respectable purposes: it makes the lights work, and it punishes the wicked. Where's your problem?'

I couldn't think of anything to say, except, 'What happens to them after they've been burned?'

'Well of course they're not destroyed – only the Annihilator can do that. We just reconstitute them in water and start the whole thing over again.'

My eyes were drawn back to the blurred images before me. This truly was suffering. Different from the relentless terror and mayhem of the battlefield, but surely no better. In my mind I found myself sharing the fate of those billions of souls, conscious through the countless years of crushing compression, conscious through the ripping and tearing of the mining process, conscious through the flames of the furnace.

And then with a metallic screech and a spray of sparks the cage slowed and then stopped.

'Ground floor, kitchen appliances, domestic electrical equipment and pets,' quipped Clarence as we stepped out into what looked like bright sunshine. A Bruiser lolled either side of a doorway. The one on the left seemed almost to smile as we passed through, unchallenged. Scrote paused to spray a jet of piss on the other. Rather than the expected kebabbing, the devil good-naturedly nudged him away with the blunt end of his trident.

'Not exactly high security, is it?' I said, bemused. Things weren't usually this simple in Hell.

'Well remember, this is a another country, and they do things differently here,' replied Clarence, rather unsatisfactorily, I thought.

I looked around. The doorway was set in a sheer black

cliff face through which the cage had plunged to bring us down from the high plateau. Before me I could see a sort of dirty, scrubby wasteland, littered with Coke cans, crisp packets, broken kettles and other rubbish. A road wound through, lined on either side with billboards on which torn and flapping posters advertised stuff that nobody could ever want: gizmos to defuzz sweaters, sandwich toasters, plates with pictures illustrating the Lives of the Great Dictators; china dolls in Marie Antoinette bonnets.

'Welcome to Gehenna!' Clarence announced dramatically. 'Next stop, Wandsworth.'

Chapter 31
Are You Ready for This?

The road led to a town, not too far distant. I saw what looked like seedy tenements and high concrete tower blocks and I heard, or thought I heard, a rhythmic beating – intense, insistent, nagging.

'Which way?' I asked Clarence, although I already knew the answer.

'Oh, onwards,' he replied. I noticed a new urgency, almost anticipation, in his manner. He looked a little bigger than I remembered. I'd always thought of him as shorter than me, but now he was definitely a head taller.

'How do you know the way? Have you been here before?'

I was nervous. I felt like a gunslinger waiting in town for the arrival of the bad guys. But we were the ones heading for town.

'All down to planning, thinking ahead. Trust me.'

We set off along the road, through the blowing rubbish of this cheap and tatty place. As we walked, the music – for music it was – became louder. Dance music by the sound of it, at skull-cracking volume.

'So Wandsworth is Party Town then,' I said.

'Mm. Could say that. All the fun of the fair. It's really rather famous in Hell. A sort of giant experiment. The regime here was one of the pioneers of deregulation. We – I mean *they* market-tested the various services, and found many were more efficiently run by agencies. The whole place has been privatized. Much less bureaucracy, more pain per pound spent, more bangs per buck. Taxpayers love it. Only a few loony Lefties complained about the end of the recycling schemes. As if we really needed a van to come round collecting used whips, tongs and limbs. And there was that scandal involving the old devils' home. And the selling off of the communal dungeons to developers for three auk eggs. Bit of a boob that. But it's all gone relatively smoothly.'

By now we were on the outskirts of the town. The buildings were mainly derelict. They all looked like they'd been used for a rave. And then raided by the riot squad. And then raved and rioted in some more.

If the buildings were ruins, then so were the few people I saw wandering through the wreckage. Hollow eyed, and as insubstantial as leaf skeletons, these were tormented by something other than the relentless, frenzied pursuit of the citizens of my first city in Hell. These souls had been sucked dry like the husks of insects trussed in a cobweb. They stood in corners, sometimes facing the street, sometimes the wall, moving their weight from foot to foot, or shuffling a few centimetres backwards and forwards.

The beat grew louder. It seemed to come from the ground we walked on, from the sky, from the buildings, from everywhere. And with the music there came a guttural groaning, a '*guh, guh, guh*', like the sound of some sexual horror being played out in another room.

'We have to go through the middle of town to get to your own little *pensione*,' smiled Clarence.

He had adopted a swaggering jive walk, which might have been cool if he'd been a black man in a beige leather jacket with matching slacks in Harlem in the 1960s, or if he'd at least had a sense of rhythm. As it was, we were strictly in the dad-at-the-disco territory. But it was no less unsettling for being silly.

The noise by now had become deafening. My fillings

started to ache; my eyeballs felt as though they were loosening in their sockets. We were approaching the epicentre. The streets now were full of people, staggering past us in both directions. Devils were mixed amongst them, but rather than harrying and torturing them as I expected, they seemed more to insinuate and tempt. I noticed that most of the souls here were bleeding and scabby. And then I saw why. Small packages passed from claw to hand and, in exchange for the packages, the claw would pinch or twist off a piece of flesh, from the arm or the cheek, leaving a moist, ulcerous wound. Other devils seemed to be enticing souls into buildings with promises. The faces of young women, streaked with dirt, looked out from dark windows.

'Rubbish,' muttered Scrote, his first announcement in pages.

'You said it,' I agreed.

'Oh, I don't know,' said Clarence brightly. 'Surely you can feel the excitement in the air, the buzz, the vibe. It's happenin', man. You should hang a bit looser.'

' "*Hang a bit looser*"? Just what I need, a Beatnik devil.'

But I kind of knew what he meant. The town stank of something horrible, something corrupt and foul and wrong, but I could feel myself being drawn to the devils with their wraps of whatever it was they were pushing. Something in me wanted to move towards the doorways that led to the rooms from the windows of which the women's faces gazed numbly.

The street had been closing in on us, sidling up like a dodgy uncle, but then with a battering of sound waves it opened out into a huge square thronged with souls. This was Hell as a Cecil B. DeMille epic: a huge orgy of writhing, groaning, naked bodies. The faces of the orgiasts were contorted, caught between drunken abandonment and disgust. Orifices were stretched, torn, violated. Embraces crushed. Lips met in savage, biting kisses. The square was lined with massive neon signs and huge screens showing action replays of what was happening in the middle.

At the heart of it all a platform had been set up, and on the platform there was the universe's biggest sound system, with stacks hundreds of metres high. And riding the tables was a colossal devil like none I had seen before. He was huge and powerful, and had horns curving over his head, but he also had a majesty and presence you just didn't get with the ordinary Bruisers or the wimps like Clarence.

'It's DJ Baal himself,' screamed Clarence.

Against my will I felt myself being drawn into the heaving crowd. I was repelled and yet attracted, and the attraction was winning. Why did I want to join the sick revellers? Let's not go there. Clarence smiled and nodded, as if to encourage me. It was Scrote, the most unexpected of moral guardians, who pulled me back, chewing at my ankle, and growling, 'Rubbish shag. Rubbish shag.'

'I suppose the dog's right,' said Clarence. He looked as if he'd have liked to stay. Instead, he guided us around the outside of the square, as DJ Baal bellowed:

'ARE YOU READY FOR THIS? ARE YOU READY FOR THIS?'

Chapter 32
Go to Your Room

Clarence led us down a narrow street off the main square.

'Almost home,' he chirped.

The street was like the one by which we had entered the town: desolate, flyblown, haunted by spectral figures wandering to or from the party. Clarence knew exactly where he was going. Me and Scrote followed as he strolled up to a tenement. A gaunt, stinking figure lay face down in a doorway. We stepped over him and entered a dingy hall.

'No point trying the lift,' said Clarence and headed for the stairs.

Inevitably they stank of piss and vomit. Syringes, their ends clotted with blood, lay on almost every step. The walls were daubed with graffiti in languages I didn't know. We carried on up the stairs for what felt like hours, the stench and squalor growing all the time.

'Clarence,' I said in despair, 'how could you have taken me to a place like this?'

'Well excuse me,' he replied, with mockery in his voice. 'Just whose idea was this? Surely you remember that it was *your* plan to swap your own, rather refined little Hell for another's? But anyway, we aren't there yet. Remember, Mr Bass would hate everything that you love, so you should find your . . . quarters to your liking.'

The logic was impeccable. After all, it was mine. But I was beginning to feel scared. Something was not right. No, I'll go all the way and say that something was wrong. Did I sense that the Malebranche had somehow followed us here? Were they right now on our trail, about to come crashing through the walls to drag me back to my cell, to Gibbon, to Proust, to the dusty musty world I had left behind? But no: of course, it would be the Annihilator, not ennui, that would await.

Finally Clarence seemed satisfied that we had climbed for long enough. We turned into a long corridor and moved along it to the sixth door on the left, number 666. I looked either side. All the rooms were number 666. A rather poor joke, I thought. Clarence turned the handle and we entered.

I almost fainted with shock. The portable telly, with a wire coat hanger stuck in the back as an aerial, the PlayStation, the ghetto blaster, the crap posters, my Spiderman duvet (hang on, hang on – that was always meant ironically, so hold that sneer), the crumpled tissues, the crusty underpants left sunny side up . . . There was a smell, somehow both musty and acrid, a palpable feeling of grease, filth, neglect, squalor. Yep. It was my old bedroom.

'Look familiar, Conor?'

'You know it does. But how can this be? I don't understand.'

'Which bit don't you understand? That Hell's designers should have modelled an adult's nightmare on your bedroom, or that you should have ended up back where you started?'

'Well, both. Please, Clarence, tell me what's happening. Is this the bit of the dream where things get so weird that you suddenly realize that it *is* a dream, and then you wake up?'

'Oh no, Conor, it's not that bit. It's not that bit at all. It's a completely different bit. It's the bit I like best.'

You know how I said that Clarence seemed to have grown? Well now, as he stood there amid the tissues and torn posters and empty CD cases (why do I always lose the CD and never the case?) and other stuff, he seemed positively huge. Where had those bulging biceps come from? Weren't those talons sharper than I remembered, those horns a touch longer? Scrote noticed it too, and had backed off into a corner, bristling and growling. And still, as I watched, Clarence continued to change. His little leathery bat-wings stretched and grew, and sprouted bronze and iron feathers. The process looked both painful and joyful; he closed his eyes, grimaced, shuddered, and let out a wolfish howl. And then he opened his eyes, which now seemed to burn with a black fire. I barely recognized the creature I saw before me. He was magnificent. He pulsed with strength and vigour, exuded authority, arrogance, endless, exquisite cruelty.

'Clarence! What the f—?' was all I could say.

But this was no longer *my* Clarence: this was some god of the underworld: a Titan; a monster; and he ignored my question. Unless, that is, you call sinking his talons into my neck and bursting spectacularly out through the window an answer. And with me dangling helplessly beneath him like a rabbit under an eagle, he soared up into the sky, high above the town, abandoning Scrote to the dubious delights of my old bedroom.

I felt myself being drawn up towards his mouth, his lips drawn back in a heartless sneer.

'Enjoy the ride,' he breathed.

I could barely speak from the pain of the talons in my neck and shoulder, and from the fear of the miles of red sky beneath my feet. But I tried.

'Clarence, you're hurting me. What is this? Where are we going?'

In reply, my own little devil, my foolish tormentor, my almost-friend, only laughed, and as he laughed lightning crackled around us. It was a laugh of scorn and mockery, and it hurt more than the talons and scared me more than the empty air and hard ground beneath.

We began to descend and I looked down. We had travelled

well beyond the city, but I could still see it in the distance, feel its insistent beat, smell the sleaze and corruption. Directly beneath me, however, I saw something more terrible. Chimneys poured forth black smoke; great, fat cooling towers sighed plumes of vapour. It was a factory of some sort. No. A power station. A hum of generators mixed with the drum beat from the city. And at the heart of the complex, surrounded by gangways and elaborate, weblike metal structures, was a colossal engine. I felt the raw power of the thing; it throbbed and pulsed like a great heart in an open chest.

At the centre of the engine I could just make out an opening. As we came closer I could see that the four sides of the opening were lined with rollers, grooved and bladed to lock together as they revolved. There could be no doubt, no doubt at all.

This was the dread machine, the Annihilator of Souls.

Chapter 33
Soul Muzak

A reception committee awaited me. There was a platform around the mouth of the Annihilator, and a decent crowd had gathered. I found myself strangely comforted by the fact that at least I would not be Annihilated in complete obscurity. Was it just because I'm a show-off, a poser even in death? Or was it because perhaps a crowd meant that there would be another trial, another chance to redeem myself?

And then, with a casual flick of his talons, Clarence tossed me towards the opening and I knew that my time was up. Goodbye, cruel Hell. For some reason the thought saddened rather than horrified me. I cannot say that my life and death, and life after death, passed before my eyes as I spun through the air. It was more that I was intensely aware of the millions of thoughts that I was never going to think, and feelings that I would never feel, and sights that I would never see. Here at last was the big black nothing, and I found that I wanted something more than nothing, even if that something was in itself really very bad.

As I fell towards my oblivion, I could see the crushing rollers of the Annihilator with a supernatural clarity. I saw the pattern of light, iridescent on the slick, oiled metal. I could hear with utter precision the grinding of the soul-mangle. Closer I fell, turning and spinning, until I felt the shadow of the mouth close around me.

And then, of course, I stopped.

Clarence had caught me by the ankles. He hovered,

flapping his miraculous wings, suspending me above the mouth of the Annihilator.

As I squirmed and spun, I saw the jeering faces of the upside-down crowd of spectators who had come to watch my destruction. They made Manchester United fans look human. These were the same dead people from the city, both lost souls and their tormentors: dissolute, craven, eager for the next fix. And the next fix was me.

At the head of them all I saw the huge figure of DJ Baal himself. He was draped in leopard and ocelot skins, and looked like the kind of devil who'd had some fun in his time: a distinct paunch protruded from between the spotted skins. But flies swarmed around him, and when he spoke the stench of death hit my face like a bucket of hot shite.

'So,' he murmured, deafeningly, 'this is the great Conor, the boy wonder, who thought he could fool all Hell. The child who tried to dupe us all, to escape his punishment. Feel clever now, boy?'

I opened my mouth. I assumed, perhaps optimistically given the circumstances, that something clever would come out. A witty put-down, maybe, or some piece of insouciant banter. But it seems the wells of wit and of banter were dry.

'What, nothing to say?' rumbled Baal, and I felt my internal organs thrum to the rhythm. 'How *very* dull.'

And then he nodded at Clarence, who let me fall a metre or two towards the Annihilator before catching me again. The turning rollers nibbled at a strand of my ever-annoying hair, teased it, and then yanked out a clump. I screamed and the crowd laughed at the funniest show in Hell.

'No, not yet, not yet,' said DJ Baal. 'Plenty of time for fun. Let me introduce you first to a few old friends.'

The crowd parted, and to my amazement I saw a magnificent Viking warrior, complete with horned helmet, battle axe and polka-dot dress. For a moment or two I completely forgot my imminent doom.

'Olaf, you great tit,' I exclaimed joyously. 'I thought you were . . . but then I thought I . . . Shag it! It's good to see you.'

'Yes, er . . . well . . . you too, I suppose,' he replied, looking from my upside-down, twirly-round perspective distinctly sheepish. 'But I'm afraid things . . . well. You know.'

'Olaf, what is it?' But somehow I knew. 'You're one of them, aren't you, Olaf?'

'No, Conor!' he said, vehemently. 'I mean, well, yes. Sorry.'

Things were starting to become a little clearer.

'What did they promise you?'

'The deal was that if I helped you out, kept your hopes up, acted as general minder, you know, just sort of looked after you, then I'd get to leave the Valhalla Caf for good, and they'd let me do a bit of pillage and stuff. They definitely mentioned nuns. And as much gingham as I could carry. What could I say?'

'They'll never keep their word, you know, Olaf. Why should they? They've got what they want out of you. What makes you think they'll keep their part of the bargain? They'll just think of loads of even shittier things for you to do.'

Olaf clearly hadn't considered that. Of course, he wasn't the brightest Viking in the longship. He looked worried, but worried soon gave way to something rather worse. Clarence pulled out a whip – no fumbling this time with brolly, staplegun or propelling pencil – which cracked out and coiled around Olaf's left leg. With a jerk, Clarence pulled him towards the Annihilator and then, with a nonchalant flick of the wrist, he dropped him down into the grinding teeth.

Olaf, his eyes wide with terror, gave one last despairing look at me and the world he was about to depart. He bellowed what sounded like, 'Odin! Thor! Laura Ashley!'

And then he was gone, but for shreds of polka-dot and his horned helmet, which bobbled about on top of the rollers like a bingo ball.

The ground trembled, the smoke from the surrounding chimneys thickened, and somehow the very substance of Hell – the grey earth and red sky – seemed to grow in intensity.

The crowd, taken by surprise, were silent for a moment, and then erupted into wild cheers. For a second time I said goodbye to my friend, the traitor.

'For once, Conor, my child,' hissed Clarence, 'you got it right. Except we prefer not to have any witnesses. This kind of subterfuge only works if there is complete secrecy. And Vikings, you know, do tend to brag. Can't allow our methods to become public knowledge.'

'Why don't you just drop me and have done with it? What's the point of continuing this bollocks? Haven't you tormented me enough? I see that the whole thing was a trick. Getting my hopes up just to drag me down further.'

It was DJ Baal who answered.

'Tormented you enough? Oh, no, not nearly enough. What do you think Hell is? A health farm, where we make life a little more . . . stringent than usual so you can walk away a pound or two lighter? Time for another friend, I think.'

I knew it was her before she appeared: the air was touched with gold and sapphire and, insanely, I felt my heart pound with joy and excitement, and fear. Had they caught her also? Or did she have the power to rescue me? She moved through the crowd like a swan through a scum-caked pond.

'Francesca.'

'Conor, my poor one, my darling.'

'I knew you wouldn't forget me. I knew it would all be all right.'

'Conor, how could I forget you?'

Her smile was as wondrous as ever, her eyes as liquidly

beautiful. But something in her, it seemed to me, something hovering just below the limits of perception, had changed also.

'How could I forget you,' she continued, enunciating each word with deliberation, and relish, 'when you are my meat?'

I felt a reeling nausea and I could not breathe or speak. The change I had detected in Francesca became clearer. Her hair shortened and darkened. Her teeth showed small and white and deadly sharp between her open, ecstatic lips. A sinuous, writhing tail burst through the seam of her provocative, ever-shortening skirt.

Of course.

Not Francesca.

Trixie.

'What have you done with Francesca?' I managed to squeak.

'Done with her? Done with her? This is more fun than I thought it would be, and I thought it would be *lots* of fun. You still don't get it? I haven't *done* anything with Francesca, I *am* Francesca. Or rather, she's an invention of mine. It's a shame you never got round to Dante. You might have appreciated my,' and then, glancing over at Clarence, '*our* little joke.'

Stupid of me. How could I have been so blind? Love, naturally. Or lust. And now the crowd were all laughing, and Trixie was laughing, and Clarence was laughing, and DJ Baal was laughing. And this, I thought, was truly to be the last thing I would ever hear: the last, at least, before the sound of my own choking screams – all the ghouls of Hell wetting their knickers at my expense.

Grinning, Clarence hissed in my ear: 'Feel the sting of it, Conor? Delicious, isn't it? Humiliation is one of our favourite toys. And you know about humiliation, don't you?'

'Of course I do. It's been one humiliation after the next ever since I got here.'

'Oh no. That not what I mean. I'm talking about dishing it out, not taking it.'

'What are you on about? What did I ever do to anyone? I'm a kid, not a concentration camp guard.'

'Conor, really! I know, and you know, and you know that I know, so let's stop this pretence.'

And you know what? I did know.

And now you have to know. So I'm going to leave me there, spinning helplessly above oblivion for the sake of this, my last ever digression. Yes, I know, the timing's bad, but it's now or never, and, like I said, you really should know this. I promise to be strict with myself – no digressing from my digression this time. Focused like a laser. Straighter than John Wayne's macho older brother, Wayne Wayne.

And the thing is that that is a great, a heroic act of self-sacrifice. Because, if you've stayed with me this long, you're not just going to wander off now, are you? Not when you can feel the end approaching (have a flick through. How many pages left? Not many, not many). So I could, if I felt like it, blather on about anything, and you'd hang on in there, just waiting for me to finish so you can find out what happens to me. I could tell you anything. I could repeat myself – drone on about Sara Peaks, or the Angels of Avalon. I could tell you my theory about Stephen Hawking. But I won't. I have too much respect for you. Love, even.

So here goes. My final confession.

Jason, Erco. Monkey-faced, feeble of limb, friendless, hopeless. When I say friendless, I suppose I mean without any friends who weren't equally slashed with the Mark of

Sorrow. There was a blimp called Jones, a rubber-lipped blubberer called Moran. One or two other smudges, indistinct, forgotten.

We called Jason 'Erco' because there used to be a crappy cartoon of Tarzan on the telly, and Tarzan had this monkey sidekick – yeah, that's right, Erco. And Jason did look just like that monkey: he was a pathetic, puny, bony, insignificant little kid.

And people seemed to hate him for being small and ugly. He was at the bottom of the pile, and got it from just about everyone. If someone kicked you, then you could always kick Erco. If someone spat in your dinner or caught you with the johnny-stick, then you could always do the same for Erco. He was the butts' butt, the scapegoat. I tended to stand aloof from the persecution. I certainly didn't join 'the line'. And what was 'the line'? Every few days the school thugs would make Jason walk slowly down a line of boys – they tried to make everyone join in – taking a punch or a slap from each person as he passed. The 'winner' was the one who made him cry. And that took some doing; Erco had more guts than you'd think. Not that it helped him. Sometimes, adding to the horror, girls would join the line. Big-boned girls with burly arms; sharp-clawed, kittenish girls.

It wasn't much fun. You could see him desperately trying not to cry as the punches came down on him. The humiliation of blubbing was far worse than the pain. But he always cracked in the end.

No, I never joined the line, but I never stopped it either. What could I have done? Me against ten of the hardest bastards in the school? Me against the *whole* school? Well, I did the sensible thing. I chickened out and let them get on with it. I had my own problems.

How could I know what was going on inside that monkey head?

Sometimes I noticed Erco looking at me. It was unsettling. I felt bad because I thought he might want to join in with my gang, play footie, talk about the telly, lech. But what did he think I was? A social worker? I'd fought hard for my status as maybe the second or third coolest kid in the year. I wasn't going to jeopardize that by letting the monkey boy in. All because I never clattered him. Next time, I thought, I'll join the line. It's that or get infected by his monkey fever.

And then it was the school summer disco. His last school disco. Come to think of it, *my* last ever school disco. The summer disco was the big one. A weird bacchanalian spirit haunted the place. It was the time when you could get drunk and talk to girls. You could snog them. Somehow everything was allowed at the summer disco that was forbidden, or just plain impossible, at other times.

Me and the Angels had been to the Rat and Scrotum earlier. I'd drunk cider with Pernod-and-black chasers. I was getting myself revved up to make a lunge at Sally Port, whose main, possibly sole, claim to fame was that she did a very good sea-lion impression.

We hit the assembly hall late – it was going on seven thirty. Nigel Sweltery, the gormless sixth-former who always dee-jayed, was working his way through his massive collection of twelve lame dance hits of the seventies, with the odd New Romantic fiasco thrown in for bad effect. His one red light bulb pulsed like a boil in time to the music.

I spotted Sally amidst a gaggle of her mates, over by the concertina screen that separated the assembly hall from the dining room. A smell of Scotch egg and cabbage seeped under or through the screen and hung in a green mist around them. Sally was doing her sea-lion routine. I moved into action, slipping her off safety, and sliding a hollowpoint round into the chamber. The Angels clustered together behind me and sighed me on towards my target. I was doing this for all of them. I was their champion: the greater glory of the group rode on my performance. I grooved my way forward, throwing some cool, if comically exaggerated shapes.

And then, as I was closing on the quarry, a figure moved out of the shadows and blocked my path.

It was Erco.

He was wearing his grey school trousers and a purple nylon shirt. He wasn't wearing his glasses and his tiny black eyes squinted up at me. But there was something else strange.

'Did you see *Top of the Pops* last night?' he asked.

I didn't know what he was doing there, at the disco, in my way.

'What?' I snapped, looking beyond him at Sally and her friends. They were looking back at me and smirking.

And then he said something else. Something I didn't quite catch.

'What?' I asked again.

'I love you.'

I must have misheard. Surely to God he didn't say that.

'What?' I said for the third time, still not looking at him. This was getting embarrassing.

'I love you.'

He now had my full attention.

'What the shag are you talking about, Erco?'

That was probably the most I'd ever said to him. He looked down and then up, pleadingly. He reached out his hand and touched me on the arm. I pulled away, violently.

I felt embarrassed, humiliated. I was blushing. I hated him. Thinking back after the event, after the terrible things that followed, I still couldn't work out what he wanted, what he thought he was doing. I don't know if it was just a way of saying that he wanted to be my friend. Or if it was some kind of sexual overture. All I'd ever done to deserve his love was not hit him.

Well now I was going to put that right. I stepped up to him and shoved my open hand into his face. I pushed hard and he fell back on the floor. I laughed, and all the other kids around laughed too. But there was something half-hearted about the laughter; somehow the world knew that my gesture had been *inauthentic*, that my act of violence was not the gleeful, thoughtless oppression of the true bully, but a sham, born of fear.

I tried to put the little runt out of my mind, but when I went to chat up Sally, it seemed as though Erco had contaminated me with his uncoolness. Sally and her gang looked through me as if I wasn't there, ignoring my quips and capering. I went back to the Angels and we found a dark corner in which to lurk. Phil had what he claimed was an e. We split it five ways. Nothing happened. I didn't tell anyone what Erco had said to me. I didn't want people to think I was a poof.

And Erco? He spent a couple of hours standing by himself and then went home. Two hours, toughing it out alone. My God, but he was a brave little sod.

The police came the next morning. Mum got me, gummy-eyed, out of bed, hissing, 'What have you done now?' I thought it must be something to do with Phil's e. I put on some tracksuit bottoms over my underpants, and pulled on a T-shirt.

There was a policeman and a policewoman. My dad had made them a cup of tea. The policewoman had red hair, and was quite pretty. She did all the talking. I was Jason's best friend, wasn't I? I wanted to laugh, but something in her face made me swallow it. I made a non-committal sort of noise.

'Did he ever talk about . . . about doing things to himself?'

'What sort of things?'

'Games.'

'Games?'

The policewoman looked at her colleague, and then back at me.

'Games with ropes.'

It must have been obvious from my expression that I didn't know what she meant, and so she told me what had happened.

Jason had left the disco at nine thirty. He'd taken the bus home. His mother saw him come in at about ten. He'd smiled at her and then gone straight to his room. In his room he took the cord from his pyjamas (what kind of fifteen-year-old has pyjamas?). He tied one end of the cord around the metal coat hook on the back of the bedroom door and the other end around his neck. He was naked. His mother found him at ten forty-five, when she came to bring him some Ovaltine (*Ovaltine!*).

I tried to explain that I didn't really know Erco – Jason – that well. They asked me if I'd ever done anything like this. I couldn't work out what they were getting at. I was glad when they went away.

Two days later there was a story in the local paper implying that Erco had done what he did as part of some sort of perversion. They made him out to be a real weirdo.

At the start of the next term nobody wanted to talk about Erco. It was as if he'd never existed among us, so deeply was that bony face and those puny arms and legs buried in our collective subconscious.

Why had he done it? Was it the rejection? Or was it because he thought I would tell everyone, mock him further? Sometimes I tried to believe that it had nothing to do with me. And sometimes it worked, for an hour or so.

So. That's it. That, I suppose, is why I ended up in Hell.

Hell, back to Hell. See, wasn't I good? I told you I'd tell it straight, and here I am delivering you back to the boy spinning above the Annihilator's gaping mouth.

Where it was time for another surprise.

I had played that particular memory tape many times, both here in Hell and as a living teenager. Something would set me thinking, and once Erco was on, I'd have to watch it through to the end. As I was playing through this same sordid little history in my head, the crowd had been silently gazing upwards. I reached the end of my interior drama and then followed their gaze, just in time to see my own memories projected onto the sky, lagging behind by a frame or two.

Cool trick.

The show finished and the spectators turned back to me, recognition and familiarity now added to their former raw antipathy. Yes, they knew I was one of them, one of the evil dead, damned rightly and eternally.

'This really is too good to end here,' chortled Baal. 'It would be a criminal waste of a soul such as yours to use it to stoke our boilers. You seem to have an infinite capacity for suffering – the ultimate unjaded palate. I can think of many more interesting things to do with you than to Annihilate you. Home with him, Clarence.'

The crowd, robbed of its entertainment, groaned and muttered.

'But, master,' replied Clarence, slyly, 'what about the Annihilator? It needs more meat. The Viking alone could not quell its hunger: his soul was thin. And, master, witnesses . . .'

'Ah. Yes, I see your point. Ever the careful administrator.' Baal looked around at the now restive clutch of damned souls. 'More meat it shall have.'

He waved his fur-draped arm at the crowd. In an instant the sly exultation on the faces of the lost souls turned to terror. Whether they were pushed by the tormentors scattered among them, or drawn by the power of Baal, they all fell sliding into the grinding maw of the Annihilator. Screams filled Hell. Again the black smoke thickened and Hell's substance grew dense, and vital and bloody.

Chapter 34
The Eternal Recurrence

I'm back in my room. Yes, Clarence took me back – not to the boredom cell in Sheol, but to my 'bedroom' in Hell's Wandsworth. I've been playing *Carapocalypse IV* on the PlayStation. You're equipped with a nuclear-powered car and you race against the other cars, which are all driven by mutant zomboids who are trying to make you crash so they can eat your brain. You lose points if they eat your brain. But you can get extra points by ploughing into pedestrians, who are all also zomboids.

It rocks.

I hate it.

I've been ruined. You see, it turns out that culture is addictive. It gets under your skin, and once it's there there's no getting rid of it. What I want to do is read Proust in French. I want to listen to Monteverdi and Berlioz and Brahms, not the relentless cacophony that pours like toxic waste from the radio: jungle, house, big beat, even punk and death metal. Yeah, you get variety on Skull FM. Oh, and the Angels of Avalon. Turns out we're big in Hell. Never toured Japan or broke the States, but big in Hell. Scrote sits in the corner all day with his paws over his ears.

The telly has eighteen thousand one hundred and ninety-two channels. I know: I've counted them. They all show Aussie and Californian soaps, with the same plot that goes round and round again, where a brainy but plain A likes a brawny, good-looking B, but B likes an evil bimbo C, until he finally realizes that C is a bitch and that A is, in fact, gorgeous as well as brainy.

Once I swam like a porpoise in those waters, and they gave me all I needed. Now, suddenly, I'm like a goldfish (sorry, for some reason I'm stuck with aquatic metaphors. But don't worry, we'll be back on dry land again soon) who suddenly realizes that he's in a stupid little bowl, and that just outside the bowl there's a million amazing things to see and do. Suddenly I'm filled (that's I, me – not I, goldfish) with the desire to know about the decline in civic government in the later Roman Empire. I want to engage intelligent people in debate on the relative merits of the second-rank Jacobean dramatists ('No, no, Professor Andrex-Himmelpfäarb-Hoffenstadter, I really can't agree with you on Middleton's use of prose; Beaumont and Fletcher seem to me . . . hold on, me pipe's gone out . . .' puff, puff . . . 'there we go, seem to me to knock him into a cocked hat. Chapman, I grant you . . .). I want to learn about philosophy, and science, and how the world works, and why Buckminster-Fuller balls are so clever and who would win in a straight fight between a samurai and a medieval knight (OK, so I've *always* wanted to know that one, so scratch it). I want to look into the origin of things, and work back through the chain of causation to the end so that I understand EVERYTHING.

But all I have is the beep and bash of the PlayStation, the mechanical clatter on the radio and the insipid pointless pap on the TV. Hell's trash, the world's trash: the empty, meaningless, boring clutter of a society without a point or a purpose (or a porpoise), except satisfying its own craving for pleasure and pain – I have it here. Once I wanted it, and it alone. Now I hate it, and want it gone.

I've also got a new tormentor. He's nothing like Clarence. He's a burly pinhead with the imagination of a turnip – a turnip so stupid it has to go to a school for turnips with special needs. He drops in once a day to beat me up. He doesn't talk to me, just sort of grunts a greeting when he comes in. Sometimes he uses a baseball bat, and sometimes a golf club (a three-iron, I think). The golf club doesn't hurt that much, but I always wail and moan and make him think he's doing some damage. That way he won't be tempted to look for something worse.

But the weird thing is that there is something much worse than the beatings or, for that matter, the flayings (more of which anon). It's the boredom. Yes, somehow my old punishment of infinite boredom still applies; it's simply that the means have changed. There's a bit in the Bible you always get at marriages or funerals or suchlike events (I last heard it at the celebratory mass held when my auntie Elsie found out the symptoms she was suffering from were not cancer of the colon, but haemorrhoids), the bit that goes, *When I was a child, I spake as a child, I understood as a child, I thought as a child: but when I became a man, I put away childish things.* Well now I'm a man, sort of, but the childish things haven't been put away. The childish things are all I have.

So when I heard a knock at the door it came as a pleasant relief from slaying zomboids. I knew it wasn't my regular tormentor, because he wasn't one of your knocking-at-the-door kind of devils; he was much more your smash-the-door-down, kick-your-head-in sort of devil, without so much as a pause to wipe his cleft hooves.

I staggered to the door, trying to shake away the images of carnage and death, and, without thinking much about who might be there, opened it.

It was Clarence. The old Clarence, my Clarence, not Scary New Clarence.

'Hi, er, Conor,' he said. He was wearing a natty three-piece disco suit in red polyester. Must be seventies revival time in Hell.

'What do you want?' I replied wearily. I did not feel any overwhelming urges towards employing the more ornate forms of courtesy.

'Oh, just thought I'd pop in to, you know, say hello.'

'Well, hello. Goodbye.'

'Don't be like that. Look, can I come in? Just for a few minutes. To have a chat.'

Reluctantly, I stood aside to let him through. I didn't suppose I really had much of a say in the matter. After all, I was the damned, and he was a devil. He always had the option of getting his talons out again and flying off to drop me in the shit somewhere.

'So, how have you been then?' he asked, still coming on like a vicar who had just popped in for a cup of tea on his way to visit his maiden aunt in the care home.

'What do you want me to say? The truth?'

'Honesty's always the best policy. Ha ha.'

I waited for a moment before I said:

'I'm in Hell.'

We looked at each other. I don't know if there was sympathy in his eyes, but I don't think I saw cruelty there, or joy in my suffering.

'So,' I said, finally, 'what was it with the big scary New Clarence, then? I mean, where did *he* come from? And why do you look normal now?' Relatively normal, I meant.

'Ah, well, I got an upgrade, I guess you could call it. For services rendered. Extra powers. But I don't want to go about looking like that all the time. Rather ostentatious. And a bit of a strain, if truth be told. Very high maintenance, those talons. I can see I must have seemed a bit . . . strange to you.'

'Evil. You seemed evil. Scared the living shit out of me.'

'Maybe the new powers went to my head a bit. But anyway, I had to finish the thing off, ride the train to the end of the track. It was all my plan, after all.'

'So you really were the mastermind behind the whole thing?'

'With some help from Trixie.'

'But how could you know what I was going to do? What if I'd turned back, or got stuck somewhere, or been blown to atoms in the war?'

'We were always looking out for you. Always there for you.'

'Like true friends.'

'Please, Conor. I don't feel too good about what I had to do. But, you know, all's fair in love and war, and damnation.'

'Come on, Clarence, you pretended to be my friend and then you buggered me over a barrel. Betrayal, treachery . . . it's just not very *nice*. And remember how keen you were on nice?'

He shrugged. 'It's my job. And anyway, most of what we did came from you. I just helped to facilitate your own plan. But let's not get bogged down in ancient history. How are things here? Are they looking after you? We had some good times, didn't we, you and me?'

'I can't do this, Clarence. I mean, chat like nothing's happened.'

I don't know why, but I found that I was snivelling. My chin fell to my chest but I couldn't hide it. And then I felt a scaly hand on mine.

'You know, Conor, I envy you.'

'Why? How much more in the shit could I be?'

'I mean you plural, you humans. You see, you have a kind of freedom we can never know, never fully understand. Since I've been promoted, I have more time on my hands, an opportunity to think more deeply about . . . things, about human beings, about the way you are. And I've had the chance to read. You know, "What a piece of work is a man! How noble in reason! how infinite in faculties! in form, in moving, how express and admirable! in action how like an angel! in apprehension how like a god! the beauty of the world! the paragon of animals!" All that stuff.'

'Very pretty. So why are we damned then, if we're so bloody great?'

'I told you, because you are free.'

'You don't seem to be able to make your mind up on that one.'

'I've worked it all out now. We angels, the dark ones and the light, have no choice about our nature. We act purely, like some perfect chemical reaction. Old Gabriel and Michael and that crowd, they have no temptation, no sordid side. But with humans, you're perfectly balanced. You have the animal nature, which wants you to eat and fornicate and murder anyone who stops you, but then you have reason, the higher urges and aspirations, the love of beauty and virtue. And the war between those two, the base and the sublime, makes you free. It's miraculous really. If you were any more animal, I mean the *tiniest* amount, then you'd be just another beast; if you were any more rational, any more like an angel, you'd be another timeless elemental being, beyond good and evil.'

'Am I supposed to be consoled?'

'I don't know. But I'm telling you something important. And I'm asking for something.'

'What?'

There was a long pause.

'Forgiveness.'

'How can I forgive you?'

'Because you are greater than me. Because I had no choice, no possibility of doing good, because you are morally free and I am a slave.'

'Then I forgive you.'

'Thank you, Conor.'

'But I'm still in Hell. And there's no way out.'

'No way out? But you know, there is.'

I looked up at him. 'What . . . ? Oh, the way that Olaf went. The escape into oblivion. It didn't seem like such a good way to go.'

Clarence looked perplexed, perhaps even flustered for a moment.

'Yes, that's what I meant. Oblivion. No escape. No return.'

'OK, Clarence. I've forgiven you your trespasses. Is there anything else?'

'Else? Ah, well, yes, actually. I was asked to give you something. No, no, sorry, don't go looking hopeful on me. It's a punishment. Your additional sentence, if you like, for your escape attempt.'

'But that was—'

'They were going to get your new guy to do it, but I volunteered. Thought I'd make a neater job of it. Could you stand up please? And just slip your clothes off.'

I did as I was told, and Clarence, with a few deft cuts from the scalpel-sharp tip of his trident, cut off my skin and tossed it to the floor. The pain was intense and exquisite and perfect: pain as a work of art. I was peeled. I was raw. I was meat. Nakedness makes us helpless, and no one is as naked as a boy without his skin. I saw that he was doing the same to Scrote, humming as he worked. And then Clarence left, closing the door quietly behind him, the way a parent leaves a room after kissing their sleeping child goodnight.

So, that's how things were. I'd been conned, manipulated and mocked. At every stage I had done exactly what they wanted me to do. I was an actor reading the lines they had written for me. I was the plaything of devils. Not because I didn't have free will, but because I was too stupid.

Perhaps Clarence was right about the glory of humankind,

but that wasn't much solace as I lay shivering on the floor, trying to grow myself a new skin.

But there are other sources of consolation.

I have a plan.

Insane, reckless, almost certainly futile. But a plan!

Let's scroll back a way. As I was spinning upside down above the Annihilator I saw something. Something that made little impression on me at the time, my mind being on other things, things such as Annihilation and so forth. It was only later, when I was lying skinless in my foetal position with Scrote whimpering in my arms, that I thought about some of the things that Clarence had said, something about a way out, and then I re-lived that spinning, trouser-filling terror.

And I saw it.

A big lever.

A big lever set in a box.

And on the box a scale, with at one end a '+', and at the other a '−'.

The lever was set at '−'.

It *had* to be the control for the Annihilator. And if it was set to '−' when it was annihilating things, surely that must mean that setting it at '+' must do the opposite of annihilating things. All I had to do, and this is the cool bit, because it's something that every kid who's ever watched *Star Trek* has wanted to do, was to reverse the polarity. Somehow I knew that if I could just reverse that polarity on the Annihilator, throw it back from the '−' to the '+', then something *really really* good would happen. It was escape. It would reunite my body and my soul.

It would get me home.

And now my preparations are all ready. Scrote and I have both re-grown our skins. Mine fits quite nicely, and I think

I've got a bit of stubble coming through. Scrote's fur has come back ginger, which is quite funny.

I'm sure I can find the Annihilator – we did not fly far from the city, and the way by foot seemed easy, by Hell's standards. Getting there shouldn't be a problem; there really is no decent security here. You see, the thing about Hell is that wherever you are, everywhere else is either just as bad, or slightly worse. So there's no need for them to guard you because if you struggle all you can ever do is impale yourself more deeply.

And now these, my memoirs, are composed. That skin of mine came in handy – made pretty good parchment when it dried out. Scrote, of course, will come with me. He doesn't know about the plan. I couldn't risk telling him: who knows what hi-tech surveillance equipment they have here? Or maybe it's just some devil with his ear up against the wall. Anyway, we all know what he'd say about it (I pause here, while you all chorus 'Rubbish!').

And so I'm to leave. Leave you who, stupid, ugly, slothful, malicious, and malignant though you may be, I've loved enough to labour through my story. Leave this Hell, a Hell I *might* have deserved. (Sorry, Erco, you poor, brave little bastard.)

When this paragraph finishes I will vanish for all time. At least as far as you're concerned. And I have to entertain the possibility that I could be wrong, and that I could vanish not just from your phenomenological field (look it up – I haven't got the time to explain now), but from everything. I mean, *reverse the polarity*! Who am I kidding? And after what I once said about something being better than nothing.

But I have a plan. And a plan's a plan. So here I go.

Goodbye.

Coda

Two devils walk together around a cloister. One devil is bent with age; long white hair flows over his shoulders. The other devil is much younger and moves with a quick, dancing step. He could be an apprentice, or a nephew, or a catamite.

Let's settle for nephew.

Both are dressed in drab monkish robes, although the older devil has a hood lined in ermine, and the tip of his tail is kept warm and snug by a knitted affair like a tea cosy or bobble-less bobble hat.

'Master' (OK, screw the nephew idea, he's an apprentice), begins the Young Devil, 'tell me of your greatest success, so that I may learn the Art of Torment.'

'Success,' answers the Old Devil, 'covers a multitude of sins. You must define your terms. Do you mean which of my many administrative reforms led to the greatest improvements in efficiency, and therefore made a major contribution to Hell-wide misery levels? Or do you mean a particular innovation – the internet, mobile phones, car alarms, et cetera – on which I worked, and which helped ensure more misery among the living, and greater numbers of damned?'

The Old Devil's face shows the mix of vanity, pedantry and cunning for which he has long been renowned.

'I was thinking more of a particular case, an individual client, master.'

'A case? A case? So many. Well, my name was made by one, ah, um, *exquisite* subterfuge. It was the first use of the

Grass-Is-Greener Pain Oscillation Manoeuvre that they teach you at Technical College. My own work is footnoted in Professor Stinkhorn's famous article in the *Journal of Diabolical Penal Theory*.'

'I have not yet reached that level, master. What is the Grass-Is-Greener Pain Oscillation Manoeuvre?'

'Oh, simple enough. Infinity, you see, is a very difficult concept to grasp, even for the most acute mind. And so the threat of an infinity of punishment – burning, scourging, and so forth and so on – lacks that certain something. It remains *vague*; it does not, of itself, *sting*. Our idea – you note by the way, the modesty of that "our" – was to give punishment a little more . . . purchase, by holding out the possibility of escape, of relief. You see, that way we set up an oscillation, a constant movement from hope to despair, and back again. That way pain is always here and now, always immediate, always cutting.

'True, with our original subject, the boy O'Neil, we invested a great deal of ingenuity, and for once a project was properly resourced. Really quite delightful, the whole operation.'

'O'Neil? Yes, I've heard of the case. But I seem to remember that something happened . . . that the project ended . . . unexpectedly.'

The Old Devil's demeanour changes. His brow wrinkles and his long tail flicks irritably from side to side.

'That was after I had passed on responsibility. I had nothing more to do with the case other than writing up my notes and reporting back to HQ.'

'But you know what happened, master? There is talk, gossip among the students, of a reversal in the Annihilator. There is talk of the possibility of . . . a return to life. Only foolish talk, I'm sure, o master.'

'THERE CAN BE NO RETURN!'

The Young Devil cowers in fear (or mock fear), pulling his hood over his eyes.

'But, master, we have heard that the Annihilator was in former times fitted with gears, and that one of those gears was set to run the opposite way, and that if a soul entered the Annihilator when it was running that way, then it would reunite the body and the soul. I mean no offence, master, but the other students, knowing of our closeness, pleaded with me to ask you about this.'

His rage over, the Old Devil now seems infinitely tired.

'My boy, my boy, such a muddle of truth and fiction. Why would the engineers have allowed such a thing? And how could the soul re-enter a body already decayed . . . ?'

'Perhaps another body, a new human child, or another sentient thing . . .'

'No, no, no. But it is true that the boy was seen approaching the Annihilator. And, yes, he threw himself into its jaws. But we have no reason to believe it was anything other than despair.'

'And the talk of a manuscript?'

'Lies. The boy is gone. And I am tired. Let us go.'

And with that the Old Devil puts his frail arm around the shoulders of his apprentice and they walk slowly from the cloister. Ah. The hand is straying from the Young Devil's shoulder to his—

Well.

Perhaps catamite was right, after all.

ABOUT THE AUTHOR

Anthony McGowan was born in Manchester,
brought up in Leeds and lives in London.

Author photo copyright © Jerry Bauer

Also available now in Doubleday hardback: